# BEFORE DEANNA COULD MAKE ANOTHER MOVE . . .

her mother was sweeping across the room.

As if he sensed Lwaxana Troi coming, Q turned. He raised a bemused eyebrow and watched her until she came to a halt barely two feet in front of him.

The true horror of the situation didn't dawn on Picard for a moment and then Mrs. Troi spoke.

"Jean-Luc, who is your charming friend?"

"Mrs. Troi," said Picard quickly, "now might not be the best time," not bothering to add that no time would be an improvement.

Then Q took a step forward and, with impeccable manners, took Lwaxana's hand. "I am Q," he said.

And Picard began to perspire.

# Look for STAR TREK Fiction from Pocket Books

## Star Trek: The Original Series

# Star Trek: The Next Generation

#18

**THE NEXT GENERATION** ™

## Q-IN-LAW

### PETER DAVID

**POCKET BOOKS**

New York   London   Toronto   Sydney   Tokyo   Singapore

An *Original* Publication of POCKET BOOKS

POCKET BOOKS, a division of Simon & Schuster Inc.
1230 Avenue of the Americas, New York, NY 10020

This book is published by Pocket Books, a division
of Simon & Schuster Inc., under exclusive license from
Paramount Pictures.

ISBN: 0-671-73389-3

First Pocket Books printing October 1991

10  9  8  7  6  5  4  3  2  1

POCKET and colophon are registered trademarks of
Simon & Schuster Inc.

Printed in the U.S.A.

Dedicated to

Gene Roddenberry—
who's given us a hell of a ride

and Gene L. Coon—
what a crime he wasn't able to
come along

## Historian's Note

*Q-in-Law* takes place approximately three months before the events in "Ménage à Troi" and significantly before "Q-pid."

# Introduction

So here it is. The one that people have been asking about, and for, the most.

I would be less than honest if I claimed that I was the first and only person to come up with this idea. A clash between two of the most formidable, and memorable, guest stars in all of *Next Generation*—and possibly in all of Trekdom—was a prospect that fans had been bandying about for ages. I was simply in a fortunate enough position to be able to execute the idea and produce the book you hold in your hot little hands.

Although the manuscript was completed late last year, I am writing this introduction in June of 1991. Everyone in fandom is massing for the celebration of the 25th anniversary of *Star Trek*.

Recently I came from the set of *Star Trek VI*, for which I gratefully thank George Takei (thaaaaank you, George), and am eagerly looking forward to what promises to be the most ambitious and the last (well, actually, I'm not that eager for it to be the last) adventure of the original *Enterprise* crew.

Since this book will be coming out in October of 1991, I like to think of this (along with my Original Trek meets Next Gen comic story, published by DC) as my own small contributions to the 25th anniversary celebration.

I was invited to no less than three conventions on the weekend of September 8th (the day *Trek* premiered), none of which I can go to since that's right around the due date of our third child. I am kind of hoping, in a fannish sort of way, that the baby's born right on that day. It would be the ultimate sort of poetic justice, considering that I met my wife at a *Star Trek* convention sixteen years ago.

That would just be the capper on a life that owes a tremendous debt to *Trek.* Thanks to *Trek,* I have a wonderful family, have been on the *New York Times* bestsellers list for three different titles (including a month's run with *Vendetta,* the virtually uniform praise for which was extremely gratifying), and have an entire group of readers that I probably wouldn't have had with just my comic book work and my other twenty or so novels.

For all of that, I just want to offer up my 25th anniversary thanks to Gene Roddenberry, whose creativity, driving force and vision have given me and mine so much. I can only hope that, in the pleasure that my novels and comic book work have given to the readers, I have managed to give back a little of what I got.

Considering that the world is currently choking in drugs, pollution, disease and decay, Gene's vision gives us something to cling to (bet you thought I was going to say "cling on," huh?) and lets us dream of a time when the madness is over, and we no longer need to worry about destroying ourselves through our own neglect, but instead about being destroyed by cybernetic dreadnoughts or superhuman beings . . .

That didn't come out right at all.

Obviously mankind's life is never going to be perfection, even in the future. But at least in the time of *Trek* when we meet the enemy, he will not (as Pogo said) be us. And if the enemy is someone else, I would be perfectly happy to trust the fates of my descendants to the capable hands of Captains Kirk, Spock, Picard, Riker (eventually) and whoever will follow in *Star Trek: The Generation After That One*.

In addition to the vision of Gene Roddenberry, I would like to thank—for the purpose of this book— Ms. Majel Barrett. Not only was Majel's powerful performance as Lwaxana memorable enough to prompt me to write a book about her, but she actually took the time to read the manuscript and offer comments, praise and support. Without her this book quite literally might never have been published, and I am eternally grateful.

I also want to thank my wife, Myra, and my 2.5 children—Shana, Jenny, and little whomever. Their support and help is invaluable as always.

Oh . . . as always, thanks to Kevin Ryan and Dave Stern, who had the exceptional good taste to hire me. And to the cover artist of this book. Aren't those great expressions on Q and Lwaxana?

And finally, to you, the readers, who have been tremendously supportive and very patient. I hope this one was worth waiting for.

# Q-IN-LAW

# Chapter One

KERIN LET OUT a slow breath, trying to calm the slamming of his heart against his chest. The stars hung suspended around him, the stars that had been part of his daily existence for as long as he could remember. He'd heard that when one stood on the surface of a planet, the stars actually twinkled because of atmospheric distortions. He wouldn't know firsthand, having never—in his eighteen years—set foot on a planet.

At the moment, the thoughts of planets were as far off as the stars. His full concentration was on the great mother ship of the Graziunas that loomed in front of him. It was dark blue, oblong, with great spires jutting out at odd angles. Swarming about it, insectlike, were a variety of single- and double-pilot ships, patrolling in a leisurely formation against incursion by any enemies who might be in the area.

Kerin could clearly see the great landing bay at the far end of the mother ship, and even if he couldn't, the array of instrumentation in front of him could easily pinpoint it for him. He scanned it with practiced ease. He knew his high-powered, single-pilot shuttle inside and out. It was a gift from his father for his twelfth birthday, and for a moment he allowed himself the luxury of remembering the thrill of the first time he'd stepped inside the shuttle, run his fingers across the controls, and sat in the command seat—his command seat. All his.

Kerin glanced at his own reflection in the viewport before him. He was amazed how much he was beginning to look like his father. His hair was cut into the widow's peak that was customary for all members of the house of Nistral. He was sloe-eyed, his pupils dark, yet luminous. His skin was a dusky silvery hue that gave him an almost metallic sheen. He had a strong jaw that was set in a determined fashion.

Glancing across his weapons array he noted with satisfaction that everything was fully charged. All engine readings were normal. He'd checked and rechecked everything a hundred times before setting off from the Nistral mother ship. The nervousness he felt and his overcaution had gotten him some good-natured ribbing and derision from his friends. He didn't care, because the redundant checks that had consumed hours before now gave him the confidence to worry about nothing except his obstacles.

The first of the patrol ships of the Graziunas family had broken off and were approaching. Only two. More than enough for a routine check.

"Approaching craft," said a crisp voice, "state your business with Graziunas."

His long, tapered finger paused over the comm controls for a moment before he flicked a switch. "This is Kerin of the house of Nistral. I go where I wish. I do what I wish. And I take what I wish."

2

There was a silence on the other end. A long, significant silence.

"If that is how it must be," the slow and measured response finally came, "then that is how it must be."

Message sent. Message received. Everything understood at both ends.

Kerin let out another breath and tried to calm himself, tried to forget everything that was at stake. Just let the reflexes take over, the long, practiced movements that had been drilled into him for as far back as he could remember.

He took one more look at the battle array, belted himself in, and slammed into overdrive.

The sleek craft shot forward, dipping just under the two wing fighters that were coming towards him for the intercept. He dropped like a stone, then levelled off quickly and angled straight towards the great mother ship.

The fighters banked around and came after him. Kerin had them both tracked, timing their pulse bolts, his fingers racing over the computer navigator for evasive maneuvers. Blasts exploded to his right and left, and his shuttle swayed gracefully, avoiding them with amazing precision. He allowed a small smile to play across his lips. "Catch me if you can," he muttered.

A shot clipped his right-hand stabilizer and he lurched wildly, scrambling to bring his bearings back on line. He muttered a low curse and went straight up in a sharp L pattern. The fighters stayed right after him.

"This is your final warning to retreat with honor," the admonition crackled over the comm.

"Noted," said Kerin briskly, and he slammed the thrusters into reverse.

The fighters shot right past him, leaping straight into his computer target sights. Kerin opened fire, the twin guns of his shuttle blasting. He clipped the wings of both of the fighters, sending them into a momentary spiral. It was all he needed to sail clear of them and dive down towards the mother ship.

More fighters were coming towards him, but Kerin's confidence was growing with each moment that brought him closer to the ship. He hurled his shuttle into a dazzling array of evasive maneuvers that seemed impossible for anything but the sleekest of fighter ships. Kerin had counted on the unassuming exterior of his shuttle to be his salvation, and thus far he had wagered correctly. He heard exclamations of surprise at the dexterity and capabilities of the little craft. Blasts exploded around him, but no one was able to pin him down.

He dove as his pursuers laid down a pattern fire after him. But he had studied every pattern that the Graziunas used and was prepared to dodge every one.

The landing bay lay directly ahead of him, and then suddenly he was hit. Obviously, he thought wryly, the Graziunas fighters had developed some new patterns.

He lurched wildly, trying to bring his shuttle back under control. Its wild flight now proved to be something of a salvation, as more shots that might have struck home now exploded harmlessly nearby him.

The shuttle hurtled into the docking bay, the walls of the bay flying past him in a dizzying blur. He was moving fast, too fast. He had brief glimpses of men who normally helped to manually guide ships in, and they were scattering madly to get out of his way. He tried desperately to bring his nose up, knowing that if it struck first, he'd flip over and crash, possibly—hell, *probably*—fatally. At the last possible second he edged it upward. The bottom of the shuttle sparked and squealed, and Kerin let out a brief shriek.

"Hold together, baby," he prayed.

The shuttle slid crazily, vibrating Kerin to the point

where he thought his teeth were going to shake loose. Reflexively he closed his eyes as he sped towards the wall at the far end, bracing himself for the impact. He knew he was going to hit, and the only question was how much impact there was going to be when he did.

The shuttle half-turned once more and the rear end slammed into the wall. Kerin was forced back against his seat, gasping, as the world spun around him. He took an unsteady breath, his head still ringing from the ear-splitting howling of metal on metal.

From his vantage point, he could see men of the Graziunas running towards him, shouting and pointing. He unbuckled quickly and ran to the door.

It was jammed. He slammed the release button a second time, but still nothing happened.

With a curse, he yanked out his blaster and opened fire. He hated having to inflict damage on his own ship, but there was no other choice. Within seconds he had blasted a hole large enough to squeeze through, and that he did immediately.

He leaped out of the ship and pivoted, simultaneously powering down his weapon. He ran around the side of his shuttle, and at that moment a guard came at him, swinging his weapon up with a blood-freezing yell. It didn't freeze Kerin, however, who—with an outward calm that he didn't feel inwardly—fired off a quick shot. It struck his attacker full in the chest and hurled him backwards, knocking the breath out of the man. He lay there, gasping, and Kerin leaped over him and out the nearest exit door. It hissed shut behind him as several blasts from behind ricocheted off it. Kerin wondered in passing if their blasters were set to a lower setting as well.

The corridors of the ship were large and elaborate swirls of blue and orange, sweeping and graceful. It was a stark contrast to the sharp black and silver that were the colors of the Nistral. Kerin looked right and left, trying to remember which way to go. He had memorized the schematics of the ship so carefully, so thoroughly, that he'd been confident he would be able to find his way. Now he wasn't so sure. He felt his blood pounding against his head and then heard another pounding—that of feet directly behind him.

He was fairly certain he was supposed to make his first right, and that's what he did. With the first decision made, the subsequent ones came faster and easier, his confidence growing with every passing moment.

A right up here, then another right, then a left and . . .

He skidded to a halt, wincing against the light.

He stood in the open doorway of the grand chamber of Graziunas.

Graziunas was the name of the house, and Graziunas was also the name of he who was head of the house. It was an inherited title.

The man who was at present known as Graziunas was massive, barrel-chested, with a shock of red hair swept back and over his gleaming blue face. He had a long moustache that hung down as well, almost down to his collarbone.

His court was crowded with retainers and other family members. Everyone was on their feet. Everyone was watching Kerin.

Next to Graziunas was his daughter, Sehra. Certainly word that Kerin was coming had reached her, and she was standing there, looking almost as nervous as Kerin must have felt. She was slim where her father was stocky, but in her eyes there was something of the same firmness of spirit that her father possessed. She was watching Kerin, taking in his every move hungrily.

Graziunas stepped down from his dais and walked towards Kerin with firm, steady steps. Kerin made no move, standing in a combat-ready position. No one was making the slightest noise. The only sound at all was the steady whisper of Graziunas' boots on the polished floor. He wore a tunic and leggings that were blue, trimmed with orange, as was the long cape that swirled about him with every step.

He walked to within a few paces of Kerin and then stopped, his arms folded.

"Yes?" His voice was deep and commanding, and yet there was a tinge of amusement to it.

Kerin's mouth moved, and nothing came out. Vapor lock.

It did not get easier under the steady gaze of Graziunas. His eyes seemed to widen, and Kerin felt himself wilting under the unyielding gaze.

Kerin looked frantically to Sehra. She was mouthing something. Words.

His words.

". . . as a supplicant . . ." he said, coming in on the middle of the sentence.

"What?" Graziunas looked as if he were trying not to laugh, and the implied condescension angered Kerin so that he promptly forgot again what he was supposed to say.

He closed his eyes a moment, took a breath to cleanse his thoughts, and then opened his eyes again. "I come to thee," he said, praying that his voice wouldn't crack, "as a supplicant . . . and as one who demands."

"Demands what?" said Graziunas.

"Demands the hand of thy daughter in marriage."

He saw her with alarm give a quick shake of her head, and then he realized his error. Mild, to be sure, but everything had to be just so. "Demands the hand of thy most honorable daughter in marriage," he quickly amended.

"And if I do not grant it?" asked Graziunas quietly.

Kerin steeled himself. "Then I shall fight thee for her. With every breath in my body, with every spark in my soul, I shall fight thee. For she shall be mine, and I hers, until all the stars burn away."

Graziunas swung a quick right that Kerin quickly dodged. There was a gasp from the people of the court. Kerin came in quickly and drove as hard a punch as he could directly at Graziunas' face.

Graziunas caught the boy's fist effortlessly.

Kerin grunted, trying to draw back, then drive forward. Neither move did him any good. Graziunas had a grip like steel, and he closed it that much tighter on the boy's hand. He waited for Kerin to cry out, smiling mirthlessly.

But the heir to the house of Nistral would not cry out, as much as the agonizing pressure on his hand urged him to. Instead he clamped his teeth down on his lower lip, to make certain that no sound of weakness escaped him.

All around held their collective breath, waiting to hear if Kerin would make some sort of noise. Nothing. His body was shaking, and blood was starting to trickle down his chin.

Graziunas laughed loudly, a sound so startling that several people jumped slightly. He released his grip on Kerin and the boy staggered back, rubbing his hand.

"Thou hast shown spirit, son of Nistral," said Graziunas grudgingly. "Spirit and fire. Thou hast spoken the words as they should be spoken, and issued the challenge. Thou hast not defeated me, but thou hast displayed thy worth." He stepped back and gestured towards Sehra. "If she will have thee, then the hand of my only daughter is yours."

Kerin couldn't believe it, and yet already there were the sounds of admiration and cheers from all around. Smiling now, he shook his hand slightly to restore circulation, a gesture that engendered a bit of good-natured chuckling. He accepted it in stride, for the pressure was off.

He crossed quickly to Sehra, who was standing there, smiling, her hands extended to him. He took her hands in his and when she squeezed his, he tried not to wince.

"You'll have me?" he said, forgetting that he was supposed to speak in the formal tongue.

Sehra didn't bother to correct him. She was smiling too widely. "Of course."

She stepped down off the dais and embraced him, which prompted more applause and laughter throughout the room.

"How did I do?" he whispered in her ear.

"Fine." She ran her fingers across his tight-cropped hair. "You did just fine."

## Chapter Two

LIEUTENANT COHEN was sitting in the Ten-Forward lounge, watching the stars glide by. He held up his glass of synthehol and watched the stars refract through the scintillating, swishing liquid. He sighed the sort of long sigh that was a clear indication—should anyone be listening—that he was depressed about something. So depressed that he desperately wanted to talk to someone about it, but likewise too depressed to get up the energy to discuss it with anyone.

Guinan glided several paces towards him, then stopped short. She raised a nonexistent eyebrow and pursed her lips. Her eyes twinkled no less than the stars through Cohen's glass as she stepped back and then moved diagonally across Ten-Forward.

She had not seen Geordi La Forge come in; her back had been to the door at the time. She didn't need to have seen him, though, to know that he was there.

"Geordi," she said softly.

He looked up at her. Or rather, he tilted his head and observed the flickering trace patterns of her body that his VISOR perceived. There was always something a little different about the way he saw Guinan as opposed to the way he saw others. A sort of—it was hard to pinpoint—coolness about her. As if her soul floated in an inner calmness that was reflected in the heat emanations of her body.

At the moment, he was alone at the table. He was expecting O'Brien and Riker to be joining him before too long, but he was already feeling in an expansive mood. "Guinan!" he said cheerfully. "Problem?"

She inclined her head slightly. "Him."

"Who?"

"Cohen."

He glanced in the direction she'd indicated. "Cohen?"

"Yup."

A smile broke across his face, and he shook his head. "We going to be talking in one-word sentences all night?"

She smiled in return. "Maybe."

"What's with Cohen?"

"He seems a little down," Guinan told him. "Since he's one of your staff, I thought you might want to cheer him up."

"Isn't that your department?" he asked, but he was already getting up from behind his table.

She took a step back. "Something tells me this might be 'man' stuff."

"'Man' stuff?" he said with a touch of amusement.

"You know," and she raised her arm in a flexing gesture. "'Man' stuff."

"Right," he agreed, flexing in return. Considering the knack that Guinan had for sweetly strongarming people into doing things, he had a sneaking suspicion he knew who had the stronger muscles.

Walking across the Ten-Forward lounge, he took notice of the way Guinan paced him a couple feet away, only to break off and head in another direction as soon as he got near Cohen. He heard Cohen sigh loudly and knew the tone of it. He'd heaved a sigh or two like that himself.

"Cohen?" he asked.

Cohen looked up at him. "Oh, Lieutenant Commander. Hi."

"Hi," Geordi replied, sliding down into the chair opposite. "Call me Geordi. We're off duty, and we're all friends here."

"Geordi," said Cohen uncertainly.

"And I should call you—?"

"Cohen."

"Oh." Geordi paused a moment. "Something got you down, Cohen?"

Cohen raised an eyebrow. It was the sort of subtle face movement that Geordi could not detect. Instead he depended on his ability to read pulse jumps, or the slight tilt of a head that usually accompanied a facial reaction. "You could tell that?" asked Cohen, impressed. "Wow. You know, I saw you come in, but you were way over there, and I didn't think you'd even noticed me. How were you able to tell from way over there?"

Somehow, *Guinan told me* wouldn't sound impressive. "Call it a knack," said Geordi. "So . . . you want to talk about it?"

Cohen looked down. "I don't think so. No. I'd really rather not discuss it."

"Okay," said Geordi, and he started to get up.

"I'm so depressed. My life stinks," said Cohen.

Geordi sat back down again.

Cohen stared into his glass, and Geordi said, "You want to elaborate on that?"

"Life in general."

"Ah."

"And women."

"Ah," said Geordi, this time with more understanding.

"Look at me, Geordi," said Cohen, and then he quickly amended, "I mean . . . I'm sorry, I didn't mean to offend you . . ."

Geordi laughed. " 'Look' isn't a dirty word, Cohen."

"Yeah, yeah I know. Look at me, then. I'm thirty-four years old today, Geordi."

"Happy birthday!" said Geordi. "I'm sorry, I should have—"

Cohen waved it off. "That's not the point. I'm thirty-four years old. My hair is thinning. I've put on some weight—look at this. My uniform's getting tight around the waist. That's embarrassing. And yesterday I broke up with Technician Jackson."

"Jackson, huh?" said Geordi. "She's cute. You two were a couple?" He was mildly annoyed with himself. Since his promotion to chief engineer, he'd been a hell of a lot more busy. He wasn't in the rumor loop as much as he used to be.

"Eight months," said Cohen sadly. "Eight months down the Jefferies tube. Look at me: I'm wasting my life. I signed on with Starfleet to explore. All I ever explore is the engine room. I never serve on away teams. I never make any sort of discovery. I'm just . . . just there. I'm a grunt. Look at what I've got."

"Yeah," said Geordi. "Yeah, let's look at what you've got. Look out there," and he pointed out the viewport.

Cohen didn't understand. "What am I supposed to see?"

"The stars."

"The stars. Great," said Cohen dismally. "So what? What do they have to do with me?"

13

"You live among the stars, Cohen!" said Geordi with enthusiasm. "Do you have any idea what that's like? Centuries ago, people stared up at the stars, their feet unable to leave the earth. They never saw outer space. Your ancestors never went to Mars, which was practically next door. The kind of life you lead—it would have been the most incredible flight of fancy to them. The things you take for granted." He nudged Cohen's shoulder. "You don't know what you've got."

"What have I got?" said Cohen. He still looked skeptical.

Geordi leaned back in the chair, his arms folded. "Why don't you tell me?"

"This is silly," said Cohen.

"Consider it an order," said Geordi, still friendly.

Cohen stared at Geordi, trying to figure out if the engineer was kidding or not. He didn't seem to be. "Tell you what I've got."

"Right."

Cohen gave it some thought.

"Nothing comes to mind."

Geordi blew air through his lips. "You help keep this ship running," he said. "That's one thing. There's a thousand people on this ship that depend upon the engineering department—more than any other—to get them where they're going. Now, maybe you consider your duties to be routine, even humdrum. But it's the ability to stay on top of those duties, even when they're tedious, that makes you a good officer."

"I suppose," said Cohen slowly. "I mean . . . I can look at it with an eye that all these people need me."

"Right!" said Geordi.

"And, well, I do get shore leave, occasionally. And with the holodeck . . ."

"Exactly," smiled Geordi. "You can simulate any-place you'd want to go. And only the very latest starships are outfitted with holodeck technology."

14

"And it's not like I've got a dead-end job," said Cohen. "I mean, there's room for advancement."

"Now you're getting it!"

"I mean, it's not like I'm chief engineer. Now *that's* a dead-end job."

Geordi opened his mouth and then closed it again.

"Oh! No offense!" said Cohen quickly.

"None taken," Geordi said evenly. "I suppose some people might perceive that job as such, but I assure you—"

"Oh, you don't have to assure me of anything," Cohen told him. "I understand fully."

"Well, good." Geordi smiled. "We were talking about you."

"About good things, yeah." Cohen was looking back out the viewport. "When I see the stars, it reminds me of Jackson's eyes. She has the most gorgeous eyes. When she would look at me in that way, with her eyes twinkling—there was nothing like it. You know what I mean?"

*No. Because I've been blind from birth, and I can see a single burning coal from thirty paces, but I can't see a woman's eyes burning with love from thirty inches away.* "Sure I do," said Geordi. "There's nothing like it, you're right."

"And I could always have something done about the hair, right?" he said, running his fingers through his thinning pate. "And just work out more to drop those extra pounds. It's not really a big deal, is it? Just self-discipline."

*Right. Dealing with his "shortcomings" is no big deal. As opposed to me. If I have my "shortcoming" attended to—my sight restored—I lose the sensory abilities of my VISOR, and that would simply be too much to give up.* "Just a little self-discipline," Geordi echoed.

"And even if Jackson and I did break up—well,

15

hell, we did have all that time together. And when we were together, it was fantastic. Fantastic woman, great conversationalist, great sex. There's nothing like a relationship when it's working, huh, Geordi?"

*I haven't had a serious relationship in close to two years.* "Nothing like it," said Geordi.

Cohen stood, filled with new confidence. "You know, Geordi, I'm going down to engineering just to run a routine systems check. I mean, it's not due for another two hours but, hell, you can't be too careful, right?" As Geordi nodded silently, he went on, "And then I'm going to see Jackson and tell her just what she's missing out on. And if she still wants to keep it broken off, well, there's lots of fish in the sea, or stars in the skies. Right?"

"Right," whispered Geordi.

Cohen got up, clapped Geordi on the shoulder, and strode out of Ten-Forward. As he exited, Commander William Riker entered. Riker nodded briefly in acknowledgment, and Cohen tossed off a jaunty salute. This surprised the hell out of Riker since salutes were hardly required, or even expected. Cohen walked away, arms swinging, whistling softly.

Riker glanced at the table where he and Geordi customarily sat, but he didn't see the chief engineer. Then he spotted him on the other side of Ten-Forward. Geordi was staring out a viewport when Riker walked up and dropped into the chair across from him, straddling it. "Geordi? Something wrong?"

Geordi looked at him. "I'm so depressed," he said.

"You're joking."

"Do I look like I'm joking?"

"Well, no," admitted Riker. "You want to tell me about it?"

"I don't think that would be—"

Riker's communicator suddenly beeped. Riker tapped it and said briskly, "Riker here."

"Commander," came the clipped tone of Captain Picard, "to the bridge, please."

"Right away, sir."

"Bring Mr. La Forge with you."

"Yes, sir." Riker didn't question how Picard knew that Geordi La Forge was with him. Somehow, his being the captain was sufficient reason. He stood and said to Geordi, "You heard the man."

"Yeah, I know," said La Forge, getting to his feet.

"You'll tell me about it on the way to the bridge," said Riker. "Whatever's bothering you, I'm sure we can shake it."

"If you say so, sir."

Jean-Luc Picard rose from his command chair the moment that Riker and La Forge entered the bridge. With a curt gesture of his head he indicated that they should retire to the conference lounge. Worf was already heading there and Riker stopped just short of the door, protocol clearly dictating that the captain enter first.

Picard glanced at his first officer and chief engineer, some instinct that was attuned to the moods of his command crew immediately tipping him that something was wrong. Geordi seemed in a chipper enough mood. Indeed, perhaps even excessively jovial, with a large smile and cheerful demeanor.

Riker, on the other hand . . .

Picard gestured that Geordi and Worf should precede him, and they did so. Picard then took a step closer to Riker and said softly, "Number One, are you quite all right?"

"I'm fine," said Riker, unconvincingly.

"You seem a bit . . . put off."

"Just a little depressed, Captain. It'll pass."

At that moment Deanna Troi entered. "I'm sorry

for the delay, Captain," she said. "My duties else-where . . ."

"You don't wish to run out in the middle of a counseling session if it can be avoided," Picard said.

She nodded gratefully. "I'm glad you understand, Captain."

"The body of a ship runs on the hearts and minds of her crew," said Picard.

"If I may say, sir, you seem unusually cheerful today," said Troi. One hardly needed empathic ability to perceive it. Picard was smiling, virtually ear to ear.

"You'll understand why shortly, Counselor."

He entered, and Riker was about to follow, when Deanna placed a hand on his forearm. "Are you all right, Commander?"

"I don't want to discuss it," he said with such firmness that she took a step back.

"You just seem a little depressed . . ."

"I'm *not depressed,"* said Riker in no uncertain terms and stalked into the conference lounge.

Troi sighed inwardly. This had the makings of a long day.

Geordi passed a cup of coffee over to Riker and took one for himself. He made sure to sit several seats away from the first officer, who gave him a glance that seemed to say, *I was having a good day today until I talked to you.* At least, that's how Geordi was inter-preting it. He would have felt guilty about it if he weren't already feeling so darn good about his life.

"Gentlemen and ladies," said Picard, for Dr. Crusher had shown up as well to join Troi, Riker, La Forge, Data, and Worf in the conference lounge. "We are going to be hosting a wedding for a very important group of people."

"How marvelous!" said Troi.

"What is the occasion?" said Worf. In contrast to

Troi's upbeat and cheery reaction, Worf was sullen and already thoughtful. Large numbers of newcomers on the *Enterprise* meant that all sorts of security questions would have to be answered. If the individuals coming aboard were among the more aggressive members of the Federation, the entire thing could be a logistical nightmare.

"A wedding among the Tizarin," Picard informed them. "Not an unusual occasion in and of itself, of course, but this is a cross-marriage between the houses of Nistral and Graziunas."

"All right, I'll bite," said Geordi. "Someone want to tell me who all these people are? I've never heard of the Tizarin or these 'houses' you're talking about."

There was dead silence for a moment.

Picard looked in surprise at Data. "That's your cue, Data."

"I am endeavoring to practice more restraint when I supply information," the gold-skinned android said in his calm, almost monotone voice. "I am beginning to perceive how an unending, and even unasked for, supply of facts can be unnerving in many situations."

"That's very good, Data," Geordi said.

"For example, there was a doctoral thesis written thirty-seven years ago, wherein a test group of subjects from four different races was barraged for twenty-six hours with sensory input ranging from . . ."

"Data," said Picard quietly. "The Tizarin."

"Oh. Yes. The Tizarin," Data continued, switching subjects without missing a beat, "are a spacegoing race of merchants, somewhat similar to the earth peoples known as Gypsies. If there is a home planet for the Tizarin, it is unknown. They are spread throughout the galaxy, engaging in trading with most races in the Federation with the exception of the Ferengi."

"Why not the Ferengi?" asked Troi.

"The Tizarin offer lower prices for their wares and engage in business in a more upright and evenhanded manner," Data told her. "The Ferengi consider the behavior of the Tizarin to be 'bad for business.'"

"They would," Worf observed, making no effort to hide his distaste.

"The Tizarin usually travel in groups of two or more houses, for mutual protection and strength," Data continued. "The two that the captain mentioned —the Nistral and the Graziunas—are two of the oldest, most influential, and most powerful. There has been something of a rivalry between the two for many years, but business has been consistently good and relations have been properly handled so that this rivalry has not developed into hostility."

"It has, in fact, developed into something far more promising," Picard now said. "The son of the head of the Nistral family has fallen in love with, and asked for the hand of, the daughter of the head of the Graziunas family."

"Oh!" said Crusher, smiling. "How sweet. Like *Romeo and Juliet.*"

"Ah, yes," said Data. "The play by your William Shakespeare. A treatise on the subjects of parental neglect and teen suicide."

"It was a bit more than that, Data," said Picard, trying not to sound as annoyed as he felt with this cavalier dismissal of the Bard. "That play contained some of the most famous and moving romantic passages in history. Why, in my youth, I took an acting class that recreated original stagings of Shakespeare. I was in a production of *Romeo and Juliet.*"

"I didn't know that, Captain," said Crusher. "Did you play Romeo?"

"Well . . . no," said Picard, suddenly looking as if he wished he hadn't brought up the subject.

"Mercutio?" suggested Geordi. "Or one of the fathers?"

"Not exactly."

"The priest?" asked Troi.

"No, not Friar Laurence. The point is that—"

"Captain, whom did you play?" asked Riker.

Picard sighed and said, "I portrayed the nurse."

"The nurse?" said Crusher. "Juliet's nurse?"

"It's a superb part," Picard said.

"Oh, I'm sure you were wonderful, Captain," the doctor said.

"In original productions, women's parts were always played by men," Picard informed them. *"The point is* that in this scenario, the houses are not feuding. The love between the two young people, although unusual considering the rivalry, is not cause for recriminations, war, or backbiting. It's all been very civilized.

"In fact, the Tizarin have a very specific ceremony that is to be followed when one member of a house wishes to propose to a member of another house. The young man accomplished this ceremony with flying colors. So you see, Mr. Data, unlike the Shakespeare play, there will be no neglectful parents and no teenage suicides.

"Now then, why don't we move on," said Picard, closing the subject. "Since it is a joining of two houses, their protocol requires that a third party perform the actual vows of marriage. Since the Tizarin are such an important asset to the Federation —and since, as a spacegoing society, they have more than the normal respect for space vehicles—the Tizarin have humbly requested that the Federation's best ship be the site of the wedding, and that the captain of that vessel officiate. Starfleet has selected this vessel to fill that need and naturally I, as captain, will perform the ceremony."

"Congratulations, Captain."

"Thank you, Number One. It is one of the more pleasant duties of being a captain, albeit one of the least performed. We are scheduled to rendezvous with the houses of Graziunas and Nistral in seventy-two hours. In addition, several races who are principal customers of the Tizarin will be sending delegates as well. Recommendations for the site of the wedding?"

"Holodeck," said Riker. "We can customize the interior to whatever they want."

"Beats the shuttle or cargo bay," Geordi added.

"Make it so," said Picard. "Mr. Data, perform an overview of Tizarin history and select several appropriate choices to offer them."

"I will need a detailed list of all the representatives," rumbled Worf, "as well as profiles on any potential security risks."

"Starfleet has assured me that we will have the list shortly," Picard said.

"Betazed does a good deal of trade with the Tizarin," said Deanna. "The Tizarin prefer not to deal with overly warlike races, Worf, so I would not be overly concerned."

"You," said Worf firmly, "can afford not to be concerned, Counselor. The safety of this ship is my responsibility."

"And you will be given every assistance in attending to it," said Picard firmly. He frowned. "Is there another problem, Worf?"

Worf's lip wrinkled in mild distaste. "Is it necessary to turn the *Enterprise* into a catering hall?"

"The mission is to promote interstellar harmony and goodwill," said Picard firmly. "I can assure you, Mr. Worf, that we are first and foremost an exploratory vessel. We are not—emphasize 'not'—a catering service."

22

Picard's communicator sounded and he tapped it. "Picard here."

"Captain, this is Guinan. I have that assortment of hors d'oeuvres you asked me to put together."

Picard felt the uncomfortable glare of the Klingon security officer upon him.

"The little hot dogs in buns are nice," said Crusher.

"I've always liked those," Troi agreed.

Worf grunted.

"Later," said Picard.

# Chapter Three

"You wish to tell me about it, Number One?"

Riker cocked his head and looked at the captain questioningly. He had been curious as to what Picard wanted to discuss with him when the captain had asked him into the ready room shortly after the briefing. "What 'it' is that, sir?"

"You seem less your usual self-confident self," said Picard, leaning back in his chair.

Riker waved it off. "It's nothing, sir. Really."

"I could order you to talk to Counselor Troi about it," said Picard slowly. He waited for Riker's reaction and got exactly what he thought he would. "Or is Counselor Troi 'it'?"

The first officer sighed. "It all comes from trying to cheer up Geordi."

"Mr. La Forge is having difficulties?" Picard half smiled. "I should have known all this was coming, all things considered."

"All things, sir?"

"One tends to lose track when one is in space, Commander," said Picard with amusement. "But obviously there are certain things which stay with us, no matter where we are. Or aren't you aware of the season that earth is currently beginning?"

Riker frowned. "I think it's . . ."

"Spring, Number One," Picard said with an expansive wave of his hands, as if addressing a stadium. The ready room echoed with the power of his voice. "Spring, when a young man's fancy lightly turns to thoughts of love, as Tennyson said."

"I don't know if that's really it, sir."

"Then what? Are you unhappy with your position in Starfleet?"

"Not at all, sir," said Riker with pleasing certainty. "I could not find a better ship, or a better commander. And I've dedicated my life to Starfleet, with no regrets."

Something seemed to be hanging unsaid in the air. "Except . . . ?" said Picard.

Riker looked down for a moment, as if suddenly intrigued by his toes. "You know that Counselor Troi and I had a relationship prior to our meeting again on the *Enterprise.*"

*If I were deaf, dumb and blind it would still be obvious,* Picard thought. Out loud, he simply said, "Yes, I was aware."

"When we decided not to . . . proceed in certain directions with that relationship," said Riker, "that was a turning point in my life. There are certain moments where you stand at a crossroads, and you choose a path for yourself. And in the other direction lies . . ."

"The road not taken," Picard finished. "And usually you leave the road not taken behind you."

"You see the problem," said Riker.

"Of course. Counselor Troi serves as a perpetual reminder of a direction you chose not to pursue. A question mark personified. Does that make you uncomfortable, Number One?"

"Not uncomfortable. Deanna's specialty is making people feel comfortable, and even if it weren't, she's too good a friend. Just maybe a little . . ."

"Wistful?" smiled Picard.

"Around springtime," Riker admitted.

"You could look at your situation as a unique opportunity," observed Picard. "All of us have moments in our life that we look back on and say, 'What if?' But Counselor Troi serves by your side, Number One, so, unlike those of us whose lost loves are dim parts of our past, you still have—if and when you feel ready—the chance to say instead, 'Why not?'"

Riker nodded slowly, his customary, confident grin gradually spreading across his face. "I hadn't thought of it that way. That's presuming, of course, that when I feel ready, Deanna feels the same way. Or is even there."

"That, Number One, I cannot help you with. In love, as with all things, timing is everything. Take that from someone who has had his share of experiences in pursuit of the fairer sex."

"Did you do anything you regret in that pursuit, Captain?" asked Riker.

Picard's mouth twitched. "I wore that blasted nurse's costume."

"Ah."

"Impetuous youth. You see, there weren't enough young men to go around, so we did indeed have a female playing Juliet. Beautiful young thing. Long, silky blonde hair . . . blue eyes, slim-waisted. I would've cut off my right arm to be near her. The part of Romeo was already taken by this annoyingly heroic-looking young man. Only the nurse had any other real scenes with her, and I was willing to go to whatever lengths to be close to her."

"What happened?"

"She wound up with Mr. Heroic-Looking," said Picard, shaking his head. "Girl had no sense at all. But she was marvelous to look at, Number One. I'll never forget her."

"What was her name?"

"Linda . . ." His face suddenly went blank. "Or was it Lisa? Lisa . . . something. Oh Lord. I wore a hot, sweaty nurse's costume for four weeks of performances, not to mention rehearsals, for a girl whose name I can't remember anymore."

"Now *you're* going to be depressed."

Picard shook his head and smiled. "No, Number One. I've long ago made peace with the untrod roads of my life. And the young lady's name, well, it's no doubt been replaced in my gray cells by matters of more import. I assure you, Will, springtime or not, I'm not going to get depressed."

Picard's communicator beeped and he tapped it. "Yes."

"Captain," came Worf's stentorian voice, "we have received the list from Starfleet of the guests who will be in attendance at the . . . festivities." The last word sounded as if he were uttering a profanity. "I will be studying it and giving my recommendations and security needs to you within an hour. I thought you might wish to examine it as well."

"Yes, absolutely, Mr. Worf."

Picard turned in his chair to face his computer screen. Names of ambassadors, their pictures, and their home planets scrolled past him, and he nodded curtly as each went past. "I have a good feeling about all this, Number One," he said. "A celebration such as this one helps to remind us that the purer emotions, such as love, are the great constants of the galaxy."

Riker smiled. "You certainly seem happier about this than any time I've seen you recently, Captain."

"This crew has been through a great deal, Commander. We can use a genuine celebration. And you," he said without looking away from the computer screen, "are seeming a bit more chipper, I might add."

"Perhaps you should consider becoming a counselor, Captain. Talking to you is certainly . . ."

And then he saw Picard go ashen. "Captain, what's wrong?"

"Oh no," said Picard softly.

"Captain—?"

Riker's view of Picard's screen was blocked as Picard muttered, "Daughter of the fifth house . . ."

"Fifth house?" said Riker in confusion, and then he realized. "Fifth house of . . . Betazed."

"Holder of the Sacred Chalice of Riix," Picard continued, ostensibly reading from the computer screen but, in fact, quoting from memory.

"Heir to the Holy Rings of Betazed," intoned Riker. "Are you saying . . . ?"

"It appears that the mother of your untaken road will be joining us," sighed Picard. "Lwaxana Troi is being sent by Betazed to be their representative at the joining of the houses of Graziunas and Nistral aboard the U.S.S. *Enterprise.*"

"Do they ever miss an opportunity to send her off planet?" Riker wondered.

Picard glanced at him. "Would you?"

"Captain, are you all right?"

"A headache, Number One," said Picard tiredly, rubbing the bridge of his nose. "Just a headache. God help us if she's still in phase."

"Yes, sir. Can I get you something?"

Picard turned to the food dispenser just behind him. "Earl Grey tea. Piping hot." Within an instant the small hatch slid open and a cup of tea extended out. Picard took it and sipped it gingerly. "Take the conn, Number One. I'm going to be indisposed for a few minutes."

"Yes, sir," said Riker, standing. He was feeling his old, confident self. Picard, on the other hand . . . "Captain, if you want to talk about it . . ."

Picard barely afforded him a glance, but what he did see in his captain's eyes was loaded with significance.

Without saying anything further, Riker turned and walked out of the ready room.

As he walked out onto the bridge, Geordi glanced up from the engineering station, where he was doing a systems check before heading back down to the bowels of the engine room. As opposed to earlier, Riker now seemed more relaxed, even jaunty. Then the door to the ready room hissed shut, and Picard did not emerge.

Geordi frowned and sidled over to Riker as the first officer took the command chair. "Where's the captain?"

"He's a bit under the weather," said Riker neutrally.

But Geordi wasn't falling for it. "He's depressed, isn't he. Isn't he?"

"A little," admitted Riker.

Geordi stared at him and then said firmly, "Don't try to pin this one on me." And he went back to the engineering station.

Wesley limped into sickbay as his mother emerged from her office. She looked at him with a mixture of annoyance and concern, trying to maintain the stern decorum that a chief medical officer should have when faced with a crew member who had clearly injured himself taking unnecessary risks. At the same time, she was still a mother who had to fight the impulse to—well—mother him.

It wasn't hard to figure out. Wesley was standing there, leaning on one of the sickbay beds, decked out in full skiing regalia. The only thing he didn't have was ski poles. Naturally not, because the holodeck would have provided those. Just as it had, apparently, provided him with—

"A twisted ankle, I think," said Wesley apologetically. "Took a wrong turn down a slope."

"Wesley," sighed his mother, getting her instruments. Wesley hoisted himself up onto the table.

Wesley rolled his eyes. He knew that tone of voice. "Mom, please. Don't give me that 'you've got to be more careful' speech. I'm not a kid anymore."

"Well then don't act like one." She slapped him affectionately on the shoulder and ran an instrument over the ankle that he had extended and propped up on the table. "What were you doing on the slopes, anyway?"

"Nothing."

"Try again."

He sighed. "Okay, I was showing off a little."

"For who?" She couldn't keep the amusement out of her voice.

"You don't know her."

"Should I?"

"I don't think there's going to be much need to," Wesley sighed again. "I didn't just turn the ankle. I kind of went heels over head into a bank of snow. With my feet sticking out and my arms every which way it was a mess."

"I can just imagine." Her instrument hummed softly, and Wesley could feel the muscles reknitting and relaxing under the sonic ministrations.

Wesley sighed. "Mom, am I ugly or something?"

She looked up at him in surprise. "Of course not. You're a very handsome young man."

"Then, what's wrong with me? Why am I having trouble getting something going with a girl?" He looked down. "Maybe it's this gray uniform. I bet things would go better if I had a Starfleet uniform. A full ensign's uniform."

"Well, they do say clothes make the man." She smiled. "In your case, though, I wouldn't worry. In gray, or red and black, or sackcloth, you'll find somebody. In this whole galaxy, there's somebody for everybody."

"You really believe that?"

"Of course I do."

"But the way things are now, I'm hoping that the somebody for me is on this ship. I mean, if she's on Rigel 6, she's not going to do me a whole lot of good."

She laughed. "Wes, don't try to outsmart yourself, okay? Trust in yourself and the machinations of fate, and let everything else sort itself out. Try the ankle."

He slid off the table, gingerly putting his full weight onto the foot. He nodded with brisk approval. "Feels great, mom. Thanks."

"Pretty girls should be turning your head, not your ankle," she told him reprovingly, putting her instruments back in their holders. "Still, showing off on a ski slope is mild, I suppose, compared to what one of our upcoming guests did to impress a girl."

"What do you mean?"

"Come on, I'll show you."

She gestured for him to follow her into her office. She couldn't help but admire the determined, confident manner in which he walked. It seemed barely yesterday that he had been nothing but knees and elbows as his long-limbed growth had outstripped his ability to coordinate his movements. Not anymore.

"The captain met with us a few minutes ago," she told him, sitting in front of her desk, "while you were busy displaying your form on the ski slopes. We're hosting a wedding for the Tizarin."

"The merchant race? The guys who are like honest Ferengi?"

"That's them." Various medical documents flashed on her screen. "Whenever we're having an assortment of races coming on board, I always review the medical profiles. That way I'm prepared should anything happen. For example, remember when we had that representative from Chumbra III on board, and he suddenly seemed to go into a deep coma? Now, if I hadn't realized that he'd simply entered a chrysalis stage prematurely, and the proper procedure was to pack him in ice, who knows what might have happened?"

"Yeah, I remember. And as it was, he came out of chrysalis as a female."

"Exactly. Now, the Tizarin don't appear to do anything quite that drastic. But I've been studying their culture as well. The would-be groom, Kerin, had to run a virtual gantlet in order to satisfy tradition that he was serious with his intentions towards his desired mate. Alone, in a shuttle, he had to get through several fighter squads—and the Tizarin are the toughest space pilots in the galaxy. Then he had to confront the girl's father."

"He must really love her," said Wes.

"And she's a girl from a rival family," his mother told him. "It's what I was telling you. There's someone for everyone, and you never know where you're going to find them."

"How old is this Kerin guy?"

She glanced at the records. "In human terms, about nineteen."

"He's *nineteen* and he's engaged to be married already?" said Wesley incredulously. "I haven't even found a girl who'll give me more than a glance, and this guy is playing fighter pilot to get to his future wife. Is he in too much of a hurry or am I just taking too long?"

She laughed and put a hand on her son's arm. Male egos were such fragile things. The slightest word could send them spiralling down in flames. The reason for this probably was rooted in adolescence, when boys had to suffer the humiliation of watching girls mature faster and with more grace, turning from approachable objects of scorn into mysterious objects of desire. It was an unexpected uprooting of The Way Things Were, and she suspected that most men never fully recovered from that jolt in their formative years.

"Everything happens in its own time, Wes. Just hang on to that."

Wesley nodded and turned to leave, flexing his ankle experimentally once more and nodding quick approval. Then he paused and turned back to his mother. "Mom, are you saying that dad was the special guy for you?"

Bev Crusher smiled. "He was certainly special, all right. You know, when we first met, he reminded me a lot of a certain teenage boy that I met in later years." And she ruffled Wesley's hair.

Automatically, extremely self-conscious of keeping his appearance Just So, Wes smoothed out his hair. "But what you're saying, mom, is that . . . if dad was the guy for you, and he's gone—"

"Am I alone in the universe?" she finished with a raised eyebrow. "I hope not. And as long as I have you and this ship and co-workers like the ones I have, it makes loneliness that much easier to handle."

He nodded and walked out of the sickbay.

And Beverly Crusher's smile slowly disappeared. She leaned against an exam bed and sighed.

"God, I'm depressed," she said.

# Chapter Four

GUINAN STARED OUT OF the viewports of the Ten-Forward lounge, and she was smiling. Just outside, seemingly so close you could touch it and yet, in fact, hundreds of kilometers away, floated the great ship of the Graziunas family. She knew that out of her view, on the other side of the *Enterprise,* was the House ship of the Nistral—powerful and bristling with weapons for their protection, for a life in space, although attractive, was infinitely filled with peril. At the same time, there was a grace and beauty to the flowing designs of the ships.

She spotted, here and there, the telltale orange-and-blue trim that were the colors of the Graziunas. And she remembered that the Nistral were silver and black. With those skin color combinations, she wondered what the children were going to look like when . . .

Suddenly her eyes narrowed.

Something was wrong. She tilted her head, like a dog listening to a sonic whistle. Her legs didn't seem to move as she glided across the room. It was a slow, careful movement on her part, as if she were searching for water with a divining rod. She knew by heart every inch of Ten-Forward, and yet she studied it now again, cautious and unsure.

There was a little tickling in the back of her mind. She couldn't place it, couldn't judge it, couldn't figure it. But there it was, just the same. There . . . *what* was?

She thought she could pinpoint what was bothering her if she just had a few more moments to . . .

"And this is the Ten-Forward lounge!" came Picard's voice.

Guinan spun like a cat and within the blink of an eye had composed herself utterly. She smiled, pushing aside her concerns, as the captain entered along with a party of four.

It was easy to tell who was who. One of the men, husky and powerful looking, was clad in bursts of orange and blue, as was the woman next to him. Another man was dressed in silver and black, as again was the woman who accompanied him. The house allegiances were clear.

"Guinan," said Picard, sounding his most suave, "may I present Graziunas and his wife . . ." and he inclined his head slightly in the direction of the silver man, ". . . and Nistral and wife, of the house of Nistral. This, gentlemen and ladies, is Guinan, the hostess of the Ten-Forward lounge. This is our somewhat relaxed meeting place, where the crew can go to interact, socialize, consume superb drinks and food, and enjoy one another's company away from the rigors of day-to-day starship life." He smiled. "Have I covered everything, Guinan?"

"I can't think of a thing to add, Captain," Guinan

told him, bowing slightly in the direction of each of the newcomers.

The orange-and-blue-clad Graziunas was quite husky compared to the silver-and-black-clad Nistral. Nistral was taller, with a powerful build but a slim and tapering waist. He had a beard but no moustache, close-cropped black hair and glistening silver skin. When he smiled he showed a lot of teeth, and his eyes were set low and back in his face. As opposed to the massive Graziunas, Nistral looked like he was built for a hit-and-run type of battle.

Now, why was she thinking of battles, Guinan wondered.

Nistral's clothing was a complex intertwining of black and silver threads that almost seemed to shift, depending upon the angle you looked at him from.

The wives of each of the men, on the other hand, seemed studiously generic, as if they'd been produced by a cookie cutter. Both women were tall and aristocratic-looking, and perhaps the Nistral woman was slightly shorter than the Graziunas, but that was about it. Most of it was in the clothing, Guinan felt. They wore simple gowns that were, naturally, tailored in their respective colors, and close-drawn hoods covered their heads, giving no indication of their hair color or even if they had any hair. It seemed as if the women had gone out of their way to obscure whatever natural assets they might have.

"I had assumed that you would wish to use this facility for the reception," Picard said.

Nistral—who, like Graziunas, was known only by the name of his house—slowly turned in place, as if taking in the entire room. "It will suffice," he said simply.

The wife of Graziunas was looking around as well. "It seems a bit spare, to be honest," she said, and it was clear she was trying to hide her distaste.

Guinan glanced around. She wasn't entirely sure she was taken with the woman's tone of voice, but her unflappable manners prevented her from making the response that came immediately to mind.

Picard, for his part, smiled tightly and said, "The Ten-Forward lounge has always served our needs more than adequately. And we have always felt, in Starfleet, that less is more."

The wife of Nistral was also gazing around. "In that case, this lounge is positively excessive."

Now it was Picard's turn to bite off a reply. In response to the woman's remark, however, Nistral laughed loudly. "What snobs we're becoming, eh, Dai?" he said to the woman, giving Guinan the first indication that she had a name other than "Mrs. Nistral." "So caught up in our own tendency to decorate every inch of space with our latest acquisitions that we've forgotten simple elegance can be as strong a statement. My apologies, Captain, and to you, Guinan. We'd be honored if you'd share the Ten-Forward with a group of ungrateful Tizarin."

"My pleasure," said Guinan, nodding graciously.

Graziunas was moving about the room, taking wide strides with his feet no less than four feet apart, even when he was standing still. His massive cape swept about him, almost knocking a glass to the floor, but an alert Guinan scooped it up just as it started to fall. "I don't see what your problem was!" he said. "I liked it from the moment I walked in. You're too obsessed with opulence, Nistral! Isn't he, Fenn?" he said, turning to address his own mate.

Nistral smiled thinly. "I've already admitted as much, Graziunas. I think it's time we moved on in the conversation, don't you?" His voice was low and calm, whereas Graziunas seemed to bellow everything with a boisterous frivolity.

"How long do you see requiring Ten-Forward for?" asked Guinan, also eager to move on. "How long will the party last?"

"A week," said Nistral briskly.

Together, Picard and Guinan said, "A *week?*"

"Of course a week!" declared Graziunas. "When the firstborn child of a house head weds, a week of celebration and festivities at the place of the wedding is mandated custom! Are you saying that our children are not worthy of that?"

"No, no, not at all," said Picard. "It's just that a week . . ."

"We don't have to keep it entirely in here, Captain," said Graziunas' spouse, Fenn. Her hands fluttered as she said, "We can certainly use the entire ship to . . ."

"No!" said Picard, a bit more loudly than he would have liked. Ever the diplomat, he composed himself immediately. "We will set aside a portion of the ship—"

"A large portion!" boomed Graziunas.

"A *portion,*" said Picard firmly, with a tone of voice that indicated he was not going to lose control of the situation. "We will be as cooperative as humanly possible, and put our ship at your disposal, but there must be limits, gentlemen and ladies. I'm sure—as ruling heads—you understand the need for it."

"Of course," said Nistral neutrally.

Graziunas shrugged his massive shoulders. "It's your ship, Captain."

"Yes," said Picard in no uncertain terms. "It is. We have a level of discipline and order that must be maintained. I welcome the idea of a celebration, especially for something as joyous as a wedding. But I cannot tolerate disruption of my ship or her crew. We are all quite clear on this point?"

There were quick nods from all concerned.

"I like you, Picard!" declared Graziunas. "A man who speaks his mind and takes a stand. The kind of man who demands respect and gets it."

"Thank you," said Picard.

Graziunas dropped down to a table and propped up his meaty hand. "Would you care to arm wrestle?"

Picard was rescued from the situation by Fenn, who in irritation slapped her husband on the shoulder. "Stop that," she snapped. "You always do that, no matter how inappropriate the time, and I can't think of a more inappropriate time than this."

He shrugged expansively as if to say *Women* and relaxed his arm. Picard couldn't help but notice that it looked as big as a slab of beef.

"Can we see the bridge?" asked Nistral abruptly. "As a spacegoing society, we are always interested in the design of other ships."

"Of course," said Picard, and they started to head to the door.

He stopped, though, when Guinan said, "Captain, a moment of your time, please?"

He smiled at the Tizarin and made a small, just-a-minute gesture, and went over to Guinan. "Yes?" he said softly, in a voice just low enough that they couldn't hear.

"Something's up," said Guinan uncomfortably.

"Up?"

"I don't know what it is," she told him. "That bothers me. Just a funny feeling that something's going to happen."

"But nothing specific." Picard was all business. If there was one thing he had learned, it was to trust Guinan's hunches.

"No, nothing specific."

"Do you think it's necessary to cancel the wedding?"

It was a display of his confidence in her. On her

say-so, he would scrap the entire affair, and even though Starfleet would raise all hell about it, he would unflinchingly take the heat.

She couldn't abuse that trust, especially when she wasn't precisely sure what was making her feel this way.

"It'll be fine," she said with a confidence she didn't entirely feel. "I'll just keep alert, and if I can lock it down, I'll let you know immediately."

He nodded curtly. Then he reapplied his best diplomatic smile, turned, and faced the members of the Tizarin.

"Now, then, you wanted to see the bridge . . ."

Kerin and Sehra stood on the observation deck of the Nistral ship, gazing at the glistening, majestic starship that hung next to them. The Nistral ship was half again as large as the *Enterprise,* but nevertheless the young people found the *Enterprise* to be most impressive.

"You nervous?" said Sehra, holding his hand. Her fingers were interlaced with his.

"Not at all," he replied, but he squeezed her hand with a firmness that seemed to indicate, if nothing else, a certain degree of anxiety. "How about you?"

She returned the grip. "Not in the least."

"When do we go aboard?" he asked.

She shrugged. "Tomorrow, I think. By that time, the last of the Federation guests will have shown up, and then the celebration can begin."

"A week," he said softly, wistfully. "An entire week. Gods. Now that we've committed to each other . . . it seems like an eternity. An eternity to wait."

"To wait for marriage?" she asked.

"For . . . everything," he replied. He smiled ruefully. "But I'll wait. As my father waited, and your father, and theirs before them . . ."

"Yes, you're right," she said. "I mean, everything has to wait for a week . . ." She paused significantly. "Doesn't it?"

He looked at her as if seeing her for the first time. "Doesn't it?"

"Well . . ." She paused thoughtfully. "We are to be married. That's definite. Nothing can change that."

"Nothing," he agreed readily.

"So if we didn't wait for . . . everything . . . maybe it wouldn't be so bad."

He paused. "Are we talking about the same thing?"

One of her fingers rubbed the inside of his palm, and he trembled. For some reason there was a pounding in his head that resounded throughout his body.

"I think so," she said softly.

"But it's not right. It's not proper. It's not tradition. What would our parents say?"

"They're on the *Enterprise*. Who's going to tell them?"

"Right. Let's go." He bolted towards his room, almost yanking her arm from the socket as he ran. She dashed after him, trying to keep up with him and with her hand, which was firmly in his, and she laughed with a joyous laugh that was like a bell.


Picard always took pride in his ship, but rarely more so than when people who were truly knowledgeable in the ways of space vessels look the *Enterprise* over with nods of approval. And who could be more knowledgeable than people who have lived, from birth, in the airless byways of space?

Graziunas and Nistral walked around, nodding briskly, running their fingers over the consoles and studying the displays. Their wives stood by impassively. Deanna Troi watched them with interest.

"Impressive," said Nistral at length. "Most impressive."

He turned just in time to see Data walk out of the turbolift, and he gasped in surprise. "Gods!" he said.

Data stopped, his head slightly cocked with curiosity. Graziunas, anticipating some problem, spun in his place and blinked. "I'll be damned," he exclaimed. "If I didn't know better . . ."

"Some problem, gentlemen?" asked Picard.

"This man is a Tizarin?" said Nistral uncertainly. "Of the house of Shinbum?"

"No, sir," Data politely informed him. "I am an android. Data. Of the *Enterprise.*"

"Remarkable resemblance. Especially the gold skin—a sure sign," said Nistral.

"That was the choice of my creator," said Data.

Graziunas nodded. "So it was with us all."

The Tizarin looked around a bit more, asking questions to satisfy their curiosity, and then took their leave of the bridge to return to their ships. As soon as they had departed, Picard turned to Deanna Troi and said, "Counselor . . . did you get any impression from them?"

"There is a continuing undercurrent of antagonism, Captain, between the Graziunas and the Nistral. It is well hidden and kept in check, however, by their determination to honor the wishes and potential happiness of their children. They have clearly resolved to make the best of the situation, and perhaps even welcome the excuse to put their long rivalry behind them."

Picard nodded. "Excellent. Most excellent. Putting their children's concerns before their own. Most definitely not, Mr. Data, a *Romeo and Juliet* situation."

"That is fortunate, Captain," said Data neutrally. "A mutual suicide on the part of the bride and groom would not be conducive to merrymaking."

"I could not agree more."

Worf suddenly looked up. "Captain—we are receiving an incoming transmission from another arriving wedding guest."

Picard mentally ran down the list of various representatives who had already shown up. He had a feeling he knew who was left.

"Put it on audio, Lieutenant," said Picard.

A moment later, a low chime sounded within the bridge. "This is the *Enterprise,*" Picard said briskly, deciding to put forward as much of a businesslike demeanor as possible, as early on as possible.

A stern male voice said, *"Enterprise,* this is the *Ambassador Shuttle* from Betazed. Prepare to transport over the delegate from Betazed . . ."

The pilot's voice hesitated momentarily as they heard a familiar whisper filtering over. When he came back on, it was with a heavy sigh that indicated he was being prompted.

"A daughter of the fifth house . . ."

"We'll bring her aboard," said Picard briskly. "Bridge to transporter."

"Holder of the Sacred Chalice of Riix," the pilot was continuing, sounding as if he'd just as soon pilot the ship into a star and be done with it.

"Chief O'Brien, prepare to transport over the representative from Betazed." Remembering the cadaverous, perpetually silent Mr. Homn, who always hovered within a few steps of Mrs. Troi, Picard added, "and her retainer."

"Heir to the Holy Rings of Betazed." The pilot sounded at his wits' end. There was desperation in his voice as he said, *"Enterprise,* I've fed you the coordinates. What's the delay?"

"Mr. O'Brien, beam them aboard. We'll be down momentarily. Make my apologies to Mrs. Troi for the delay."

"Yes sir," said O'Brien, who didn't sound especially thrilled.

A moment passed, and then the pilot's voice said, with overwhelming relief, *"Enterprise, they're gone. You've got them or don't, I don't care."*

Picard glanced at Deanna Troi, who was endeavoring to cover her chagrin and not totally succeeding. "Was there difficulty, Betazed pilot?"

"First off, I'm not Betazoid, I'm Rigellian," came the pilot's voice. "I just run a ferry service, specializing in transporting diplomats. But that's the last time I take that woman. I sympathize about her being in mourning, but she never shut up about it the whole trip . . ."

"Mourning!" Deanna's dark eyes widened.

Picard turned to Deanna. "Has there been a death in your family, Counselor?"

"Not to my knowledge, Captain," said Deanna, getting quickly to her feet. Her green skirt swished around her long legs. Right behind her was Riker.

Picard's glance skimmed the bridge crew. "Mr. Data, you come with us too."

Data obediently got to his feet as Picard said, "Pilot—might I ask for whom she was in mourning?"

And Deanna Troi came to a halt as the pilot's voice came over the speaker.

"Yeah," said the pilot. "She's in mourning for her daughter."

# Chapter Five

"Son?"

Kerin jumped a couple of feet in the air when he heard his father's voice. He had been leaning against a corridor wall on board the Nistral ship, totally lost in thought. "Yes, father!" he said quickly.

Nistral looked down at his son. "Something on your mind, Kerin?"

"No, sir."

"How's Sehra?"

For a moment a dreamy expression passed over his face as he said, "Great." Then he quickly composed himself and cleared his throat. "She's . . . uhm, she's fine, father. She was here earlier. But she's gone now. She went back to the ship of Graziunas."

The head of the house of Nistral started to walk down the corridor, his son obediently falling into step alongside him. Nistral studied his son thoughtfully. "And what," he asked slowly, "did you do together while she was here?"

He wanted to boast. He wanted to shout. He wanted to . . .

"Nothing, father. Just . . . talked," said Kerin.

Nistral raised an eyebrow. "Indeed."

"Yes, father. Just . . . talked."

"Your mother and I . . . we also just talked, shortly before our wedding."

"I'm sure you did, father."

"We had some very . . . intimate conversations," his father said.

He said it with enough significance and meaning that it managed to penetrate even the romantic haze that had covered Kerin's brain. He looked up at his father—really looked—for the first time since the conversation had started.

"How intimate?" asked Kerin.

Nistral stopped in front of his chambers. The doors hissed open as he said, "Where do you think you came from, Kerin?"

Kerin's mouth moved but no sound came out.

"I certainly hope you were more cautious," his father said dryly and disappeared into his room.

Kerin leaned against a wall. "Me too," he said.


Picard, Troi, Data, and Riker hurried toward the transporter room where Lwaxana Troi awaited in all her opulence. It was clear from Deanna's expression that her mind was whirling, trying to sort out what the Rigellian pilot had told them.

Picard empathized with her. There was something about the presence of one's parents—the ones who nursed you through sickness, who wiped your nose and your bottom—that caused all the childhood traumas and insecurities to come racing back to you, no matter how accomplished and secure you were. Probably, he reasoned, because parents know where all the skeletons are buried, and one never knew when a parent would unearth that skeleton for the purpose of taking one down a peg.

Suddenly an image of Lwaxana Troi endeavoring to change diapers flashed into his mind. Not likely.

He did not ask Deanna any further about the mourning reference on the assumption that if she knew, she would tell him.

Riker, on the other hand, didn't hesitate. "Deanna, you don't have a sister, do you?" he was asking in confusion. Troi had the shortest stride of any of them, and yet she was a good four paces ahead of them.

"Not that I know of," she was saying. "I don't understand. In mourning, for her daughter. Could she think I'm dead? What could have happened? How could she—?"

Then her voice trailed off and she slowed down. In an instant the hurrying officers had gone right past her. They stopped, looking at her in confusion.

"Counselor—?" Picard prompted.

"I think I know what it is," said Deanna. "I'll tell you, but . . ."

"But what?" said Riker, concern etched on his face.

She looked up at him with those luminous eyes. The road not taken.

"You have to promise," she said, "not to laugh."

O'Brien's fingers strayed over the transporter controls. He was running the possibilities through his mind. Could the beams be reset, he wondered, so that they would transport someone not from the platform, but instead from a location, say, precisely five feet in front of him? Yes, certainly they could. And then be made to rematerialize somewhere else in the ship? Like at the farthest possible point from the transporter room.

As these thoughts ran through his head, Lwaxana

Troi stood precisely five feet in front of him, expressing her distaste for being kept waiting.

She was dressed entirely in black, although her dress was covered with elaborate spangles that gave it a shimmering, undulating appearance. The one dash of color was a circle of blazing red, an amulet that was positioned directly above her heart.

Her luggage was at her feet. O'Brien looked at it nervously. Lwaxana Troi's luggage was legendary. One might even say . . . feared. No one had ever seen what she packed in it. The consensus was that it was anvils.

Near her was the looming form of Mr. Homn. O'Brien couldn't remember Homn ever having said anything. Perhaps he simply couldn't get a word in. Perhaps he felt it better just to maintain silence and, in so doing, draw as little attention to himself as possible. For whatever reason, he was simply there, ever present, ever patient.

"A true hardship," Lwaxana was saying, "that at a time when I am undergoing this personal tragedy, I must still put on a pleasant face in representing my people at a joyous occasion. But I do not shirk my duties, or cringe from my responsibilities. That was not how I was brought up, and that's not how I brought up my daughter . . . the gods bless her soul."

O'Brien, against his better judgment, cocked his head slightly and said, "Something wrong with your daughter?"

The transporter room doors hissed open, the sound neatly covering O'Brien's own sigh of relief. Deanna Troi entered first and stopped a couple of feet short of her mother. Her hands were on her hips and she was regarding Mrs. Troi with a look of stern annoyance.

"Mother," she said in a reproving tone.

If Lwaxana Troi took notice of it, she gave no sign.

Instead she extended her hands to Deanna and spoke in a voice laced with grief. "My little one . . . I'm so sorry."

Deanna sighed mightily and took the extended hands. "We will discuss this later," she said firmly.

"I imagine we will. Jean-Luc!" she said cheerfully, brimming with anticipation. "As handsome as ever."

Picard raised an eyebrow. For a woman in mourning, she was certainly capable of turning it on and off. Here was someone who was in consummate control of herself, which is why the business with phase was so disconcerting.

"Mrs. Troi," he said, bowing his head slightly. "I extend my sympathies in your time of grief."

Deanna shot her captain a look, which he caught, but he shrugged slightly. Counselor Troi had explained precisely what was on her mother's mind, but nonetheless, protocol required Picard making some indication of empathy—no matter how much he might disagree with the state of mind of the . . . mourner.

"Thank you, Jean-Luc. I knew that *you*," she said, glancing significantly at her daughter, "would understand."

"You remember Commander Riker," said Picard, "and Commander Data."

She barely gave Data a glance, but she looked Riker up and down. "Commander," she said. "You're looking fit."

"Thank you, ma'am," he said.

"Oh, please, not 'ma'am,'" she protested. "'Ma'am' makes me feel positively old. Do you think I'm old?"

"Yes," said Data briskly.

They all looked at Data who, utterly unaware that he was supposed to lie in order to spare feelings,

50

continued, "In comparison to the average Betazoid life span, you are—"

"Exhausted!" said Picard, stepping in. "You and Mr. Homn— Oh, good day, Mr. Homn." He had momentarily forgotten the manservant's presence. It was remarkable how someone so huge could seem simply to fade into the background. "You look exhausted. Let us show you to your quarters."

"Excellent idea, Captain," said Lwaxana Troi, still looking daggers at Data. Data, for his part, remained serenely oblivious.

Mr. Homn bent to take her bags, but Lwaxana immediately put a hand up. "Now, Mr. Homn," she scolded, "we are guests on this ship, and as I know from experience, the captain wouldn't dream of allowing guests to carry their own luggage."

"Want me to transport it to their quarters, sir?" said O'Brien.

Picard glanced at his transporter chief. From the look in O'Brien's eyes, Picard had the distinct impression that O'Brien might "accidentally" materialize the luggage in orbit somewhere.

"Not necessary, Mr. O'Brien," said Picard with relaxed pleasantness, because he had anticipated this. "Mr. Data, if you wouldn't mind . . ."

"Not at all, Captain."

Data stooped and easily hefted all the luggage. "Is there any more?" he asked politely.

Lwaxana shook her head in amazement. She knew that Data was an android, but nevertheless, his build was so unassuming that it had never occurred to her just how strong he might be.

Picard smiled inwardly. The only other person who could have so easily handled Lwaxana Troi's formidable wardrobe was Worf. Somehow he couldn't see asking the Klingon to carry Mrs. Troi's luggage.

Picard did not doubt for a moment Worf's loyalty or dependability. By the same token, it was madness to tempt fate.

The first time he'd encountered Mrs. Troi, he had graciously offered to tote her bags and almost thrown his back out as a result. The second time, Riker did the honors, and Picard had never heard his first officer grunt in quite that way. This time, Picard was prepared.

As usually happened when Deanna's mother showed up, it appeared that a chesslike battle of wits was about to begin on the *Enterprise.* In a perverse sort of way, Picard almost welcomed it. It was stimulating to try and keep one step ahead of the formidable Lwaxana Troi.

By the same token, he could have done without the effort, and certainly hoped that nothing else would arise to further distract him from the pleasant business of uniting two young people.

Deanna barely waited until Riker, Picard, and Data had left her mother's guest quarters before she turned towards Lwaxana, her slim body shaking with barely contained fury. "Mother," she began dangerously.

Lwaxana barely seemed to be paying attention as Mr. Homn began to unpack for her. "Now, what for the first reception?" she wondered out loud. "The black with the green stripe or the black with the red stripe?"

Deanna walked around to face her mother. "This is intolerable."

Now Lwaxana looked at her, a mixture of bemusement and tragedy in those large eyes that were so like her daughter's. *I am sorry you're so upset, Little One,* her mother thought at her.

"Stop calling me 'Little One'!" said Deanna fiercely. "You owe me an explanation!"

*I didn't quite hear you.*

Deanna blew air through thinned lips. *You owe me an explanation,* she projected to her mother.

Lwaxana gave a small smile. "So you can still send. Just wanted to make sure."

"You wanted to quiet me down," Deanna told her.

"Whatever. Now, Lit—Deanna—you have to understand, my hands are tied. There's nothing I can do. Tradition is tradition."

"It's a tradition," Deanna said, sitting down nearby, trying to compose herself, "that hasn't been really in use for two centuries. It's provincial, even archaic."

"I have certain responsibilities, my dear," Lwaxana informed her haughtily. "Perhaps others can ignore the Ab'brax, and heaven knows I would if I could. But being a daughter of the fifth house carries with it tremendous responsibilities. And one of those responsibilities is to uphold all the traditions of Betazed."

"No matter how ridiculous, or how embarrassing. Mother, the Ab'brax . . . !"

Lwaxana shrugged. "Take it as seriously or frivolously as you wish, Deanna."

"How am I supposed to take something where you're telling total strangers that you're in mourning for me!" Deanna said in exasperation.

"I can tell all your associates as well, if it will make you feel more comfortable."

Deanna brought her palms together, fingers steepled, to try to compose herself. "What will make me feel comfortable," she said, "is if you stop acting as if I'm dead!"

"Not dead in the physical sense, Little One!" said Lwaxana consolingly. She gently stroked Deanna's cheek. "Just dead in the hope that you will contribute to the propagation of our people, and to the hope that you will ever find a mate to share the rest of your life."

"Oh, that's all."

"Why, yes. That's not so terrible, is it?"

Deanna sighed and leaned back, softly thudding her head against the wall. "I don't believe this."

"You had your opportunity," Lwaxana said with a shrug. "Several opportunities. I found you a mate, but that didn't work out . . ."

"Are you blaming me for that?"

"No one's to blame, precious. These things happen. Then, of course, there's that lovely Commander Riker." Her lips twitched in amusement. "He still wants you, you know. Would give his left eye to have you. I can read him clear as glass."

Deanna thudded her head a couple more times. "You're still in phase, aren't you," referring to a time during which older Betazoid women's sex drive is quadrupled, or more.

"It's in remission," said Lwaxana blithely. "My abilities to read minds are as sharp as they ever were."

"Yes, that's what I thought," said Deanna ruefully. "Mother, the Ab'brax was from a time when life spans were shorter, and when a woman's niche in society was to be married, have children, and tend house. So if you weren't married by a certain age, it was anticipated that you would never marry and the family would go into mourning . . ."

"Precisely," said Lwaxana.

". . . generally in order to raise such a fuss that people would be forced to realize that someone the family was eager to marry off was in the house. This would, in theory, attract someone who needed a good wife in the same way that he needed a good farm animal, and he knew that the family would not protest overmuch."

Lwaxana gave a shrug of her elegant shoulders. "That's one interpretation."

She got up and stood before her mother, trying to be as calm as she could. In a way, the anger that she had initially felt was now mutating into a dim amusement. "Mother, I'm living a full and happy life. I have opportunities that women of centuries ago didn't have. You have those same opportunities. Why are you saddling yourself with this artificial bereavement? It's a pointless tradition."

"My dear," said Lwaxana archly, "anyone can uphold traditions that have meaning. Upholding the pointless traditions—that, Deanna, takes style."

Deanna shook her head, and her mother patted her on the shoulder with genuine affection. "Oh, my darling, I just hate to think of you going through life unfulfilled."

"I *am* fulfilled, mother."

"Lonely, then." Lwaxana sighed. "No one should have to spend their life by themselves, without the comfort of a loved one beside them. No one to share their achievements with, the high points and low points. When I think of you, day after day, in this sterile environment—alone, unmated, chaste—"

Deanna coughed politely.

Her mother continued, "I become as depressed as when I . . ."

Surprisingly, her voice trailed off. Deanna looked at her mother with curiosity. "As when *what,* mother?"

"Nothing."

But Deanna had caught the stray thought from her mother and she said softly, ". . . as when you think of yourself?"

Lwaxana glanced at her from under shaded lids. "I am perfectly fine, Little One. At least I had my opportunity with your father, and those pleasant memories are more than enough to sustain me during my long, empty nights. Nights where my own body and mind are haunting me to find a new husband, and I still can't . . ."

She actually seemed to choke on the words for a

moment, and then she immediately pulled herself together. She drew herself up and said confidently, "So . . . which do you think?" and she pointed at the two dresses she'd been considering.

Deanna brushed both of them aside and picked up a dress that was a dazzling combination of colors, like an aurora borealis. "How about this one?"

Mrs. Troi shook her head. "Now, how did that one get in there? Mr. Homn," she said scoldingly, "what's that one doing there?"

Mr. Homn tilted his head slightly.

"Oh, of course," she said. "To wear on the actual festive day, since it would be considered the height of bad taste to be in mourning garb at a wedding. Bad luck and all that. I'm sorry, daughter. I appreciate your feelings, but tradition, I'm afraid, is tradition. Even . . ."

"Pointless tradition," they said together. Deanna gave a small chuckle and consoled herself that at least she was starting to be able to laugh about it. "All right, mother—the black with red, then. It's more festive." She stood. "I have things to attend to before the reception."

"Then by all means, don't let me stop you, Deanna."

Deanna turned and was almost to the door, when a voice in her head said, *Little One, aren't you afraid of growing old alone?*

Deanna paused for a moment and then thought back, *No, because I'll always have myself.*

Mrs. Troi sighed. *I envy you.*

She turned back to her mother, but Mrs. Troi was already busy bustling about the cabin, and Deanna didn't need to be empathic to realize that her mother considered the discussion closed.

Deanna walked out but couldn't help but consider the fact that no matter how much children seemed to object to their parents, somehow, when they grew up, they wound up turning into their parents. Despite her blithe confidence in her completeness, was Deanna really looking at herself in the future? Lonely? Depressed? Regretting directions in her life, and the possible solitude of old age?

Would she be in the service forever? Would she be who she was forever? Now, now she was young, attractive, vibrant. She had her choice of men, if she so desired, or none if she desired. But eventually her looks would fade. The vibrancy would leave her. Her hair would gray and then whiten, her limbs become heavy with age, the sparkle and vitality leave her eyes.

She touched her face, imagining wrinkles creasing the soft skin.

"Deanna?"

She jumped slightly and turned. Riker was directly behind her.

He smiled the handsome, confident smile of the young. "Is something wrong?"

She went to him and embraced him so hard he thought she was going to crack a couple of his ribs.

"There's definitely something going around," he muttered.

# *Chapter Six*

THE TEN-FORWARD LOUNGE was crowded to bursting and, with the glitter of the different skinned races side by side, did not look too dissimilar to a Christmas tree.

Picard moved through the throngs, smiling and tilting his head slightly in acknowledgment as various Tizarin, or their guests, expressed their approval of the festivities or the good ship *Enterprise* herself. He thought he saw Riker for a moment on the far side of the lounge, but then his first officer vanished in another wave of partygoers.

Music filled the air, mingling with the voices of everyone around. The music was provided by a group of junior officers who, several months ago, had discovered a mutual proficiency for horns and had formed a group calling themselves the Federation Horns. At the moment, they were playing some sort of fast-paced tune that Picard vaguely recognized as swing. Picard's personal taste leaned more towards classical, although there were those—Commander Riker among them—who would argue that swing was every bit as classical as Mozart.

He bumped into Graziunas, literally. More precisely, Graziunas bumped into him, and only a quick maneuver by Picard prevented the captain from spilling his own drink.

"Sorry, Picard!" boomed Graziunas. He was shouting to be heard above the music, but it wasn't very difficult for him. His normal speaking voice was practically a bellow. "Crowded here!"

"Yes, I know," Picard replied.

"What?!"

"I said, *Yes, I know,*" Picard shouted, disliking having to shout but not seeing any other way out of it. "Perhaps we should have had this celebration in a larger area."

"Oh, no!" protested Graziunas. "No, this is perfect! This is ideal!" He laughed and pointed. "Look at them, Picard!"

Picard turned and followed where Graziunas was indicating. There were Kerin and Sehra, seated opposite each other at a table, holding hands and gazing dreamily at each other.

"Amazing," said Graziunas. "For all they're aware of the rest of the world, this room could be empty! The joyful blindness of youth, eh, Picard? Remember it?"

"I was never young," said Picard with a hint of a smile. "I was always as you see me now."

Graziunas laughed boisterously at that and clapped Picard on the back. The captain staggered slightly and hoped that the bear of a man hadn't dislocated his shoulder.

"Monopolizing the father of the bride? Shame, shame, Jean-Luc."

Picard glanced around to see Lwaxana Troi standing uncomfortably close to him. She had every reason to, of course. The music was sufficiently loud that no one could hear anything if they were more than a foot apart. What made Picard edgy was what else might be motivating her. Nevertheless, he smiled and said, "My pardon, Mrs. Troi. Graziunas," he said quickly, "do you know—?"

Graziunas took her hands and smiled broadly. "Who could forget the holder of the Sacred Chalice of Betazed! Lwaxana, how are you, my dear?" He graciously took her hand and raised her knuckles up to tap them lightly against his forehead. "You are never far from my thoughts."

"Graziunas, you old flirt, you," replied Lwaxana, allowing him to retain her hand. "You'll make Jean-Luc jealous."

Graziunas looked from one to the other. "Captain! Are you and the exquisite Lwaxana—?"

"Oh, just friends," said Picard quickly. "Just friends."

"Close friends," said Lwaxana Troi, "with a certain . . . understanding. Isn't that a fair assessment, Jean-Luc?"

Picard, trying to find some gracious way out of the situation, was abruptly given a reprieve. The lights throughout the Ten-Forward lounge flickered, and there was an odd sound, as if there had been a temporary power drain. Everyone looked around in a vague, but not terribly alarmed, manner. They were all too much the space veterans to become especially upset over a power surge. The Federation Horns, in fact, did not miss a note.

Nevertheless, Picard seized the opportunity, especially when Lwaxana said in confusion, "Now, what caused that, I wonder?"

The lights went back to normal, but Picard wasn't about to let that be an excuse. "I will definitely find out," he said. "In fact, I see my chief engineer over there. Yes, I must check into this. You'll excuse me. Duty calls."

"But, Captain," began Mrs. Troi.

He put up a hand. "I'm sorry. I cannot stand about and enjoy myself when there's the slightest hint of a problem." He turned quickly and started to make his way towards La Forge, who had sought safe haven near one of the viewing ports.

"Now, there is one dedicated man," said Graziunas approvingly.

Lwaxana frowned. "Yes," she said, not entirely able to hide the sourness in her voice. "He's dedicated enough to be three dedicated men."

Behind the bar, Guinan's eyes went wide. The lights had just gone back to normal—it had been so minor a flickering that under ordinary circumstances, it wasn't cause for the slightest concern.

But Guinan knew, knew immediately. She looked around quickly, trying to pick *him* out in the crowd. Damn *him*. Where was *he?* Maybe *he* hadn't even materialized in the crowd, but instead, just outside Ten-Forward, and *he* had just entered . . .

Her head snapped around in time to see the doors hiss shut. Someone had indeed entered, but it was so mobbed that she couldn't see where *he* was.

"Captain!" she called out, but there was so much noise that she couldn't make herself heard. She didn't wear a communicator, so she couldn't get his attention that way. She could have shouted at the top of her lungs, but she didn't want to do anything that might result in general alarm or even, God forbid, a panic. There were too many people in Ten-Forward, way too many people.

She glanced around and saw Picard on the other

side of the room, getting farther away by the second. He definitely was on the move, and his target seemed to be Geordi La Forge.

Guinan took a deep breath and started to push her way through the crowd, all the while looking around with barely controlled desperation, trying to pick out the being that she knew was there.

Geordi glanced around as Picard walked up to him. "I don't do well in crowds, Captain," said Geordi, feeling the need to explain. "All the images, and keeping them sorted . . . gives me a headache."

"Quite all right, Mr. La Forge. To be honest, you gave me a much-needed excuse. Those lights flickering before . . ."

Geordi gestured towards his communicator. "The moment it happened, I called down to the engine room. They're running a systems check now."

"Any idea what caused it?"

"A mild energy flux like that?" Geordi shrugged. "Could be any one of a dozen things, all of which are purely routine. Still, it's the kind of thing we should be preventing through standard diagnostics checks. I'll make sure my men stay on top of it."

"Yes, see that you do. However," Picard smiled thinly, "if it had to happen, at least it happened when I needed a break from—"

"Mrs. Troi!" said Geordi quickly in a very hearty, greeting-sounding voice.

Picard turned, immediately understanding the clear warning of his engineer. "Lwaxana," he said, as Mrs. Troi swept up to him.

"Graziunas found someone else to talk to," said Lwaxana. "And although I know most of the people here, frankly, I can't think of anyone else I would rather speak with, Jean-Luc. We have so much to catch up on." She idly dabbed her little finger in her drink and swirled the liquid. "So much to discuss. We really never . . . connected . . . the last time I was here."

La Forge was watching the ebbing and flowing of body heat and color that his VISOR was sending him. The captain was clearly disconcerted. It was fascinating to watch, since the last time he'd seen the captain this way was . . . well, when Lwaxana Troi had made her last visit.

It was fascinating. It was as if Lwaxana was sending out some sort of waves to Picard, and Picard was doing his level best to ignore them.

Picard heard a burst of laughter carrying over the voices of the other revellers, and even above the music. It was Graziunas, all right, and the voice of Nistral was joined in it. Both men were laughing as if they had heard some sort of tremendously funny joke.

They sounded so boisterous that even Kerin and Sehra looked up for a moment, and then they smiled and went back to gazing at each other.

"Sounds like the fathers of the bride and groom are having a good time," observed Geordi.

"Counselor Troi says that they have some innate hostility towards each other that they're trying to sublimate," Picard said, gazing out over the crowd. He noticed the people reacting with annoyance about something, as if somebody were shoving at them. He raised an eyebrow. He certainly hoped it was none of his people. He counted on them for better behavior than that.

"Sounds to me like they're doing a pretty good job of sublimating it," Geordi said.

The men laughed raucously again. "Whatever is keeping them happy," said Picard, "I only hope it keeps going. We have a week of ceremonies and such, and the last thing we'd need is for the fathers to suddenly remember that they dislike each other."

Then his voice hardened in annoyance as he saw more people shoved out of the way by someone in the crowd. "Who the devil is that?"

And then he was astounded to see Guinan push her way out, getting more nasty glances from others in the crowd. "Some hostess," one person muttered. Guinan ignored it and went straight to Picard.

The thought of scolding Guinan for her behavior never even crossed Picard's mind. He would have staked his life on her manners.

"What's wrong, Guinan?" he said immediately.

She wasted no time on preamble. *"He's* here," she said in a low, intense voice.

Picard frowned for a moment, not able to understand . . . and then he did. With startling clarity, he knew exactly who and what she was referring to. Mostly it was her reaction. He had never seen Guinan respond to anyone else in the galaxy the way in which she was now.

She was . . . tense.

No one, and nothing, made Guinan tense, except for one being.

*"Merde,"* said Picard. "Deep *merde."*

"What's wrong?" said Geordi. All he knew, from the way that the captain's thermal readings had reacted, was that something was seriously wrong.

"Jean-Luc? You're upset," said Mrs. Troi with authority. She didn't sound like someone expressing concern, but rather a doctor making a diagnosis.

"Nothing to concern yourself over, Lwaxana," said Picard, making the faintest attempt to cover. He turned back to Guinan. "Where—?"

"You're concerned over a letter of the alphabet?" said Lwaxana.

Picard flinched as if struck. He could not believe he'd forgotten with whom he was dealing.

He turned and faced Lwaxana and, in a command

tone of voice that he had never taken with her, said, "This is not the time for mind reading."

"You think powerful thoughts," she replied with amusement. "If you're knocked over by a powerful gust of wind, do you blame the wind or yourself?"

Gently, but firmly, he sat her down in a vacant chair. "Stay here. We're all in terrible danger," he told her in a low, intense voice. "If you read anything from my mind, read my genuine concern for you and for this ship. Stay *here.*"

She nodded indifferently, never taking her eyes from him. "Yes, sir."

He turned back to Guinan. "Where is he?"

"I don't know."

There was even louder laughter from the center of the room, where the two fathers were rocking with mirth.

And then he heard Nistral say, "A cigar in his mouth! Oh, that must have been priceless!"

"Oh, it was," came another voice, as familiar as the sound of nails on chalkboard, and about as soothing.

Without a word, Picard immediately started through the crowd. He toyed with the thought of summoning security, but dismissed it. What in the world could they possibly do, besides get themselves injured or transformed?

The crowd parted for him, since he was the captain, after all. Guinan was right behind him, followed by a still-confused Geordi. Picard heard three men—well, two men and something else—laughing loudly, and then he made it through and stood there facing Graziunas, Nistral, and . . . *him.*

"Oh, Captain!" said Graziunas, pointing. "Your admiral was just regaling us with some stories about your past adventures, although I'm sure they're things you'd rather have kept quiet."

"I know precisely what I'd like kept quiet," said

Picard, and he stabbed a finger. "And what I'd like kept quiet is this . . . person . . . right here!"

"Now, Jean-Luc," said Q, raising a scolding finger. "Temper. You may not respect the individual," and he smiled ingratiatingly, "but you have to respect the uniform."

# Chapter Seven

Deanna Troi and Worf were on the bridge. All had been calm thus far, so although a security team was ready in case they were needed, it had been decided that the presence of security was not needed at this first reception for the Tizarin. Picard had felt that it was imperative to try and set a relaxed atmosphere for the proceedings in order to encourage the air of cooperation and goodwill that was necessary for this gathering. Worf had agreed, albeit with some reluctance. To the Klingon, there was no such thing as too much caution.

Rather than sit in the captain's chair, however, he hovered nearby at the security station, keeping abreast of routine developments through the quadrant via Starfleet communications. He performed this function in much the same way that twentieth-century automobile drivers kept themselves apprised of developing traffic jams. Forewarned is forearmed, and if the Ferengi or any potential troublemakers were to wander into the area, or if anyone had declared war on somebody else, then Worf wanted to be prepared.

Deanna Troi sat in her customary seat on the bridge. She was there for two reasons—first, because she knew that her mother was down at the reception, and she was still uncomfortable enough with this Ab'brax business that she wanted to give her mother some distance. The second was that crowded parties tended to be uncomfortable affairs for her. The barrage of empathic waves could practically be battering to her.

She envied her mother's superior and formidable telepathic abilities. Lwaxana could easily erect powerful screens that shielded her from the thoughts of others. She could pick and choose as she saw fit, since she was a full Betazoid, and a strong one at that. Deanna was half-Betazoid. She had her carefully trained empathic skills, and she could receive from a skilled sender such as her mother. Still, how much more could she accomplish as a counselor if only . . .

*Little One* sounded in her head.

Deanna blinked in surprise. Usually her mother didn't broadcast unless they were face to face. Something must be up. She called upon her rarely used projection talent, and sent back, *What is it, mother?* For the moment she chose to ignore the annoying *Little One.*

*I'm curious, dear. Does the letter Q have any meaning for you?*

Deanna's eyes widened. "Q!"

Worf's head snapped up immediately. His voice dropped a tone lower in register. "Q?" he said cautiously. "Counselor, what are you—?"

*Mother, why did you bring it up?* Deanna demanded.

68

*There's the oddest individual here, and Jean-Luc associated him with that letter . . .*

Deanna immediately got to her feet. "I'll be right down," she said to thin air. "Worf, hurry," and she bolted into the turbolift. Worf had no idea what was going on, but he immediately followed her into the lift. The rest of the bridge crew stared at each other in confusion.

In the turbolift, she said, "Ten-Forward deck," and then turned to Worf as the turbolift started towards its destination. "I believe Q is at the party."

"He picked the wrong one to crash," rumbled Worf, touching his communicator. "Worf to security. Meet me at Ten-Forward. Q is there."

"Why hasn't the captain summoned you?" she asked him.

"Perhaps Q is blocking his transmission. In that event, I do not wish to do anything to warn Q we are coming. That way, we have the element of surprise on our side."

"Somehow, Worf," said Deanna Troi ruefully, "I tend to think Q always possesses the element of surprise, because he is Q."

Worf checked the level of his phaser. "Then I'll borrow it," the Klingon said curtly.

"What are you doing here, Q?" demanded Picard.

Q actually looked hurt at Picard's tone. It was, Picard thought, a splendid bit of acting. "I? Merely enjoying your hospitality, Picard. Am I not entitled?"

"No, you are not," shot back the captain.

Graziunas was looking from Picard to Q and back again. "Captain, is there some problem here?" he asked.

"Yes," said Nistral, also looking confused. "Do tell us. The admiral was being most entertaining . . ."

"He's not an admiral!" said Picard. "He is—"

And Picard thought, *What now? I tell them he's a super being who can accomplish anything with pure thought? Let them know we have a creature who can punt us light years into the middle of Borg space if he's of a mind to, standing here in the middle of this party? Start a complete panic for no purpose?*

He also realized, at that moment, that he had just graciously filled in Lwaxana Troi on the true nature of things, if she was of a mind to have been listening in. He hoped she wasn't.

Without any visible hesitation, Picard said, "He is not welcome on this ship."

The majority of the partygoers were Tizarin, but there were enough *Enterprise* regulars around to spot Q and promptly start to back away. They knew that whatever was going on, it was definitely the captain's ball to run with. Commander Riker, however, immediately pushed his way to Picard's side. The Federation Horns, sensing the abrupt mood switch in the room, slowly lowered their instruments.

"Captain, I beg to differ," said Graziunas.

"Yes, Picard, he begs to differ," Q told him. Picard glared at him, but Q serenely sipped the synthehol from his glass. He glanced at it with a frown and abruptly the clear liquid turned a deep purple. He continued to drink.

"This is a Tizarin celebration," Graziunas continued, unaware of what was happening. "It is Tizarin tradition that all who peaceably attend a wedding celebration must be welcome."

"He is absolutely right," said Nistral, wavering slightly. Clearly he had been drinking a bit too long.

"That may be," said Picard, "but this individual is not welcome aboard this ship."

"We can't ask him to leave," said Graziunas, looking shocked. "That would be a formidably bad omen.

70

Why, we couldn't allow the wedding to proceed if that happened. Everything would be canceled, and the marriage deemed hopeless."

Picard looked from one to the other. "You can't be serious."

"Yes, Captain, quite serious," said Nistral.

"Face it, Picard. I'm back," said Q serenely.

Picard turned to face him, planting his feet firmly. "What do you want, Q?" he demanded.

"Why do you assume I want anything?" Q replied. Suddenly he took a step back as Guinan approached him. She crossed her hands in front of herself, palms upward, as if trying to ward Q off in some bizarre fashion. Q tensed like a cat. "This is no way to welcome a guest, Picard."

"You're no guest here, Q," Picard told him.

"He is if he's attending our gathering," Graziunas stepped in.

Picard turned to face him, a rage burning so hot in him that Graziunas unwillingly took a step back in deference, even though he towered a good two heads over the *Enterprise* captain.

"This is my ship," he said with barely controlled anger. His voice was carrying in the sudden silence, and various partygoers were starting to back up and give this sudden tension some room. "I say who stays and who goes."

Graziunas rallied and drew himself up. "Starfleet says, Captain. And they say we're to be here, and I say that he's supposed to be here."

"Picard," said Q calmly, never removing his eyes from Guinan. "We can settle this amicably."

"Is that a fact?"

"Yes. If you're so certain of your command over this ship, then try and make me leave."

Q displayed a row of teeth and smiled in that incredibly irritating way that he had.

Worf chose that moment to make his entrance, backed up by four security guards. The crowd immediately parted as Worf knifed through them like a shark.

"Worf!" Q greeted him jovially. "Still struggling up the evolutionary ladder?"

Worf stood before him, a snarl emerging from him.

Whereas the argument between Picard and Q was merely drawing a great deal of curiosity and interest from the partygoers, the sound of an angry Klingon, on the other hand, was more than enough to frighten a goodly number of people.

Virtually the only one who was not intimidated was Lwaxana Troi. She watched the entire confrontation unfold with overwhelming interest, and she never took her eyes off Q. Deanna was at her side now, and she took her mother's arm.

"Mother, come quickly," she said. She wasn't quite sure where she was intending to go. The power of the Q knew no boundaries, and there was certainly no place on the ship that she could bring her mother that would be safe. Nevertheless, she felt compelled to try and do *something* to safeguard her mother, even if it was something as trivial as getting her away from ground zero.

Lwaxana didn't budge. Nor did she stop watching Q. "I am fine, Little One. Leave me be."

"Mother, you don't understand the danger—!"

Lwaxana made a dismissive gesture. "I've never run from anything in my life. I'm not the least bit intimidated by the thought of danger."

"But, mother—"

"Hush," said Lwaxana in no uncertain terms.

Picard, in the meantime, was desperately trying to keep a lid on things. He had no idea how Worf had known to come down here, but it was exactly the situation he was hoping to avoid.

"Permission to bounce uninvited guest, Captain," rumbled Worf. His great hands flexed, clearly aching to reach over and throttle Q.

Q, for his part, merely stared disdainfully at Worf. In a loud voice he called out to the others at the party, "You'll have to forgive Worf. He just discovered opposable thumbs and he's feeling overly confident."

Worf took a step towards him.

"Worf!" said Picard.

"Heel," Q told him. He raised a hand up and Picard suddenly had a vision of Worf being hurled to the ground, made to heel and roll over, beg and fetch, and whatever humiliations the all-powerful alien might care to put him through. The loss of face, in front of all those people, would be so devastating that Worf might never recover.

Guinan stepped between them, her eyes blazing. Q's lips drew back in a sneer. Graziunas and Nistral were talking at the same time, protesting this treatment of a guest. Everything was happening much too quickly, and matters were spiralling completely out of control.

*"Enough!"* shouted Picard, his voice cutting through the conflicting chatter from all around and the combative mood of his own people.

There was dead silence. Riker had just shown up from somewhere within the crowd, and now he was standing next to Worf. He had placed a restraining hand on the Klingon's shoulder, and Picard was grateful for that.

"Captain, Tizarin tradition is quite clear," said Graziunas.

"We can discuss Tizarin tradition later," Picard told him. "For now, Q, let's discuss this outside."

Q shrugged extravagantly. "As you wish, Picard."

Picard and Q headed for the door, the crowd parting to let them through. Few people there were entirely sure of what was happening, but they knew better than to try and interfere.

Picard's officers started to follow, but Picard turned and snapped, "Stay here. See to the guests. Number One, try to explain matters to Graziunas and Nistral. Everyone else," and Picard tried to force an amiable smile that wound up looking more like a desperate grin, "enjoy yourselves. This is a party. I merely have to straighten out a small misunderstanding. It will take only a moment." It sounded lame, he knew. Even absurd. But he was trapped in an absurd situation, and he had to say and do *something*.

The doors hissed open, and Q gestured grandly. "After you, Picard," he said in that silkily irritating voice.

Picard had a momentary glimpse of Data about to enter the room. "Captain," began Data.

"Later, Data," said Picard, and he and Q stepped outside . . . the ship.

# Chapter Eight

WESLEY CRUSHER had never screamed at his post before.

He didn't scream this time, really. More like yelped in astonishment.

He had just come on duty. Actually, he wasn't really due to be up on the bridge. But he didn't feel like going to the party, because he had been unable to get a date and he was feeling self-conscious about that. So he figured that he would come up to the bridge and spend some time with Worf and Counselor Troi, but neither of them was there. He found that odd, since neither of them was really a party type. Nevertheless, he shrugged it off, and took his post.

He ran a quick systems check, satisfied himself that everything was in solid working order, and then glanced up at the screen.

Picard was on it.

Wesley practically leaped from his seat, crying out in alarm. Heads snapped around on the bridge in response, and questions of "What's the problem?" "What's wrong?" and such died in throats as they saw what Wesley was looking at.

"Oh, my God," said Lieutenant Clapp. Nearby, Lieutenant Burnside was trying to make sounds, but none were coming out.

Picard was floating dead ahead ... not just floating, but moving, since he was pacing the *Enterprise,* and the starship was proceeding at a leisurely one-half sublight. Leisurely for a starship, that is. There was no record of a human being moving at one-half sublight unassisted, as Picard was doing. Then again, there was no record of a human being surviving for any length of time in airless space with no protective garb, and Picard was doing that too.

"What the hell?" muttered Ensign Chafin, who had stepped in at tactical. "You guys are seeing this too, right?"

A thousand questions leaped into Wesley Crusher's mind. One answer was rung up.

"Q," he said.

Showing remarkable presence of mind, he immediately hit his communicator and said, "Bridge to transporter."

"Transporter," replied the calm voice of O'Brien.

"O'Brien, don't ask, though it sounds crazy. The captain is dead ahead at," he glanced at the forward sweeps, "101 mark 1."

"The *captain?*" said O'Brien incredulously.

"Lock on and beam him back in here."

There was a moment of dead silence.

"O'Brien?"

"Something's wrong," said O'Brien's alarmed voice. "Transporter is totally nonfunctional! I don't understand. Readings are all correct, energy's at the proper levels, but it simply refuses to work. Like there's some sort of short-circuit."

"I was afraid of that," said Wesley. "Work on it." He was barking orders, he realized, to someone who distantly outranked him, but he spoke with such authority that O'Brien's only reply was a simple, "I'll let you know. O'Brien out."

"Bridge to Commander Riker," Wesley now said.

"Riker here," but Riker sounded definitely distracted. Wes had a feeling he knew why. He could hear the sounds of babbling in the background. Riker was clearly in a crowd. "Bridge, can this wait—?"

"It's the captain."

Riker's tone immediately snapped to full attention. "Where is he?"

"Right in front of the ship."

*"What!"*

"He's dead ahead, pacing us at sublight. Commander, would Q by any chance—?"

"Good guess, Mr. Crusher. Riker to trans—"

"I already tried that, Commander," said Crusher with frustrated urgency. "Transporter nonfunctional."

"Great. Riker to shuttle bay. Prepare to launch a shuttlecraft. I'm on my way down. Bridge, keep me informed if anything changes. Riker out."

Other members of the bridge crew were gathering around Wesley, all staring out in total befuddlement. The captain was waving his arms about as if trying to move. He was clearly not in control of the situation.

Wes tapped his communicator. "Bridge to Picard," he said, just to see what would happen. There was no response. He wasn't entirely surprised.

Burnside leaned forward, her long, reddish-orange hair brushing against Wesley's back. "What," she said in stupefaction, "is the captain doing out there?"

* * *

The turbolift shot towards the shuttle bay deck as Riker and Worf turned to Data. "What did you see, Data?" he demanded.

"It happened very quickly," said Data. "I was about to enter the Ten-Forward lounge, when the captain emerged with someone who appeared to be Q. That surmise would seem to be supported by the fact that the captain dematerialized, virtually instantaneously. Q did as well."

"By all rights, the captain should be long dead by the time we get there," said Riker.

"Then Q dies immediately after," said Worf, with more determination than common sense.

"I doubt that will be the case," Data said. "From past behavior, it would appear that Q receives far more enjoyment from subjecting the captain to various difficult situations than could possibly be derived from merely killing him. I suspect that Q is making sure the captain is unharmed."

The turbolift doors opened as Riker said, "Why do I derive little comfort from that?" They bolted towards the shuttle bay.

"Tell me about him."

Deanna Troi stared into her mother's eyes. All around them the party was resuming a subdued, if steady, buzz, as various Tizarin and guests tried to figure out what had just happened, and the handful of crewmen present who knew of Q's history tried to be noncommittal. Fortunately, the sliding doors had blocked from everyone's view the sight of the captain and Q vanishing into thin air.

"About whom?"

"That intriguing-looking gentleman who had Jean-Luc so nervous."

She stared at her mother.

She didn't have to ask.

"You can't be serious," she said to Lwaxana.

Lwaxana laughed lightly. "Can't a woman even ask a simple question?"

"There are no simple questions when it comes to that . . . person. Mother," said Deanna firmly, "do not think it. Do not contemplate it. Do not toy with it in your wildest imaginings."

Lwaxana Troi patted her daughter's face in a screamingly patronizing fashion. "Don't worry about me, Little One. I can handle myself. Mister La Forge!" she called out and moved off to try and pump Geordi for information.

Deanna stood, quietly fuming.

Guinan stepped up to her. "Deanna—?"

"Don't call me 'Little One'!" Troi practically exploded, and she stormed away from Guinan.

The Ten-Forward hostess, who was still preoccupied with Q, merely shrugged. "Okay. No 'Little One.' Got it."

The *Enterprise* loomed in front of Picard.

Intellectually he knew how large his ship was, and certainly he had been outside her enough times in a shuttlecraft. But that was altogether different from floating unassisted in a vacuum, looking up at the massive spacecraft gliding effortlessly through space.

Picard allowed himself to be impressed for a long moment by the glory and majesty of his ship. He was also impressed that instead of the numbing cold that he knew should accompany free-floating, the imminent death that would come, he felt as warm as if he were in his cabin.

That he wasn't already dead was a good indication to him that he wasn't going to die, at least not

anytime soon. By the same token, the utter silence—
and the utter helplessness of his situation—
threatened to overwhelm him.

"All right, Picard," came that voice. "Shall we
chat?"

He tried to spin in place, but moving about in zero g
did not come easily. It had been something that was
part of his academy training, certainly, but he had
never been very proficient at it at the time. Now, years
later, it didn't come any easier. "Q!" he shouted, not
even wondering anymore how he could possibly hear
voices in an airless vacuum. Undoubtedly he was
hearing and speaking within his own head. "Q, show
yourself!"

Q appeared in space next to him, arms folded,
looking quite comfortable with the situation. "You
wished to step outside, Picard. You get what you wish
for. Part of my new policy."

Picard was doing everything he could to ignore the
horror of his situation. He was totally at Q's mercy,
floating there helplessly as he was. Then again, the
simple and frustrating fact was that whenever the
superpowered entity chose to make his noxious presence felt, Picard was always at his mercy. But the
*Enterprise* captain had never backed down from him
before and was not about to start now.

"What new policy are you talking about?" demanded Picard, making no effort to hide his irritation. He noticed with dim interest that small pieces of
hurtling space particles ricocheted away from him the
moment they got near.

"To try to be more like you," Q informed him airily.

"Rubbish," said Picard. "You've made your disdain
for humanity all too plain."

"And is someone not permitted to change their
mind?"

"There is nothing in your past behavior that gives

the slightest indication you would do so," Picard snapped.

"You seem overly irritable, Jean-Luc."

"I'm floating in empty space outside the *Enterprise!*"

"So am I," said Q reasonably, "but you don't see me carrying on about it."

Q glided over to him, looking serene and totally in control, which of course he was. Picard had to admit to himself that the last time he'd seen Q look this sincere was when he appeared on the *Enterprise* bridge, naked and bereft of powers. It had taken a long time for Picard or anyone else to believe that Q was genuinely helpless. And he had, in fact, proven to be useful. Even God help them all—possessing a touch of self-sacrifice.

But still . . . Q, for pity's sake . . .

"Listen to me, Jean-Luc. Are you listening?"

"Raptly," said Picard. He folded his arms, making an effort to appear nonchalant and trying not to think about the deadly vacuum that surrounded him and could crush him at Q's slightest whim.

"My powers were restored, as you know. But I am, in your human terms, on parole. My fellow members of the Q," he said, allowing more than a hint of irritation to show through, "are of the opinion that my quest for knowledge was accompanied by bullying tactics."

"Really!" said Picard, voice dripping with sarcasm.

If Q noted it, he chose to give no sign. "Frankly, I think they're being unfair in their assessment. Humans did experiments on lab animals for far more pointless reasons than gaining cosmic knowledge. No one accused humans of being bullies for those actions."

"Yes, they did," replied Picard, "and all such experiments were discontinued by the beginning of the twenty-first century. We humans are capable of recognizing inappropriate and brutish behavior and of acting to rectify it."

"And I am not, is that what you're saying?" asked Q.

"Q, I'm floating in deep space, against my will, becoming angrier by the second. What does that tell you?"

Q pondered it a moment. "That you have absolutely no sense of humor."

"That you *are* a bully!" exploded Picard. "You do what you want, when you want, to whomever you want! And all the while, you claim that you want to understand us better. Fine! Understand this, then— we don't like to be treated in this fashion!"

"What can I say, Jean-Luc?" sighed Q. "You bring out the worst in me."

*"I* bring it out in *you!"*

"Yes," said Q testily. "When I arrived, did I stop your ship in space? No. Did I disrupt your bridge? No. Did I attempt to harass you? No. Instead I show up, relatively quietly, at a party. I mingle. I mix. I tell entertaining anecdotes, and give absolutely no indication that I am infinitely superior to the life forms milling about in your dreary little Ten-Forward. And my reward for my restraint? You challenge me, you berate me, and you order me to leave. I ask you, Jean-Luc: Is that fair? Is that just? Is that the open-minded behavior of a starship commander?"

"That is the behavior of a starship commander who has been burned more than enough times by an unpredictable and uncontrollable individual." And yet, Picard couldn't rid himself of the nagging irritation that Q—for all his bluster—had a point. He had indeed been behaving in a fashion no different than anyone else at the party. But Picard had singled him out.

But this was Q, dammit! Q . . .

Who, as an ally, might be the Federation's first, best hope against a Borg invasion.

Who, as an enemy, could destroy them with a thought.

But he was on parole.

But he was . . .

"We're getting company."

At first Picard didn't know what Q was talking about. Then the shuttlecraft seemed to separate from the looming background of the *Enterprise* and swoop towards him.

Q turned back to him, and speaking with amazing restraint, said, "Jean-Luc . . . you would give the lowest of the low the chance to redeem himself. To show that he is capable of fitting in. And yet I, the most supreme of supreme . . ."

"There you go again! Humans don't like to be reminded of how superb you are in comparison to us! If you want to be like us, understand us—stop patronizing us and elevating yourself!"

Q shrugged. "It's reflex, Picard. I've been godlike for centuries. You can't expect me to go from omnipotence to incompetence overnight. If a human tries to break the habit of a lifetime, no one expects immediate success. I've lived thousands of your lifetimes, so how can you expect more of me? Just because I can work miracles, don't assume I can do everything."

Picard sighed in airless space.

"It's a party, Jean-Luc. A celebration. You heard them. If you insist I leave, they'll consider it bad luck. A pall will be cast on the festivities, and it will be your fault, Picard, not mine. You won't be able to lay this failure of yours at my feet. Not this time."

Picard blinked.

And he was in the shuttle.

"He's gone!" he heard Worf say, and realized that

he was standing directly behind them. They were looking out the front. "He just vanished! And so did Q!"

"Mr. Data—" Riker was ready to start barking orders.

"No need, Number One," Picard said.

Riker and Worf jumped slightly as they turned with whiplash speed. Worf's eyes widened, then narrowed. "He's toying with us," rumbled Worf.

"Captain, are you all right?" said Riker.

Picard patted himself down. "Apparently fit, Number One."

"It may be a trick," Worf warned them. "Perhaps Q is waiting for us to turn around, and then he'll steal the captain again."

"It would hardly seem that Q would have need for such bait-and-switch motives," observed Data.

"I tend to agree," said Picard, and admitted, "I *did* demand we step outside. In his own strange way, Q was trying to show he wanted to cooperate."

"Strange is hardly the word for it," said Worf.

Riker informed the *Enterprise* that the captain had been retrieved, and Data brought the shuttlecraft about. It hurtled back towards the *Enterprise*, and all the way back Riker and Worf suspected that at any moment Picard would be whisked away once more.

Picard, for his part, had a feeling that wasn't going to be the case. It was verified when shortly before they reached the shuttle bay, Q's voice sounded within the shuttlecraft.

"So, Jean-Luc?" they heard. "I approached you in good faith. How do you—seeker of new worlds, greeter of new life forms—how do you respond to my peaceful overtures?"

"I do not trust him," said Worf shortly.

"Such grudges. Give us a kiss, Worf," came the disembodied voice.

Worf issued a growl that seemed to start from the bottoms of his shoes.

"Nor do I trust him," said Picard shortly. "But what if he is sincere? Think of the ally he'd make."

"Think of the corpse he'd make," Worf said.

Picard let it pass.

"I leave if you say, Jean-Luc, and stay if you say. It's up to you, *mon capitaine.*"

Picard sighed softly.

"Q," he said, "since it is the wish of the Tizarin that you be welcome—and since you are asking to be accorded the same privileges as other alien emissaries—I am hereby inviting you to the wedding festivities aboard the *Enterprise.*"

"Captain!" said Worf, as shocked as if Picard had just casually announced that a Romulan was going to be the new first officer.

Picard understood Worf's indignation. But the bottom line was that Q could do what he felt like, and despite his statements to the contrary, Picard had a feeling Q was going to stay whether Picard told him to or not. So he might as well extend the invitation.

There was a dead silence. "Q—?" asked Picard.

"You didn't say the magic word, Jean-Luc," came Q's faintly scolding voice.

Riker looked at Picard with mild amusement. Picard had expected it. Riker was clearly taking a perverse amusement in his captain's discomfiture. If he didn't know better, Picard would think that Riker enjoyed seeing his commanding officer taken down a peg. But no—Riker had more class than that. Didn't he?

"Magic word," Data said thoughtfully. "Alakazam? Presto chango? Hocus pocus?"

"No, Data," said Picard. "The magic word is 'please,' and if that is what Q is interested in, then what would 'please' me is if we never saw him again.

Somehow, though, I don't think we'll be that fortunate. Will we, Q?"

There was no answer.

The rest of the way to the shuttle bay, there was still no answer, and for a time Picard and the others entertained the notion that they'd seen the last of Q.

This notion held until they walked into the Ten-Forward lounge, where Q was standing, regaling listeners with embarrassing moments that Picard would much rather have forgotten. At the moment, Q was mentioning how Picard had tried to maintain his dignity with hot chocolate poured all over his uniform.

Q turned and gestured to Picard. "Jean-Luc!" he said. "Won't you join us? Oh, and Worf, just to show there's no hard feelings, I've got a present for you."

Worf's eyes narrowed. "I want nothing from you."

"Oh, but you'll love this."

He stretched out a hand and there was a soft, purring, round creature in it . . .

Which took one look at Worf and started to screech ear-piercingly.

Worf took two steps back and his face twisted in nausea. "Get that disgusting thing away!"

"Picard!" bellowed Graziunas. "Don't tell me your big, brave security officer is afraid of a tribble?"

The tribble, for its part, shook violently in Q's hand. Worf fought down revulsion upon seeing the loathsome vermin's gyrations.

Picard snatched the tribble from Q's hand. "Is this how you begin your friendly overtures, Q?"

"Gift giving seems traditionally friendly to me, yes," Q replied, looking hurt. "He didn't like it. Ah well . . ." and he gestured. The tribble vanished from Picard's hand.

There was delighted laughter in response to this

marvelous trick. *They still don't realize,* thought Picard. *Still don't understand the extent of his powers.*

"No more of it," said Picard. "Understood, Q?"

"Of course," said Q, and smiled most ingratiatingly.

And across the way, Lwaxana Troi was eyeing Q in a way that had Picard seen it, might have prompted him to shut down the entire celebration no matter how much Starfleet wished to keep the Tizarin happy. Shut it down and be done with it.

But he didn't. Because some horrific meetings are too much for anyone to have to contemplate.

# Chapter Nine

O'BRIEN SIGHED WITH RELIEF as the transporter circuits came back into full, normal activation.

Wesley Crusher and the bridge crew sighed with relief upon the return of the captain to the safe confines of the *Enterprise*.

Geordi La Forge sighed with relief when Lwaxana Troi thanked him graciously for what little information he was able to provide her regarding the awesome entity known as Q.

Deanna Troi, whose expertise was getting people to relax, was tense as a whip.

"Mother," she said firmly, in the crowded Ten-Forward lounge—as she tried to ignore the distant pounding headache that so many minds in close proximity gave her—"I forbid you to talk to him."

Lwaxana turned and looked at her daughter with amazement. "Very well, Little One. I forbid you to be unmarried any longer. Wed Commander Riker."

"If I thought for a moment that it would prevent you from making a hideous mistake, I would strip naked and perform the Betazed marriage rituals right here."

Lwaxana raised a speculative eyebrow. "That would certainly be the highlight of the party."

"But I know not even that would stop you if you put your mind to something. So instead I'm trying to appeal to plain, old-fashioned common sense. Do not do what you are contemplating."

"I am contemplating," said Mrs. Troi firmly, "performing my duties as an ambassador of Betazed and daughter of the Fifth House. No more and no less than that." She turned and regarded Q for a moment, who was still under the watchful eyes of Picard, Worf, and Riker. For his part, he was cheerily chatting with the fathers of the bride and groom, apparently oblivious of any undue attention being cast his way. "Although," she said slowly, "he is a most intriguing individual. I can't read him at all."

"Neither can I," admitted Deanna. "He's too powerful and unusual an entity for me to perceive."

"Yes, but I'm more powerful than you, my dear," Lwaxana said. It was true, of course, but Deanna still wasn't thrilled with the matter-of-fact way that her mother had put it. "And I can't detect him either." She frowned. "He's not one of those abominable holodeck things, is he?"

"No, mother." In spite of the difficulty of the situation, Deanna couldn't help but smile. One of the more amusing moments in her life had been her mother's trying to cozy up to a holodeck-generated bartender. Deanna cherished the memory. "I wish it were that simple."

"The most complex matters in life are the most simple," said her mother in that infuriating manner she had of making sweeping statements which, when analyzed, made no sense. "If you'll excuse me . . ."

Before Deanna could make another move, her mother was sweeping across the room.

As if sensing her coming, Q turned. He raised a bemused eyebrow and watched her until she came to a halt barely two feet away from him.

The true horror of the situation didn't dawn on Picard for a moment, so distracted was he by trying to anticipate what Q might do in the near future. So the recollection that Lwaxana Troi was in phase—and was still in search of a mate—did not come immediately to him.

"Jean-Luc," said Lwaxana. "Who is your charming friend?"

Then Picard remembered.

"Mrs. Troi," said Picard quickly, "now might not be the best time," not bothering to add that no time would be an improvement.

But Q took a step forward. "I am Q," he said.

"How intriguing. Are there any more letters like you at home?" She laughed lightly.

Q smiled graciously.

Riker moaned softly.

Worf's eyes widened and his fingers strayed near his phaser.

Picard began to perspire.

"How charming you are," said Q. "You seem familiar for some reason, but I don't believe we've met."

"Possibly you're familiar with Deanna Troi . . . ?"

"Of course!" said Q. "Your sister, no doubt."

Riker glanced around, hoping to locate a blunt object.

"Oh, honestly!" said Mrs. Troi, and coquettishly batted Q on the shoulder.

Q's eyes widened for a moment, and Picard took an

urgent step forward, certain that disaster was about to befall and not entirely sure what he could do to forestall it.

And then Q laughed.

It was not a pleasant sound, for it was a noise that was laden with disaster. And yet Lwaxana Troi was utterly charmed by it. "You flatter me," she said, "and deliberately so. I'm her mother, Lwaxana."

"Her mother!" said Q in astonishment. "I admit that humanoid aging is somewhat of a subtlety to me, but nevertheless, I believe I speak for all present when I say that it's hard to believe Deanna Troi is your *daughter*." He turned to the *Enterprise* men for verification. "Do I not, gentlemen . . . and Worf?"

Worf clenched a fist, but Picard said quickly, "Absolutely. You speak for all of us, Q. Mrs. Troi, why don't we go for a walk?"

He was certain that would pull her away. Picard had been her favorite target when she was last aboard the ship, and he was going to have to use that infatuation to get her away from Q. He saw Deanna's pleading look from several feet away. The counselor was terrified as to what could happen if her mother kept moving in the direction that her phasing was driving her.

*How far do you go, Picard, to keep her away from him,* mused Picard. It was a question, the answer to which he didn't like to contemplate.

Unfortunately, or fortunately, depending upon how one looked at it, Picard mused, it wasn't a question he would have to worry about.

"Not now, Jean-Luc," said Lwaxana. "Can't you see I'm talking? Honestly, where are your manners? You could take lessons from Admiral Q here."

"Yes, Jean-Luc," said Q agreeably. "You could take lessons from me."

"He is not an admiral," said Picard in no uncertain terms.

"Now, now, Picard . . . don't let your jealousy get the better of you. You'll get that promotion someday, as long as I'm there pushing for you," Q assured him.

*Mother, this has gone far enough.*

Lwaxana, without turning, replied to her daughter, *Are you under the impression that I cannot take care of myself?*

*I'm under the impression that if you were thinking clearly, you'd have an idea of the trouble you're letting yourself in for.*

*Trouble, Little One, is no stranger to me.*

Lwaxana then shut down communications and said to Q, "You know, this room is getting very stuffy."

"Wherever Jean-Luc is, stuffiness cannot help but be nearby."

This drew a laugh from the other partygoers who were within earshot. Picard flushed slightly, and he could sense behind him that Worf was ready to charge. He saw Riker take a short step to his right, blocking a direct path between Worf and Q, and was grateful for this. He didn't want to think about what Q could do to the infuriated Klingon if he were of a mind to.

"But you're right, Mrs. Troi," said Q. "Would you care to step outside?"

*"No!"* said Picard.

In a low, even embarrassed voice, Lwaxana said, "Jean-Luc, please. Now is not the time for jealousy. You had your chance."

"Yes, you had your chance, Picard," Q informed him, smiling. "Don't worry, though. We'll stick to the corridors of the *Enterprise.*" He turned back to Lwaxana. "The captain was concerned that I was going to take you for a stroll outside the ship."

Lwaxana laughed. "What a sense of humor! That's so rare in a man."

"Yes, it is," agreed Q. "But then, you'll find I'm a fairly rare individual."

"That I can attest to," said Picard.

Q extended an elbow. "Coming, my dear?"

Lwaxana took it. "Absolutely."

Deanna, Picard, Riker, and Worf all started to move forward to try and prevent Q from walking away with Lwaxana.

None of them made it more than a step, and then they froze in place. Smiles were plastered onto their faces; even onto Worf's, where it looked grotesque.

*Mother!* Deanna's mind called out.

*Later, Little One,* Lwaxana sent back and, with eyes only on Q, swept out of the Ten-Forward lounge.

The moment they were gone, Picard and the others unfroze. Unaware of what had just happened, Graziunas was shaking his head and grinning. "Trust a sharp devil like Q to waltz out of here with the best-looking and most formidable woman on the ship. She is something, isn't she, Picard?"

"Something," echoed Picard, and his officers were gathering around him quickly.

"Orders, sir?" said Worf.

"Alert all security teams," Picard told him in a low voice. "They are to keep an eye out for Q and Mrs. Troi, and report their whereabouts and activities at all times."

"And what else, Captain?" asked Deanna urgently.

"That's all for now."

"But, Captain!" Deanna began in protest. "My mother—!"

"Is a grown woman, Counselor," Picard replied, sounding more testy than he would have liked. "And Q is a grown . . . whatever. Do you have any reason to believe that Q is exerting an undue influence on her?"

"He doesn't have to," admitted Deanna.

"No, he does not," Picard said firmly. "The bottom

93

line is, Q has promised to behave with restraint. And your mother is free to do as she pleases, within reason."

"And who determines what is 'within reason'?" asked Deanna.

"I do," said Picard.

## Chapter Ten

LWAXANA WALKED NEXT TO Q, eyeing him thoughtfully and appraisingly. Other crew members went
past and when they saw who was walking down the
*Enterprise* corridor, made sure to give them a wide
berth.

"Tell me about yourself," said Lwaxana Troi.

"Are you certain you can handle the truth?" asked
Q.

"I can handle anything," she said with conviction.

"Very well. Picard was correct when he said I'm not
an admiral. I am, in fact, a god."

"Oh, really?" she said with amusement.

"Yes. I am a member of an entity known as the Q
Continuum. I can do anything."

"Anything?"

"Anything."

She eyed him speculatively. "Can you bend your
knees backwards?"

"I beg your pardon?"

"Can you bend your knees backwards? You know. Like that Earth bird called a flamingo."

Q flexed his legs and found that they bent only forward. "Not in this body, no. I'd have to change form."

"So you can't do *any*thing."

He sighed. "I can do anything except bend my knees backwards like a flamingo in this form."

"Can you bend your entire body backwards?" She gave a partial demonstration. "So that your head touches the backs of your feet?"

Q stared at her. "Why would I want to do that?"

"You said you could do anything."

"I'm a god, not a contortionist!" said Q in exasperation.

"But what is a god," put forward Lwaxana, "except a moral and ethical contortionist. Claiming that a universe of confusion and chaos actually fits together into some sort of divine plan."

"That is not a god's job. That's what philosophers do. They try and determine what that divine plan is."

"But you know?" said Lwaxana. "You know what the secret of the universe is?"

"Of course."

"And what is it?"

He regarded her thoughtfully. "You really wish to know?"

"Of course."

He glanced around, right and left, as if concerned that someone was listening in. Then he stopped his walking, drew her close and said, in a low voice, "This."

There was a brief flash and then something appeared in his hand.

She stared at it and took it slowly from him. She studied it. She turned it over with meticulous care.

"A nectarine?" she asked.

He nodded. "Don't spread it around. Especially don't tell Jean-Luc. He and his kind would kill for this sort of knowledge."

"But . . . it's a nectarine."

"Yes."

"The secret of the universe is a nectarine?"

"Sublime, isn't it. I wouldn't expect someone like you to understand."

Lwaxana's lips thinned and she said in sharp tones, "Someone like me?"

"Someone who is not a god," he told her airily.

She drew herself up. "I will have you know," she said archly, "that I am as close to godlike as you will encounter on this ship. Possibly in this galaxy."

"Is that a fact?"

"Yes," she said, and to his utter shock, she pushed past him. "Excuse me."

"You touched me," he said incredulously. "No one dares touch me!"

She took a step towards him, looking him up and down. "I am Lwaxana Troi, daughter of the fifth house. I . . . am *not* . . . no one."

She tossed the nectarine at him. He caught it effortlessly and watched Lwaxana stalk off.

And he smiled.

Unpleasantly.

And then his communicator beeped.

He looked down at it in surprise. Certainly he had created it to be identical to those worn by the men of the Federation, but this was the first time anyone had the temerity to actually summon him.

He hesitated for a moment and then tapped it. "Hello?" he said, his curiosity piqued.

"Mr. Q to the conference lounge," came the crisp voice of Jean-Luc Picard. "Immediately."

"You can't be serious," said Q.

"Dead serious."

Q shrugged and vanished.


"Mother, you have to listen to me."

Lwaxana Troi was in her quarters, lounging and snacking on a small bunch of grapes. Deanna was seated in front of her, trying to get her to listen to something that made eminent sense to her. What was distracting, however, was that each time that Lwaxana popped a grape into her mouth, Mr. Homn would stand resolutely behind her, tapping that annoying Betazoid gong. Deanna wondered how her co-workers would react if she were to start doing that every time she ate meals with them.

"You worry entirely too much, daughter."

"And you, mother, worry entirely too little. And about the wrong things."

"I don't follow you, dear."

"You give infinite care and attention to the most minute of Betazoid customs, from the Ab'brax to the going of thanks. But me, your living, breathing, concerned daughter—me, you don't heed at all. You're not the least bit worried about Q, when you most definitely should be. Mother, you have no idea what he is capable of. You have no idea what he is."

"Of course I do. He's a member of the Q Continuum."

Deanna put her hands on her hips. "And what does that mean? Do you know?"

Lwaxana made an impatient gesture. "Oh, it doesn't matter. Men always have their little clubs and such. Your father had his own organization that met once a week. They gave it a fancy name, and it was really just an excuse to get together weekly and play cards." She smiled fondly. "He thought he had me fooled."

"The Q Continuum is a bit more than a group of card players," said Deanna. "Q has immense power . . ."

"Yes, I did sense that," said Lwaxana thoughtfully. She ate another grape, and another gong sounded. Deanna closed her eyes and tried not to think about breaking that blasted gong, because her mother would just scold her for what was on her mind. "I did sense that about him," continued Lwaxana. "I wasn't able to read his thoughts, but he had a sort of aura about him—power that you could almost touch."

"You didn't touch it, did you?" demanded Deanna.

"Dear!" said Lwaxana in mock horror. "Just what do you think I am?"

"We know what you are," said Worf.

Q was lying, totally relaxed, across the conference lounge table. Picard had chosen not to waste valuable time and energy angrily telling Q to get himself off the furniture. Privately, he was amazed that Q had shown up at his summons at all.

However, Q's deliberately casual manner was clearly annoying Worf, and Riker didn't seem any happier about it. Only Data sat and watched, thoughtfully, contemplatively.

"Oh, do you?" said Q, casually studying his fingernails. "And who explained it to you, Worf? Did they find enough one-syllable words to do the job?"

"You have an angle, Q," said Riker. "You always do. You always show up acting as if you want to be the benefactor of humanity. And then, sooner or later, your true motives become evident. So why don't we get past all the nonsense, and you tell us what the real story here is."

"All I'm trying to do," said Q, sounding exasperated, "is blend in and learn the wonders of humanity. You're so insistent on expounding upon the marvels of your race, but when I express an interest in studying you close up, you suddenly get defensive. You're sending mixed signals, Jean-Luc. And your antagonistic reception puts the lie to your claims of brotherhood and peaceful coexistence."

"In addition to those traits," said Picard, "is our ability to learn from the past. And in the past, Q, you have presented exceptional difficulties."

"Captain," Data said slowly, "it is possible that Q is telling the truth." Worf made a derisive noise and Data noted it, catalogued it, and filed it for future reference should that noise seem to be appropriate. He continued, "Certainly my time among humans has had an impact on myself. Is it not possible that Q has been similarly affected by his contact with us?"

"No," said Worf sourly.

"There's possible, Data, and then there's likely," said Riker. "You came into humanity with no preconceived notions, willing to learn. Q already made up his mind from the first time he saw us. Since then, he's just looking for excuses to shore up his opinion."

"And with your belligerent attitude, you're certainly providing them, aren't you?" replied Q. "I knew that at least Data would be on my side."

"I am not on 'your side,' sir," said Data. "I am merely more willing to concede the possibility that you may be sincere. That is because I am inclined to take people at their word whenever possible."

"You're a hopeless optimist, Data," said Q.

"If by hopeless you mean unlikely to change, you are quite correct," said Data.

"But I, gentlemen, can change," Q said, sitting up on the table. "Shame on you, gentlemen, for allowing Data to be the only one among you with true compassion. I've shown compassion for you time and again."

"You *are* joking," said Worf.

"Not at all," said Q. "Have you forgotten that I've saved your lives on several occasions?"

"Saved them after you endangered them," Worf pointed out.

Q shrugged. "A minor detail. Captain, I must admit I do not understand this sudden grilling. You did, after all, give me your imperial permission to attend the festivities."

"But not," said Picard firmly, "to fraternize with guests."

Q's eyes narrowed. "Sooooo . . . that's it, is it? This is about Lwaxana Troi."

"It's not about her in specific, but rather—"

"You don't lie especially well, Jean-Luc," Q informed him. "Depending upon your point of view, that could be either a benefit or a weakness. You are concerned," and he seemed most amused, "because I find Lwaxana Troi intriguing."

"Intriguing?" said Picard incredulously.

"Even captivating, for one of the humanoid species."

"Now I *know* something is going on," said Riker.

"Really?" Q looked amused. "I'll tell you what, Riker. If you have the nerve to go and tell Lwaxana Troi that she is incapable of being intriguing and captivating to someone, then I will never speak to her again. Well?" He made shooing gestures towards the door. "I'm waiting, Riker. You go off and tell her that. We'll wait here for the call from sickbay, where they'll be picking up the pieces that she leaves of you."

"I don't find this amusing at all," said Riker.

"We'll add it to the lengthy list of things you don't find amusing," said Q. "Your problem, Riker, is that you lack perspective. It's a common enough trait among humans. Only your greatest minds and philosophers are capable of realizing just what a pathetic little species you are. And yet you constantly boast to me of your superb nature. Let's see some of that famous humanity at work, eh? The love for your fellow man."

"You're not our fellow man," Worf informed him.

"No, I'm not," said Q, "and I am tiring of this persecution. I have been straightforward in all my discussions with you. I did not have to be. Fellow man, eh? I could have done *this*—"

There was a sudden rippling of the air in front of them, and in Q's place were the form and features of an absolutely stunning blond woman. Riker arched an eyebrow in amazement. Even Data seemed impressed. She was wearing a dress cut low at the top and high at the hem. When she spoke, the room temperature increased by about ten degrees.

"What do you think?" she asked in a low, silky voice.

She was stunning in a way that surpassed earthly beauty, and Picard momentarily found himself at a loss for words.

She slid across the table, revealing a generous expanse of tanned thigh, and hovered only a few millimeters from Picard. "I could have come aboard like this, Jean-Luc. I could have made myself irresistible to you. Seduced you, if I'd had a mind to. After all, the form I've chosen is purely an arbitrary one. Can you imagine, Picard, if you'd woken up the next morning, after a night of passion, rolled over in bed . . ." And there was a sudden flash, and Q was back in his more familiar form. ". . . and seen me lying next to you?" he finished in an amused male voice. "It would have been meaningless to me—I transcend your paltry notions of gender. But what would it have done to you, I wonder?"

Picard looked positively ashen, but nevertheless he

kept his composure. "Are you saying I should be grateful because you chose to avoid deceit?"

"Precisely."

"Lack of deceit is common courtesy. Not something to be applauded in and of itself."

Q shrugged. "I would like to take my triumphs where I can find them. Now, if there's nothing else . . ."

"Why Mrs. Troi?" demanded Riker. "If you're so above primitive concepts of gender, why are you displaying such interest in her?"

"I find her mind most intriguing," said Q. "And I'll tell you something more, gentlemen. I doubt if I would have given her overt attention beyond our casual meeting and discussion. But now that you've raised such a ruckus over it, well, she must be something truly special. You've piqued my curiosity, Jean-Luc. Prompted me to further investigate this woman. Thank you for taking such pains to draw her to my attention." He nodded his head slightly and vanished.

They looked at each other.

"Great," said Riker.

"Little One, I appreciate your concern—"

"No, mother. I don't think you appreciate it at all," said Deanna, her arms folded. "I don't think you realize the purpose of it. Your judgment is clouded . . ."

"My judgment is as sharp as it ever was," said Lwaxana, "and frankly, my dear, I'm becoming a little tired of being lectured to, if you catch my drift."

"*You're* tired of it!" said Deanna incredulously. "I've spent my entire life being lectured by you, and you cannot sustain five minutes from me? Five minutes discussing a subject that I can assure you I know more about, namely Q."

"Oh, really," said Lwaxana frostily.

"Yes, really. I'll say it again, mother—you have no idea what you're becoming involved with. Do you know what always follows Q?"

"R?"

"Mother!"

"I'm sorry. Should I have said U? But there are some words that end with Q, you see, so technically—"

"I was going to say that trouble always follows him. He's brought us into some of the greatest dangers that we've ever faced."

"They couldn't have been too great. You're still here. You worked your way out of them?"

"Well . . . no, actually," admitted Deanna. "Q usually saved us."

"Now *there's* a stinging indictment."

"It's not that simple."

"Nothing simple is ever simple," replied Lwaxana. "The reason that I lecture you, Deanna, is because I know best."

"Not about Q."

"You don't exactly sound unbiased," Lwaxana informed her. "To be specific, you seem long on bias and short on experience."

"He's not the man for you!"

"And you base this on what? Your successful love life?"

Deanna's face fell. "That was a cheap shot, mother."

"The truth hurts, Little One."

"That's why you don't want to see it."

"Very well," said Lwaxana, drawing herself up. She stood and faced her daughter with quiet authority. "I'll tell you what I see. I see someone lecturing me on my love life when she hasn't been able to get her own sorted out. Someone who has not been able to put together one permanent relationship. Perhaps, Little One, you might want to consider getting your own house in order before you start rearranging the furniture in mine." She turned away from her daughter. "I'll have you know that Q and I—'Q and I,' what a charming way to put it—had a bit of a tiff earlier. He was coming off a bit too high-handed for my taste. But I'll tell you right now, that seems minor compared to the way you've been presenting yourself."

Lwaxana glanced down at the fruitbowl and her eyebrows arched in surprise. There was a nectarine sitting there. It definitely hadn't been there before. She picked it up and stared at it. "He's a fascinating individual," said Lwaxana. "There are depths to him waiting to be explored. If he's everything you say he is, why, I might be doing a service to the cause of humanity by exploring a relationship with him."

"He doesn't know how to become romantically involved!" Deanna tried to explain. "He's not human!"

"Really? Then I would be his first. That's unusual to find at my age."

Deanna moaned and sank into a chair.

Lwaxana turned and looked at her, not without compassion. "Little One," she sighed, and ran her fingers through Deanna's hair. "I understand what you're going through. But I can take care of myself, I assure you."

"Mother—" Deanna looked up at her, making one final effort to get through to her. "Mother, he thinks of us as insects."

"I doubt that," said Lwaxana. "But even if that's the case, well . . . he's never met a queen bee before."

## *Chapter Eleven*

KERIN AND SEHRA stared in amazement at the glorious tropical forest that stretched out before them. It seemed to go on and on, with caves and grottos carved in towering cliffsides. Far, far below them, a narrow river wended its way through, and the air was thick with mist.

Wesley Crusher stood next to them, his arms folded, smiling at their wonderment. So many of the miracles aboard the *Enterprise* were taken for granted, that it helped Wesley feel greater appreciation for them when he ran those miracles through their paces for the benefit of visitors.

"It's . . . it's like a planet that's new," breathed Sehra.

Wesley nodded. "It's based on an actual place—well, a place that isn't there anymore—called the Genesis Planet."

"Why isn't it there anymore?" asked Kerin. He

thought he saw something moving far in the under-brush.

"Kind of complicated," Wesley said. "I'll tell you later. So, do you think you might want to hold your wedding in some place like this?"

"It's magnificent," said Sehra. "But . . ."

Both of the young men turned to her. "But?" said Kerin.

"Mother will say it's too damp."

Kerin made an impatient gesture. "Sehra, there's been some problem with the last four environments that Wesley's shown us. And every time, you've said that it's something your mother isn't going to like! Don't you have any opinions of your own?"

She looked at him, surprised. "Of . . . of course I do, Kerin! But I want to make everybody happy."

"Just worry about making yourself happy," he told her. "That's what's important here. What would make you happy?"

"What would make me happy is making everyone else happy."

"*Sehra!*"

"Don't shout at me," she snapped. "I don't have to stand here and be shouted at."

"Look," Wesley said quickly, "I can always find someplace else. The computer has more environments than you can—"

"This is fine," said Kerin.

"This is *not* fine," Sehra shot back.

They were facing each other, fuming. Wesley was starting to get nervous. He'd been given a simple assignment by the captain: Bring the bride and groom down to the holodeck and let them choose the world they would most like for their wedding. If the entire thing degenerated into an argument, how in the world was that going to make Wesley look to the captain?

"Look, guys," said Wesley slowly. "I'm the same age as you two are, and I can tell you that if I were taking the same big step you are—marriage and all—I'd be a nervous wreck right now. And I'd probably be arguing about all sorts of incidental things—like holodeck backgrounds, for example—rather than bringing up what was really on my mind. Namely, that I was scared and that I'd want to know that my fiancé was there for me, to provide support."

They stared at him.

"Or not," finished Wesley, weakly.

They looked back at each other, and then Sehra sighed. "I'm sorry, Kerin."

"No, I am," he said so fast that he almost overlapped her. "You're trying to be considerate and everything, and I'm just being difficult."

"Really, you're right. I should be thinking about what's right for us, not what's right for my mother."

"Whatever you think is best."

"Whatever you think."

They went back and forth like that for a minute, and Wesley patiently waited it out. Finally Sehra turned and looked back out at the Genesis Planet. "This really is beautiful," she said. "If only the humidity . . ."

Kerin sighed loudly.

"Look, this isn't a problem," said Wesley. "I can adjust the climate however you want."

"Well, you should have said that immediately!" Sehra exclaimed.

"I didn't think the climate was your biggest problem," said Wes. "As I said, I thought you guys mostly had a case of pre-wedding jitters."

Kerin looked at Wesley thoughtfully. "Have you ever been married, Wesley?"

"What? Oh, no!" laughed Wes, although it was an uncomfortable laugh.

"Do you have a special girl?"

"No one special," admitted Wes.

Kerin tilted his head slightly. "Have you ever had sex?"

Wes cleared his throat loudly and said, "If you guys are settled on this, then I really have to get back up to the bridge."

"And I must be getting back home," said Sehra, with a sigh. "Mother is having yet another fitting for my dress. So much to do, so many preparations to make."

Kerin took her hands in his and smiled. "I know how it is. Your mother can be quite a handful, I guess. Wesley—do you mind if I stay here awhile?"

Wes frowned and shifted his weight on his feet. "I'm not sure if I should—"

"The captain said we should feel at home," Kerin said. "I've just never had an opportunity to explore something like this before. This is just so remarkable, I hate to leave so soon."

Wesley looked out over the scene and smiled inwardly. He remembered how exciting it had been for him the first time he had explored the parameters and possibilities of the holodeck. "Well . . . I guess it wouldn't be a problem. Look, all you have to do is remember this: If you get into any sort of problem, all you have to do is ask the computer to help you out. For example, if you say," and Wesley raised his voice slightly, "Computer . . . Door!"

Ten feet to their right, a waterfall parted and the gleaming exit from the holodeck was revealed. Sehra and Kerin gasped in amazement. The illusion of the holodeck was so perfect that it was always amazing to have the hard edge of reality jolt you.

"And if you really have problems, just instruct the computer to end the program. You'll be fine," Wesley said, as much to assure himself as to assure Kerin.

Wesley and Sehra walked through the door, which obediently hissed open and then closed. An instant later, it vanished. Kerin shook his head. Even though he now knew precisely where the door was, the illusion was still so compelling that his mind was completely fooled.

He climbed down slowly over the cliffside, hand over hand, exercising extreme caution. He knew that it was all an illusion, and yet he could not tell himself that it was anything except a huge drop should he lose his grip.

He drew in great lungfuls of air, finding the tingling sensation quite remarkable. The Nistral ship had nothing, absolutely nothing like this. Far in the distance, there were creatures that soared through the air without the need for ships of any sort. He remembered from his readings that they were called "birds." He found himself envying them immensely. With a flap of graceful wings, they cut their own glorious arc through the sky. White clouds hung against a sky of glorious blue—blue, like one of the twin colors of the Graziunas.

He thought of Sehra and then smiled to himself. He must be in love, all right. Here he was, rock climbing down a cliff in a veritable wonderland, and still his thoughts flew back to his love—his lover. His body tingled at the remembered sensations, of the skin against skin and—

A piece of rock came off in his hand, and with a cry of alarm, Kerin fell.

He tumbled but did not cry out again. He was a son of Nistral, and a son of Nistral would meet his end—if the end had come—with bravery.

The cliffside flashed past him—a blur—and far away were the sounds of birds screeching.

And then Kerin stopped.

His arms and legs flailed about in confusion for a

moment, but he continued to hang there, in midair. He wondered if this were part of some sort of computer failsafe.

"Well! It appears you've gotten yourself into some difficulty."

Kerin twisted himself around.

There was a man standing there against the side of the cliff. Standing at an impossible angle, for he was parallel to the ground far below. He was simply jutting out from the cliffside, defying gravity. His arms were folded across his chest, and he was smiling sideways . . . well, all of him was sideways.

"Need some help?" asked Q.

Wesley and Sehra approached the transporter room, and Sehra turned and faced Wesley, smiling. "You've been far too cooperative, Mr. Crusher. I really want to thank you."

"That's quite all right, really," Wesley smiled. "Just glad to help out."

"Still, I feel I should give you something to thank you. We of the Graziunas believe very strongly in gifts as a symbol of appreciation."

"That's not necessary."

"To refuse a gift would be a grave insult," Sehra told him sternly. "You wouldn't want to insult us, would you?"

"Of course not," said Wes quickly. "But it's not proper for members of Starfleet to accept gratuities for the performance of duty."

"Showing us the holodeck was duty," Sehra said. "Calming Kerin and myself down and reminding us that we love each other—those were the actions of one I would like to call friend. It is a friend that I wish to reward."

Wesley shrugged. "Whatever would please you," he said diplomatically.

Sehra bowed slightly. "I shall find something suitable," she said, and went into the transporter room.

"Nice kid," said Wesley, allowing himself to wonder briefly whether the blue faces of the Graziunas were some sort of makeup to show affiliation, or whether they were blue-skinned all over and it was something genetic. He shrugged, thought no more of it, and headed up to the bridge.

"Watch your step there."

Kerin carefully picked his way around what was apparently the burrow of some animal. "Thank you, Q," he said graciously. "And thank you also for helping me out of my predicament. Your powers are quite impressive."

Q put up a hand. "No problem, I assure you."

They came to the edge of a small river that was teeming with life. Kerin watched it with rapt attention. "I've never seen anything like it," he whispered.

"Running water?" said Q with curiosity. "Something as trivial as that, and you've never seen it?"

"When you've lived your entire life in space, nothing having to do with nature is trivial."

Q nodded approvingly. "I like you, young man. You have a true appreciation for life. More so than your hosts, I tend to think."

Kerin looked at him with curiosity. "Why do you say that?"

"Oh," Q snorted disdainfully, "they are so full of themselves, these humans. Always going on and on about their higher qualities, about their compassion and generosity and thoughtfulness—it's all a lie, you know."

"A lie?" Kerin found it hard to believe. "But they seem friendly . . ."

"Ah, they *seem* friendly, true enough," agreed Q. "But they're hypocrites, every one. They profess such high and mighty beliefs. Take their leaders—do they lead by example? I should say not! Here's a ship," and Q lowered his voice to a confidential tone, "that is supposed to be a haven for families and couples. Do the leaders approve of this? They do not."

"What do you mean, they don't approve?"

"If they thought love and marriage were so wonderful, then they would have pursued that avenue," said Q. "But have they? Look at the senior officers." He ticked off on his fingers. "Is Picard married? Is he a father? No. Riker? No. La Forge? No. Troi? She can't even get along with her own mother. Data?" He sighed. "Pity. Data is the most fortunate of them, since he is not human, and that which he most desires is what would most destroy him. Like a moth to flame. And Worf—?" He paused. "Well, he has a son, but he doesn't know it yet. He'll find out soon enough."

"He does!" said Kerin in surprise. "How do you know?"

"I'm Q," said Q simply. "If there were things I did not know, I'd be less than what I am. You're not to tell anyone."

"Not a word," Kerin assured him.

Q shook his head. "Ironic, isn't it? Of all of them, Worf is the one who goes and reproduces. There's something supremely silly about the workings of the cosmos. And you, my new young friend! You are the most impressive of all."

"I am?"

"Yes," said Q firmly, "because whereas these others give lip service to the concept of love, devotion, and parenting, you actually are dedicated enough to pursue it."

"Thank you," said Kerin, genuinely flattered.

"Even though . . ."

Q let the comment hang there, and Kerin was confused. "Even though what—?"

"Oh, it's nothing," said Q. He sat on top of what appeared to be a roughly rectangular black casing, about large enough to fit a man inside. "Nothing at all."

"No, really," smiled Kerin. "If you have something on your mind . . ."

"What can I say?" said Q. "After all, I shall go on and on, long after you have fallen into dust, and your descendants have no recollection of your name. But you, who have such a limited time in this galaxy . . . it's impressive to me that you choose to spend that brief span you call life tied down to one person."

Kerin didn't understand what he meant at first. Then he smiled. "Oh, Sehra's a very special girl."

"I'm sure she is," said Q. "Of course, many your age have married solely to experience the physical side of relationships. I assume that's not the case with you and your intended."

"No, not at all. Actually," and Kerin smiled, "we have experienced the physical side already, if you know what I mean. And now you have to promise not to tell anyone."

"Oh, not a word," said Q. He rapped on the black casing absently. "Comforting to know that the physical aspect is not important to you, all things considered."

"All things," echoed Kerin, but now he didn't quite understand. "Uhm . . . what 'all things,' specifically?"

"Well!" said Q. "She's not going to stay young forever, is she? The bodies of humans and humanoids are somewhat like time bombs. The years tick away, and sooner or later—usually sooner—everything goes off. I'll show you, if you don't mind."

"Not at all," said Kerin uneasily.

Q gestured and Sehra appeared in front of them, clad in a diaphanous white dress.

Kerin stood in confusion. "Sehra—?"

She smiled beatifically as Q said, "Oh, it's not her. Not really. Merely a simulation in order to illustrate my point. Again, I am merely trying to show my respect for you."

"Of course," Kerin said, suddenly wishing that Q had respect for someone else.

"It may happen gradually or it may happen slowly," said Q. "Usually the hair starts to go first . . ."

Sehra didn't move, her lovely smile never fading, but her long, red-streaked hair began to whiten.

"You'll notice the first few strands, and she'll make a fuss over them, but after a time there'll be far too many to count," Q said. "Then the smiling, youthful face will begin to wrinkle. The eyes that sparkled at you in the bloom of your romance will develop crow's-feet, and her gaze will turn from love to suspicion."

The image of Sehra obediently followed Q's narration, and Kerin's blood chilled as he saw Sehra regarding him with lack of trust. It was—Gods!—it was just how Sehra's mother looked at him! And her face was creased, years of concerns and adult worries puckering the skin.

Relentlessly, Q kept going. "Her breasts will sag, her skin will shrivel and become hard and coarse. Her smooth neck will hollow out, her round cheeks become high and severe. She will go from being full of grace to lack of grace. Her body will become stooped, her suppleness a distant memory. That is how the companion that you have chosen in your youth will appear to you in your later years—years that could come sooner than you think."

Sehra, a wrinkled, ancient crone, took a step towards him on a quavering foot. Her skin was so thin he could practically see her skull. Slowly she brought an arm up, an arm that had sagging skin hanging from it, covered with wrinkles and age spots. She pointed a long, withered, accusing finger at him.

Kerin shrieked and fell back, stumbling over a rock and landing—on his butt—in the water. The water wasn't high at all, but it was cold, and it splashed up into his face, dousing him. When he blinked, that ghastly image of Sehra was gone. Only Q was there.

"That," said Q, "is only a worst case scenario, of course."

"Why did you show me that!" demanded Kerin, pulling himself to his feet.

Q looked stunned. "To show you how much I respect you!"

"If you really respect me," said Kerin tightly, "then you'll respect when I say that I never want to see an abomination like that in the future. Never show it to me again!"

Q inclined his head slightly. "I'm dreadfully sorry if my efforts to compliment you served to upset you. That was the farthest thing from my mind. Not being human, I'm not always capable of fully anticipating how humans will react. I will never show it, if that's your wish, my young friend. But that you'll never see it again . . . that I cannot promise. You see . . . you're the one who's marrying her."

And with a burst of light and sound, Q vanished.

When Wesley finished his shift, he went down to his quarters. He'd been falling behind on his studies for the Academy, and now seemed a good time to catch up.

He had been disturbed by the way Deanna Troi had looked on the bridge. Usually she was the picture of calm and certainty, an emotional rock from which others drew strength. Now, though, she seemed distant, concerned. She was not at peace with herself.

Wesley had been nursing something of a crush on her since he had first seen her. Like most teenage boys, he had a fantasy life that far outstripped his reality. Every so often he'd imagine coming back to his quarters and finding Counselor Troi, or perhaps one of the more attractive teenage girls he saw around the ship, waiting for him . . .

God, he hoped that the empathic Troi couldn't pick up on that. He wouldn't have been able to look her in the eye if she had. He didn't think she knew. He hoped she didn't. He sighed inwardly. If he had to go through life worrying about every good-looking female on board being able to tap into his head, he'd go out of his mind.

He entered his quarters, took two paces, and stopped dead.

A young woman was there. She looked to be in her late twenties. Her face was blue, with short red hair and long red eyelashes.

She was wearing a robe that she allowed to drop to the floor. As if in response to his unspoken question of earlier, Wesley saw that she was indeed blue-skinned, all over.

"I'm a gift from Sehra of the Graziunas." She smiled.

In all his fantasies, Wesley had always wondered what he'd say if he found himself in a situation like this one. What was the perfect line, the perfect icebreaker.

In a voice about an octave higher than his normal tone, he said, "Help."

That wasn't it.

# Chapter Twelve

DEANNA TROI rang the chime at her mother's quarters, gamely determined to take yet another stab at explaining the situation to Lwaxana. At first there was no response, and Deanna knocked firmly. "Mother!" she called out. And then she thought, *Mother.*

*Ah, Little One,* came the reply. *How good of you to join us. Enter and be welcome.*

And Deanna thought, *us?* as she entered.

She had had a feeling she knew who was part of the "us" that had been mentioned, and it turned out she was correct. She stood there, just inside the doorway, shaking her head.

Q and Lwaxana were there, each holding a glass of wine. "Deanna. I believe you know my companion," said Lwaxana.

"Better than you do, mother. I can assure you of that," said Deanna tightly. "Q, I would like you to leave."

"And I," said Lwaxana, equally firmly, "would like him to stay."

"If this is a bad time . . ." Q began innocently.

Deanna was about to make reply, but Lwaxana cut her off with a sharp, "Deanna, I'll not have such rudeness. Q is a guest."

"I thought you had a fight."

Lwaxana smiled. "We made up. Didn't we, Q?"

"Yes, indeed. Your mother is quite a woman, Counselor Troi," Q informed her. "She's like none I've ever encountered."

"Or will again, I daresay," Lwaxana laughed. She and Q clinked their glasses.

It was more than Deanna could take. Her fists balled, and with her heart racing, Deanna turned and virtually ran out of Lwaxana's quarters.

Q shook his head sympathetically. "Poor girl," he said.

"Yes," said Lwaxana. "It's so difficult for a child when a parent becomes involved with someone else."

"Are we involved?" asked Q.

Lwaxana eyed him coquettishly over the top of her glass. "I would say we're definitely something. Unless you have a problem . . . ?"

"Certainly not," said Q stiffly. "I find you a most intriguing individual, Lwaxana Troi. You speak forthrightly, and you don't prejudge me. They're envious, you know."

"Who is?"

He gestured with his head. "Picard and the others."

"Jean-Luc!" She made a dismissive wave. "Posh. Jean-Luc Picard is the most non-jealous male I've ever encountered. Although he does tend to harbor some rather tawdry thoughts in regard to me."

"The brute!" declared Q. "He thinks, because he is the captain, he can take such liberties!"

"Oh, he can't be held responsible for that," said Lwaxana. "After all, he is only human, and I am . . . me. Besides, all he's done is *think* about it. He hasn't actually done anything. Thought is not the same as deed."

"It is for me," said Q. "That's probably where my confusion set in."

Deanna wasn't really paying any attention to where she was going. Instead she just barrelled down the hallway, her arms pumping, her thoughts racing.

How? How was it possible that an empath and a telepath were having communications problems? It was insane! It didn't make any sense at all.

Suddenly Wesley Crusher was in front of her, and she almost bumped into him. He had just exited from his quarters as if shot from a cannon. If she'd been remotely interested in anything except her own problems, Deanna would have noticed. Instead she said briskly, "Excuse me, Wesley," and started to continue down the hall.

"No! Counselor!" He grabbed her by the arm with such force that Deanna thought it might have been wrenched from the socket. He was grasping her like a life preserver. "Counselor, wait!"

Waves of anxiety were flooding from him, almost overwhelming her. She gasped as much from the mental barrage as from the physical grabbing. "What is it, Wes?" she said, trying to re-attune herself from focussing on her own problems to those of someone else.

Other people were walking past and glancing their way, and Wesley quickly pulled her close. In a low, urgent voice, he said, "I need you."

She looked at their physical proximity, heard the words he had spoken, and in spite of herself, the edges of her mouth went up slightly in amusement. "Some people might misinterpret that," she said.

Wes was so distracted he didn't even realize what she was saying. "Listen, I have to talk to you," he spoke in a rushed whisper. "I can't talk to Commander Riker, Captain Picard, or Geordi because they'll think it's funny, and Data wouldn't understand, and I *sure* can't tell my mother . . ."

She put calming hands on his shoulders. "Wesley, slow down. Talk to me. Tell me what the problem is."

"Promise you won't laugh."

"I'm a trained counselor, Wes," said Deanna, becoming more grateful by the moment that something had happened to take her mind off her immediate problem. Also, she'd made that selfsame request of her fellow officers not too long ago, when explaining the Ab'brax. Riker broke his promise and snickered. She'd almost decked him. "I've heard a great deal in my career. I assure you I won't laugh."

"All right."

He entered his quarters, pulling Deanna in behind him. The doors hissed shut.

Deanna's dark eyes widened when she saw the naked blue woman on Wesley's bed. The blue woman smiled sweetly.

"Uhm . . . hello," said Deanna uncertainly. She stared at the girl but spoke to Wesley through teeth that were clenched in an uncomfortable smile. "Is she a friend of yours?"

"We just met," said Wesley.

Deanna turned and looked at Wes. "Commander Riker would say you're a fast worker."

"That's why I didn't want Commander Riker here," Wes said pointedly, and quickly crossed the room to the girl. He hurriedly drew a sheet around her. "Look, go wait in there, okay?" he said in exasperation.

121

She nodded and went into the bathroom. Wesley pushed a button and the door slid shut. He turned to Deanna. "She's a gift," he said, feeling tired already.

"Obviously you unwrapped her."

*"Deanna!"* he howled. "I told you, I could've gotten Commander Riker down here if I wanted jokes!"

"I'm sorry."

"And you promised not to laugh!"

"I'm sorry," she said again, covering her mouth and now empathizing with Riker's earlier amusement at her expense. She waited a moment to compose herself and then looked up at him. "A gift, you said? From whom, may I ask?"

He ran fingers through his hair. "From Sehra of Graziunas."

"Why would Sehra of Graziunas give you a naked young woman?"

"She didn't know my shirt size! *I* don't know!" He started to pace. "What do I do with her?"

"What does she expect you to do with her?"

Wesley looked at her.

"Oh," said Deanna. "Are you certain that that is . . . yes, I guess it would be somewhat evident, wouldn't it?" She shook her head. "And how does that make you feel?"

"Kind of stupid. I mean . . . I can't make love to her." He looked at Deanna. "Can I?"

She folded her arms. "You're asking my permission?"

"No! I mean . . . no. It wouldn't be right, that's all. I mean . . . I tried talking to her, Counselor. Tried to find out about her background, find out who she was. She's a few bricks shy, you know?"

"She didn't seem very shy," said Deanna, glancing over where the woman had been moments before.

"Never mind. It's an old saying," said Wes. He was perched on a chair, his legs drawn up under himself.

"She's *too* willing, you know? Kind of vacuous. It's just not right, that's all."

Troi smiled. "I admit I'm impressed, Wesley. There are quite a few teenage boys I know of who would not pass up this sort of opportunity. It takes a certain type of young man not to take advantage of a naked, willing, empty-headed young woman who is offering herself to him."

"Yeah," said Wes ruefully. "The type being a stupid young man."

"Your mother would be proud."

"Ohhh," moaned Wes, putting his head in his hands. "That's the worst thing you could say. Commander Riker would probably laugh at me for not taking advantage of her."

"Wesley!" said Deanna. "You make it sound like Commander Riker will go after anything that's female, good-looking, and has a pulse!"

Wes looked up at her.

"Rather than explore that," Deanna said quickly, sensing that she was abruptly on uncertain ground, "let's move on to the main problem. If you are deterred by the prospect of this 'gift,' what do you intend to do?"

"I don't know! I can't give her back. It would be insulting. Do you think," he said hopefully, "that Captain Picard would let her stay on board?"

"In what capacity?"

"As my . . ." and Wesley's voice trailed off. "Guess not," said Wesley. "She can't stay here, though."

Deanna stood. "I will talk to the captain," she said, trying to sound as serious as she could, "about finding quarters for the young lady until such time that things can be sorted out."

"Thank you. Maybe you could hurry . . . ?"

"Warp speed," she said with a smile, and uncrossing her legs, she stood.

"Deanna . . . you don't think less of me, do you?"

She raised an eyebrow. "Less of you? Because you consider sex to be an act between two people who feel, at the very least, a deep and mutual attraction based on a variety of factors? Rather than displaying a 'She's here, she's willing, let's do it' attitude? What do you think I am, Wesley? A typical human teenage male?"

He actually smiled at that. "Hardly."

"Good." She patted him on the shoulder and walked out.

The blue woman stuck her head out of the bathroom. "Wesley? Do you want me now?"

Part of him definitely did. He waved weakly and said, "Tell you what. Go back in there and wait until I call, all right?"

"All right, Wesley," she said agreeably, and withdrew from sight.

Wesley softly thudded his head against a wall.

Lwaxana slowly circled her cabin, regarding Q with interest. "Have you ever been married?" she asked.

"No," said Q. "Marriage is a very human concept. Being together forever takes on quite a different meaning when eternity is one's reality rather than an abstraction."

"You never die?" she asked in wonderment.

"Not unless I wish it," said Q, "and even then, not in terms that you would understand."

"Try and explain it to me."

"I can't," he said simply. "There are no words. Only concepts."

"You forget. I'm a powerful telepath."

"Powerful for human terms, perhaps," said Q. "But in my terms . . ."

She put the glass down. "Try me," she said firmly.

He regarded her thoughtfully. "You become more and more intriguing, Lwaxana Troi. You are only the second individual whom I have encountered that I hold out any hope for."

"Who's the first?"

"Data."

She frowned. "You're serious."

"Oh yes. Quite. Are you certain you're serious about dealing with the Q concept of death?"

"Dead serious."

"Very well." He put down his own glass and moved towards her. He extended a hand, then hesitated, looking at it for a brief moment as if he were surprised that it was there. Then he reached out and touched the side of Lwaxana's head with a single finger.

For a brief moment, Lwaxana felt an inhuman coolness in his touch, and something more . . . something that both attracted and frightened her.

And then she was overwhelmed.

Picard didn't glance up from his desk as the signal sounded from the door of the ready room. "Come," he said briskly.

Deanna Troi entered and said, "Captain, I need to talk to you for a moment about . . ."

And then she gasped and staggered against a wall. Picard was immediately out of his seat, supporting her. He helped her to a couch and was surprised to see that she had gone deathly white.

"Mother . . ." she whispered, and then she passed out.

# Chapter Thirteen

"PICARD TO SECURITY," he snapped. "Security team to Mrs. Troi's quarters, immediately."

Deanna was sitting up already, which was a good sign. She looked shaken nonetheless, and for a moment she actually seemed frightened. "Mother . . ." she said again.

"It's all right, Counselor," said Picard firmly. "A security team is on their way to ascertain your mother's safety."

"I have to go to her!" said Deanna, and tried to get to her feet. But her legs gave out and she sank back onto the couch. "I have to . . ." she whispered.

"What happened?" he demanded in the sort of no-nonsense voice that indicated he had better get a brisk, efficient answer. It was like being doused with cold water, and Deanna composed herself so that she could give the sort of response her commanding officer required.

"I'm sensitive to my mother's moods and feelings,

as you know," she said. "And there was some sort of—I don't know how else to say it—overload. As if she had been exposed to something that was too much for her mind to cope with."

"Q?" asked Picard.

"It would seem likely," admitted Deanna.

With a scowl, Picard said, "We'll know soon enough."

Lwaxana felt strong arms around her and she blinked in confusion. "Q . . . ?" she murmured.

The world fell into focus around her, and she found that she was looking up at Mr. Homn. On his normally impassive face was an expression of concern.

She drew herself up and took a deep breath to clear her head. "I'm all right, Mr. Homn," she said, although she did allow him to help her to her feet. She allowed herself to be impressed once more by his strength as he moved her, as if she were weightless, over to a chair.

She looked around. "Where's Q?"

Homn made no reply. He didn't need to.

"Yes, obviously he left," said Lwaxana. "Why? After what happened—"

And she frowned. What had happened, anyway?

There was something, some sort of images in her mind. The barest flickering of concepts and ideas that she could just sense, at the outskirts of her consciousness. As if she had learned something, seen something, that was more than she could handle. It was wonderful, frightening, orgasmic and more. And her mind, in self-defense, had shut down. Protected her. Protected her from . . . what?

There was an urgent buzzing at her door. "Come in," she said distractedly.

Worf entered, with two security men backing him up. They had their phasers out. They were automatically scanning all corners of the room. "Are you all right?" rumbled Worf.

"I'm fine," said Lwaxana. "Perfectly fine." She smoothed out the front of her dress. "Why do you ask?"

Worf didn't seem satisfied. "We were alerted that there might be some sort of difficulties."

"None at all."

"Are you quite certain?"

"I'm not accustomed to having my word questioned, Mr. Worf," said Lwaxana archly.

Worf drew himself up straight. "I am not questioning your word, Mrs. Troi. Merely circumstances."

"The circumstances are just fine, thank you. You may leave now."

Worf seemed to glower at that. He turned to his men and said, with just the faintest touch of sarcasm, "We may leave now."

They backed out of the room slowly, as if on guard for some last-minute attack. Worf nodded slightly and the door closed.

"Women," he growled. Then he tapped his communicator. "Worf to Captain Picard. There is no disturbance in the quarters of Mrs. Troi. And if there was, she is not telling us about it."

"Thank you, Mr. Worf," came the captain's reply.

Worf grunted, then tilted his head slightly. "Let's go," he said sourly.

"Worf reports all is well," said Picard rather unnecessarily, since Deanna had heard Worf perfectly. She was seated opposite the captain, her hands still moving in uncomfortable fidgets.

"Yes, I know."

"You disagree with that assessment?"

Deanna paused, uncertain of what to say. She looked terribly vulnerable, as if the slightest harsh word would cause her to crack and shatter. Finally, all in a rush she said, "Captain, I am truly, truly frightened for my mother. I'm afraid that she has let herself in for more than she can handle."

"Counselor," said Picard slowly, "you, of course, know your mother far better than I. But I must say that in the time that I have known her, I consider Lwaxana Troi a woman who is perfectly capable of handling anything."

"With all due respect, Captain, the last time you talked of people being capable of handling anything, you were speaking of this crew as a whole. That was right before we were tossed light-years from home and the Borg almost killed us. And you will recall that Q was involved in that instance too."

She sounded surprisingly brittle. It was an indication to Picard of just how much her concern was weighing on her. "Deanna—" he began.

"All she has to do is say the wrong thing!" said Deanna. "One wrong word, and Q could wipe her out of existence."

"He won't do that."

"How do we know that?" she demanded. "Q does as he pleases, whenever he pleases. He's like an . . . an anti–Prime Directive. My mother is a very forceful and demanding personality, and who knows what she might do to set Q off. And I can't persuade her to use caution! I can't convince her that it's madness." She looked up from her wringing hands. "Perhaps you could."

"Me?"

"Yes. She looks up to you. She respects you."

"She wants me," Picard said testily. "Not that I've ever encouraged her, as you well know."

"I'm aware of that, Captain."

He pulled slightly on his uniform top. "She was absolutely fixated on me when she was last here. Made me so uncomfortable I had to retreat to the holodeck." His eyes narrowed as he pinned Deanna with a look. "I do not retreat lightly. I've faced down angry Candellian pirates and berserk Ferengi, and have not retreated. But your mother drove me into hiding. That was not a course I undertook lightly. And that is the sort of personality that is going up against Q. I'd say that Q has his work cut out for him. Now, I've told Q that I am not pleased with the current state of affairs, but to be blunt, if your mother is welcoming him with open arms, it puts me on somewhat shaky ground. She is a guest and—God help us all—so is Q. Her wishes have to be considered."

"What about *my* wishes, Captain?" she said. "What about *my* concerns? Captain—you would help me if I gave such strong advice on any crew member here. Certainly my mother deserves at least that much consideration. I understand if she intimidates you—"

"Intimidates!" said Picard sharply.

"Well, perhaps 'intimidates' is not the right word—"

"I should say not!" Picard told her. "And I'll have you know that . . ."

He was stabbing an index finger at her, and then his voice trailed off. He began to smile, and shook his head. "Reverse psychology, Counselor?"

She shrugged. "Whatever works, Captain."

He sighed. "All right, Counselor, if it means that much to you that you're resorting to obvious psychological ploys, would you ask your mother if she would do me the honor of dinner this evening? I will . . . discuss matters with her."

Deanna let out a breath of relief. "Thank you, Captain."

"Don't thank me yet," Picard cautioned her. "Your mother can be a very determined woman. Even single-minded, sometimes."

"Single-minded women!" Deanna suddenly remembered. "There is another topic I must discuss with you. It involves our Mr. Crusher."

"Teenagers," said Picard ruefully. "So tell me, what has he gotten himself into?"

"Odd that you should put it that way . . ."

Picard pulled uncomfortably at the collar of his dress uniform and wondered for perhaps the hundredth time in his career exactly who the sadist was that had designed it. He stood in front of Lwaxana's quarters and nodded formally at crewmen who happened to wander by.

Picard spotted a few raised eyebrows at the sight of the captain lurking outside the quarters of Mrs. Troi. Her pursuit of him when she was last aboard was something of an open secret. So seeing the captain now, apparently the lamb being led willingly to the slaughter—well, it was certainly something to be questioned. Nevertheless, it wound up adding to his discomfort.

"Come in," came the voice of Lwaxana Troi.

He sighed deeply. "Into the jaws of death rode the three hundred . . ." he murmured, pasted a smile on his face, and entered.

As before, the first thing that assaulted him was the heavy scent of perfume that hung in the air. It was so powerful that it was practically a physical thing.

Standing across the room, Lwaxana Troi was decked out in a long, flowing yellow-and-green gown.

"No black?" asked Picard.

"I still mourn for my daughter," said Lwaxana sadly, and then her face brightened. "But for a reunion of such old and dear friends . . . Jean-Luc, I had to dress properly." She extended a hand and Picard suavely kissed her knuckles. "Imagine my surprise when Deanna said you wanted to dine with me."

"Imagine mine as well," replied Picard.

She frowned slightly, not understanding, and Picard said quickly, "I'm pleased that you were able to make time for me."

"Always time for you, Jean-Luc."

She gestured towards a table that was already laid out with Betazoid delicacies. Mr. Homn stood by, gong at the ready.

Picard and Lwaxana sat down opposite each other, Picard trying desperately to feel comfortable in a situation that definitely had him ill at ease. Mrs. Troi watched him with that aggravating look that made it seem as if she were peering straight into the back of his head. Which, for all he knew, she might very well be doing.

"So," said Picard briskly.

"So," said Lwaxana in return. She cupped her hands and rested her chin in them, looking remarkably girlish and even—heaven help him—attractive. Picard cleared his throat as Mrs. Troi said, "Jean-Luc . . ."

"Yes, Lwaxana?" he said gamely, preparing for an evening of romantic overtures on the part of his counselor's mother.

"I believe that I've found . . . the one for me."

"Lwaxana," began Picard, "that's very flatter—"

But he wasn't able to get the rest of the sentence out, because she wasn't paying attention. Instead she continued as if he had not spoken, "Tell me everything . . . and I mean everything . . . that you know about . . . Q."

Wesley stood in the doorway of the quarters that had been assigned to his "gift." At his insistence, she was wearing the robes that she had come with. He reminded himself to personally "thank" Chief

O'Brien for going along with the transporting of the girl over to the *Enterprise* and for her subsequent entry into his quarters. Undoubtedly it was O'Brien's whimsical idea of a joke. Ha Ha.

"Are you sure you don't want me in your quarters, Wesley?" she sighed.

"Yes, I'm sure," Wesley told her. "Just stay here until I can get this all sorted out, okay?"

She cocked her head and regarded him curiously. "Sehra's other serving girls were so envious of me when Sehra decided to make a gift of me to you. You clearly impressed her in quite a short time."

"It's a knack," said Wesley quickly. He glanced down the corridor and spotted Walt Charles, a tall and handsome young ensign, heading his way. Charles slowed and raised an eyebrow and inwardly Wes moaned. "Look, go on in, okay?"

"Whatever you say, Wesley," she said, and suddenly she threw her arms around him and kissed him fiercely. He was caught completely off guard, and despite himself, he found himself returning it.

*You're in a corridor of the* Enterprise, *you moron!* his mind screamed at him.

He peeled her off him and pushed her, harder than he would have liked, into her quarters. The doors hissed shut before she could get another "Whatever you say, Wesley" out.

Wesley turned to face a clearly astounded Charles, who was shaking his head in wonderment. "Go on," sighed Wesley. "Say it."

"You know, Crusher," said Charles slowly, "my respect for you has just gone through the roof. Getting a beauty like that—"

"I didn't get her!" said Wes. "I didn't do anything with her!"

"Nothing?"

"No!"

"Oh." Charles's face fell. And he walked off.

Very softly, very slowly, Wesley once again knocked his head against the nearest wall.

*Thud.*

*Thud.*

*Thud.*

It was kind of relaxing, in a way.

"All-powerful, you say?"

Picard was leaning forward, trying with as much patience as he could to talk sense into her. "As near as we can tell, there is nothing that is beyond Q's powers. And that, Lwaxana, should be more than enough to make you realize that this cannot possibly work."

"I don't realize any such thing," said Lwaxana. She took a bite of the meat that lay neatly sectioned on her plate, and Mr. Homn obediently sounded a gong of thanks. Picard would have been ready to offer thanks had that blasted gong cracked with the next stroke. "You may find this odd, Jean-Luc, but I find powerful men exciting."

"I'm sure they can be exciting," Picard said with deliberate clarity. "Defusing a bomb rigged to the matter/antimatter mix can also be exciting. But one wrong move, and you can end up a rapidly fading memory."

"Oh, that's not going to happen," she said dismissively.

"You don't know Q . . ."

"You sound just like Deanna. It's patronizing, Jean-Luc, and I thought better of you."

"The reason I sound just like Deanna is because we're both right. Q is not what he appears to be, either in body or in intent. He has something up his sleeve."

"Yes, it appears to be a fairly muscular arm."

Picard steepled his fingers, composing himself, trying to find an angle that would get through. "Mrs. Troi . . . Q has regarded this ship and her crew as nothing more than laboratory animals, to play out experiments for him. He is constantly trying to show that humanity is some pathetic, barbaric, violent, sadistic race."

"And your response to charges of barbarism and violence is to try and throw him off the ship."

"Yes—no!" said Picard quickly, and then sighed, "Well . . . yes. But only because of the damage and chaos that his earlier visits have caused. Deanna told you of how he hurled us far into unknown space . . ."

"I thought exploring unknown space was your mission," said Lwaxana in carefully contrived confusion.

"Well . . . yes, but—"

"So he used some of that remarkable power of his," she said with that breathy voice, "to aid you on your mission."

"He left us at the mercy of the Borg, a race that has no mercy!" said Picard. "They carved out a section of the ship! Over a dozen of my people died because of Q!"

"It seems to me that they died because of the Borg," pointed out Lwaxana.

"A race we would not have encountered for years yet, if it weren't for Q!" Picard said in exasperation. "A race of unrelenting conquerors . . . , destroying everything in sight."

"But they didn't destroy you."

"Yes, well . . . after making me grovel somewhat, Q brought us back to safety."

"Hmm," said Lwaxana. "It seems to me that Q did you something of a service. By giving you that initial exposure to the Borg, you have that much more time to prepare defenses against their arrival. An arrival which, I would think, was somewhat inevitable in any event."

"That may be," admitted Picard, "but—when he first met us, he put us on trial! He treated us terribly!"

"It's not a capital offense to make a bad first impression," she said.

"He did similar things the second time we met!"

"He does take a while to get to know," she allowed. "Although, of course, with my abilities, I can attain a rapport with greater ease than you."

A part of him wanted to feel that Mrs. Troi deserved whatever she got and the hell with it all, but Picard couldn't do that to Deanna. He had to give his counselor every effort on her behalf.

Something warned him, though, not to mention to Lwaxana about the time Q had given the Q power to Riker. The last thing Mrs. Troi needed to know was that Q could share the power that was his.

"This will give you some idea of his gall," said Picard. "The last time he came here, he had no powers. He materialized on the bridge, stark naked . . ."

"Really?" Her interest perked up. "Would you have a visual record of that, by any chance?"

Picard ignored the comment as he continued, "He expected us to give him safe haven from a race that wanted to dispose of him for the tortures that he had inflicted on them. To save his own miserable hide, he thoughtlessly endangered the ship and then he . . ." Picard's voice trailed off.

"He what?" prompted Lwaxana.

"It was nothing."

"What did he do?" she demanded.

"He . . . got his powers restored because he was willing to give up his life to save ours," sighed Picard.

Lwaxana stared at Picard with amusement. "The monster! He should be hanged!"

"Lwaxana—" he made one more desperate effort to get through to her. "It's all in his attitude. In the way he views us and our relation to him."

"He's all-powerful and we're not."

"That's about correct, yes."

"But he's right!" said Lwaxana. "He is all-powerful. You've said as much yourself. And we're not. That's obvious. But perhaps what attracts him to me is the allure of my powerful mind. Not to mention my status," and she primped slightly, "as daughter of the Fifth House, and Holder of—"

"Yes, yes, I know all that," said Picard impatiently. "What it boils down to . . ."

"Is that you're jealous."

Picard tried to respond to that, but nothing came readily.

Lwaxana comfortingly patted his hand. "I never believed it when Q suggested it, but imagine that. He was right. I never should have doubted."

"I am not jealous!" said Picard.

"Envious, then. It sounds to me, Jean-Luc . . . and, of course, I can gather impressions from more than just words . . . it seems to me that by and large, you're envious because Q has shown you up on several occasions. You feel inferior. But dear Jean-Luc, don't you see? It's all right to feel inferior when you genuinely *are* inferior. There's no shame in that. No shame in being aware of your limitations. As long as you recognize these feelings for what they are."

Each word dripping with frost, Picard said, "I—am *not*—jealous—of Q!"

"Oh, Jean-Luc, you can be honest with me," said Lwaxana coyly.

"He is dangerous! I'm concerned for your safety! From my understanding, he caused you turbulent, emotional distress and then vanished when it overwhelmed you!"

"He shared things with me that I wasn't ready for," she admitted. "That was my fault for asking for too much, too soon. As for his not staying, well . . . he knows what a woman finds attractive."

*"What?"*

"If there's one thing a woman loves, it's a man of mystery. A man whose comings and goings are abrupt and whose encounters are tinged with danger. A man who—"

"He's not a man!" said Picard in total vexation. "He's Q!"

Lwaxana shook her head, and she spoke with a slightly scolding tone. "Jean-Luc, you are so obvious to me. I know that you've never given up your somewhat ribald thoughts about me. I admit I found them terribly attractive before, but now—with Q in my life—I don't think they're terribly appropriate, do you? You really should keep a closer watch on your thoughts. It seems to me that you are simply out-of-control jealous over this situation. You can't stand the thought of me in the arms of another man."

Picard stood. "I can see this is proving fruitless. Good night, Mrs. Troi."

"Now, Jean-Luc, don't be like that. Can we still be friends?"

Without another word, not trusting himself to speak, or even think, Picard turned and walked with quick strides out of Mrs. Troi's quarters.

She sighed and bit into a wafer. "Poor dear," she sighed. "The better man won, and it's just destroying him."

Mr. Homn gonged.

# Chapter Fourteen

DEANNA WAS IN Ten-Forward when Picard entered. She looked up, and the *Enterprise* captain did not even have to say a word.

"It did not go well, I take it," she said.

Picard sat down opposite her. Guinan, behind the bar, chose not to approach at this time. She sensed that she would only be intruding.

"Her mind is made up," said Picard.

Deanna looked down and sighed. "I appreciate your efforts, Captain."

"Deanna, as unlikely as it may seem, perhaps we should entertain the possibility that Q is sincere."

She looked up at him. "How likely do you think that possibility is?"

"Not very," admitted Picard. "But in many instances of love, merits that would escape the casual glance can frequently . . ."

"You think she's in love with him?" she asked with more dread than he'd ever heard from her.

"I think there is that very distinct possibility," he said dryly. "As a matter of fact, she thinks I'm jealous."

"Why won't she listen?" said Deanna.

"She doesn't want to, Deanna. Your mother is a very lonely woman. She wants so much to believe that she's found the right mate, and she will do anything—reject advice of esteemed colleagues, of loved ones—rather than admit to the possibility that this man is not right for her."

"Q isn't a man."

"Yes, I pointed that out. It didn't seem to have much impact." He sighed. "To some degree I can sympathize with her, Counselor. Growing older alone is difficult enough. To do so—and be under a hormonal imperative to do something about it—that sounds like a very difficult situation indeed. I don't envy you."

"Me?" said Deanna, arching her eyebrows.

"I don't envy her," Picard repeated slowly.

"You said that you don't envy me," Deanna told him. "A Freudian slip, Captain. You don't envy my eventually falling into phase and searching out—"

"Counselor, I know what I said. I said that I do not envy your mother."

She shrugged. "Whatever you say, Captain."

He rubbed the bridge of his nose. "I must admit to some degree of fatigue. If I did misspeak, I apologize. The Tizarin have made every effort to behave themselves, but they still make something of a racket now and then, parading up and down the corridors. Security is hard-pressed to keep up with them. If it were up to Worf, he'd blast them all out the nearest photon tubes."

"And if it were up to you, Captain?" she asked, amused in spite of the difficulty of the situation.

"I would probably help him load them in," Picard

140

admitted. "Tomorrow is the celebratory grand dance. I've reserved Holodeck C. Attendance is not required, but highly suggested. An escort is mandatory. I would assume Commander Riker—?"

"Of course . . ." Deanna smiled, then sighed. "It's been ages since we've been dancing. Perhaps that would be nice. And perhaps it will give me the opportunity to step back and let matters take their course."

"As you say, Counselor. If we can't alter the tide of events, at least we can be nearby with towels to mop up."

Picard stood, inclined his head slightly towards Guinan, and then turned and walked out. A moment later, Guinan glided towards Deanna. "You going to be all right, Counselor?"

"Guinan," said Deanna, turning towards the hostess, "you know Q better than anyone. You have a long history of animosity."

"A fair assessment."

"What are the chances," said Deanna, "that Q really has changed? That his intentions towards my mother are honorable? That he is genuinely trying to absorb and live by human concepts of love and understanding? Is there any chance of that at all?"

Guinan gave it some thought. "Anything is possible," she said at last. "In this whole, great galaxy, that is always true. And Q did go through a rather humbling experience the last time he was here. It's possible that changed him."

"Possible . . . but not likely," said Deanna.

Guinan shrugged. "I don't know. I honestly don't know. You don't want me to try and lie to you, do you?"

Deanna wanted to shout, *Yes! Lie to me! Tell me my mother will be all right. Tell me this will all turn out for the best. Tell me something I can take mindless comfort in, instead of dwelling on all the worst possibilities.*

"Of course not," said Deanna.

Wesley was at his station early, taking comfort in going through the procedures that were, to him, automatic. It helped to take his mind off his confusion.

He wanted her. She was gorgeous. She was willing. She was all his. But an annoying, irritating streak of morality was getting in the way. He didn't want to take advantage of some girl who was under a cultural imperative to be submissive. Where was the joy in that?

*Who cares about that?* an inner voice demanded. *You think too much! You're too smart for your own good! Don't make everything a morality play! Just take her and—*

"So, Crusher!" came a familiar voice.

Wesley flinched inwardly. He didn't even have to turn around. "So, Charles," he responded evenly. "Shouldn't you be in engineering?"

"Just came off shift," said Walter Charles, coming around to the front of Wesley's station. "There's a big shindig tonight in Holodeck C. You going to be bringing your girlfriend?"

"She's not my girlfriend," said Wesley tightly.

"Yeah, so I heard. Look, Wes . . ." Charles leaned forward. "If you're not interested in her . . . how about letting me take her?"

Wesley felt his cheeks burning. "No."

"No?" Charles looked surprised. "You said . . ."

"I said," Wesley told him, "that she's not my girlfriend. Not now. That might change in the future." He looked back down at his console sullenly. "In the very near future."

\* \* \*

In the family ship of the Graziunas, Sehra regarded herself in the full-length mirror and did a quick pirouette. Her long blue-and-orange dress, cut provocatively low down the back, swirled around her. She stopped and then started to experiment with her hair to see whether it would look better up or down.

She wanted to look her best that evening for Kerin. She had spoken to him briefly earlier in ship-to-ship communication with the Nistral. He had seemed distracted, even edgy. His conversation with her was brief and forced, and he didn't even really seem to want to look at her. It was the oddest thing.

She mentally chalked it up to nerves. It was understandable. Kerin was taking a major step, the same as she was. Some nervousness was to be expec—

She whirled suddenly. Something had caught her eye, just for the briefest of moments. Something that didn't make sense.

She looked at her mirror and saw only her own reflection. Yet a moment earlier she had thought she had seen . . .

She could have sworn she had seen . . .

A man in a Starfleet uniform. He even looked passingly familiar, as if she had seen him before. It was hard to be sure. Most humans looked alike to her, and she had met so many thus far. But that was crazy. What would a reflection of a Starfleet officer be doing in her mirror? It was nonsense.

Kerin was obviously not the only one who was nervous.

Beverly Crusher turned at the brisk footfall behind her and was surprised to see the captain standing at the entrance to her office. Picard never visited the sickbay unless there were injured crew members in residence, or if he had an appointment for a physical, but never for reason of personal illness. He was a strong believer in the healing powers of tea, not to mention bullheaded determination in refusing to accept the notion of being sick.

Yet now, here he was, actually looking uncomfortable. "Yes, Captain?"

"There is a gathering tonight in Holodeck C," Picard said without preamble. "Part of the grand celebratory process of the Tizarin. A dance, actually. Escorts are mandated by custom, and I was," he said, taking a breath, "I was wondering if you would do me the honor of attending with me."

She put down her padd and looked at him with unabashed amusement. "Why, Jean-Luc, are you asking me for a date?"

"Not at all," he said stiffly.

"I see. You're just going to pick me up at my quarters, bring me to a dance on your arm, twirl me around the floor—you'll insist on leading, no doubt, because no man would be insane enough to dance backwards—and then you'll bring me back after an evening of pleasant company and conversation. What would you call that?"

His lips twitched slightly. "I would call that enchanting." When he said it so formally, it came out "enchawnting."

She smiled. "I'll be waiting."

## *Chapter Fifteen*

WHEN KERIN MATERIALIZED in the transporter room of the *Enterprise,* Sehra was there, waiting for him. The sight of her took his breath away. She stood there, her hands folded in front of her, looking very much the girl that he had fallen in love with. Kerin's parents stood on either side of him, as Sehra's did with her. All were looking on in approval.

And then, for just a moment, the image of what Q had shown her flashed in his mind. And there was that look of lingering distrust from Sehra's mother . . .

Just like that, the mood was broken, and the confidence that Kerin felt evaporated. The others in the room could almost sense the cool formality that fell over him like a cloak.

Kerin bowed slightly and extended a hand, just as protocol demanded. Sehra took it, studying his face, trying to understand what was wrong. But his look was inscrutable, and Sehra clung to the belief that sooner or later, when he was ready, Kerin would tell her what was on his mind.

They walked out of the transporter room in silence, the two young people did, leaving the four parents and Chief O'Brien staring after them.

"Trouble in paradise," suggested Nistral.

"They'll work it out," boomed Graziunas. "Young people are good at that. Better than their elders, sometimes."

"Are you implying," said Nistral's wife, Dai, "that we are being at all difficult about this? That we've been hard to work with in planning this wedding?"

"Not at all," said Graziunas slowly. "I'm not saying that at all."

"*We* know that *we* have been more than cooperative," said Dai.

"Oh, and we haven't?" Fenn, the wife of Graziunas, now spoke up. "I can't say I like your tone of voice, Dai."

"I am most sorry," said Dai icily. "In the future I shall *try* and speak in a tone *more* to your liking."

With that, Dai turned her back and walked out of the transporter room. Fenn tossed a significant glance at her husband and marched out a moment later.

The two men looked at each other.

"Quite a firebrand, your Fenn," Nistral observed.

"The same might be said of your Dai," replied Graziunas. "A pity you don't have a bit more control over her."

Nistral's eyes narrowed. "I didn't exactly see you keeping Fenn in line. I can see why. She is a rather aggressive woman, after all. Very much a leader and decision maker."

"Are you implying that she is the true power of the house of Graziunas?" There was a dangerous undercurrent to Graziunas' question. A line had been drawn.

Nistral refrained from crossing it. "I am not implying it. You are inferring it. I've said what I've said, no
more, no less. If you read insult into that, Graziunas,
then that is your choice, not mine."

"You are saying, then, that insult was not intended."

"As you wish," said Nistral deferentially.

The two men exited the transporter room, each
watching the other carefully. O'Brien let out a sigh the
moment they were gone. This whole business was
becoming more difficult with each passing day, and
O'Brien, for one, couldn't wait until it was over.

Lwaxana adjusted her elaborate headpiece, a large
affair with exotically upswept sidepieces of gleaming
black metal. It was traditional, having been handed
out from generation to generation. Truth to tell, the
damned thing weighed half a ton. She felt like she was
wearing a satellite on her head. But once again,
traditions had to be attended to.

Her glimmering black dress hugged her, and she ran
her hands along her hips and along the flatness of her
stomach. Not bad. Not bad at all. Not quite the body
of her youth, she reasoned, but what slight deficiencies
there might be were more than made up for by her
years of acquired experience, grace, and sophistica-
tion.

She went to her jewelry box and opened it, examining the contents. What to wear, what to wear . . . ?

"I have just the thing."

She whirled. Q was standing directly behind her. He
was wearing a formal Starfleet uniform.

Lwaxana folded her arms and adopted a stern look,
not immediately willing to let him back into her good
graces. "You left me in the lurch earlier," she said.
"That was not very polite."

"I sensed that you were overwhelmed," Q replied,

circling the room, his hands behind his back. "I felt my continued presence might intimidate you."

She pointed her chin. "I can be surprised, Q. Even overwhelmed. But never intimidated."

"My apologies," he said suavely. "I hope this will help."

From behind his back he withdrew a pendant that was glorious beyond belief.

The breath left Lwaxana as her eyes widened. All of her archness vanished in the unadulterated amazement of what she was seeing. The pendant hung from his hand in front of her. Within the glittering jewels there seemed to be suns, exploding and being formed continuously. "Will you accept this small token?" asked Q.

Lwaxana was shocked to see that her hands were actually trembling as she reached for it. "I . . . I'm honored," she breathed as she took it. She held it reverently and then whispered, "Would you mind . . . putting it on me?"

"It would be *my* honor," said Q.

She turned and presented the back of her neck to him. He did not have to touch her, though, because a split-instant later the necklace was around her neck. She drew a hand over it, and the pendant seemed to throb with a life of its own.

She turned to face him. "It's the most splendid thing I've ever seen . . ." She paused significantly, then added, "aside from you."

"You're right," said Q.

Picard, once again clad in that irritating formal uniform, smoothed out the front of his jacket and rang the buzzer of Beverly Crusher's quarters. "Right out," came her voice.

Wesley Crusher walked past and slowed when he

saw Picard. "Captain," he said in polite greeting. Salutes were long outmoded, but courtesy required some sort of acknowledgment when encountering the ship's most senior officer.

"Mr. Crusher," replied Picard. "Will you be in attendance this evening?"

Wesley appreciated that the captain did not broach the subject of the girl. He took it as an indication of Picard's trust in him that he would resolve matters in short order on his own. It seemed that everyone else, however, was not hesitating to voice an opinion, or at the very least give him an amused look. Wesley's private little matter was all over the damned ship.

"I'm not sure yet, Captain."

Picard raised an eyebrow. "You don't have much more time to decide."

"I know, sir."

The door hissed open and Picard turned. Both Picard and Wesley gaped.

Beverly Crusher stood there, her red hair elegantly displayed in a stunning wave. Her expression was soft, and she wore a long, dark blue formal gown that was slit provocatively up to mid-thigh on the left.

"Jean-Luc," she said, her voice sounding deep and throaty.

Picard cleared his throat, which suddenly felt congested. "I am without words, Doctor."

"Do you think when words are found, one of them might be 'Beverly'?" she asked, her gleaming lips parted in a small smile.

"Of course, Beverly," said Picard.

She turned her luminous gaze to her son. "Wesley?" she said. "Will we be seeing you tonight?"

Wesley looked at the way Picard was regarding his mother, and the way his mother was looking at her son, and he started feeling emotions that he couldn't

149

identify. But he knew what he was going to do about it.

The blue girl looked up as the doors opened. "Wesley!" she said, upon seeing who was at the door. She stood and immediately dropped her robe.

"What is your name?" he demanded. He hadn't wanted to know because, somehow, he would have felt that it was implying interest on his part.

"Karla," she said.

"Get dressed, Karla," said Wesley. "We're going out."

The buzzer of Deanna's quarters sounded. "Come," she called, and when she turned, there was Will Riker standing in the doorway. Like Picard, he was dressed in his formal uniform.

"Counselor?" he said.

"Yes, Commander?"

He took a step in. "I had thought you would be accompanying me to the festivities tonight. You don't seem ready."

She sighed. "If it's all the same to you, Commander, I think I'll stay in."

"It's not all the same to me," he said firmly. "Escorts are required, and as first officer, it's incumbent upon me to be in attendance."

"I'm sure that you can easily find a young lady to accompany you," said Deanna. She went back to her computer screen and stared at text that she hadn't really been paying attention to for the past hour.

"I'm sure I can," said Riker. "But I had intended to—and wanted to—go with the most stunning, personable, and pleasant woman on the ship. That, Counselor Troi, happens to be you. Now, get dressed, or you'll force me to remove your clothes and dress you myself."

She looked up at him, smiling in spite of herself. "Now, that sounds like a chore you would simply detest."

"A dirty job," agreed Riker. "But that's why they pay me the big money."

"All right," she sighed. "Give me a few minutes."

"Whatever you say." He leaned back against the wall, his arms folded.

"Outside," she said.

"You're a tough customer, Deanna."

"Tougher than anyone knows," she informed him, as he stepped back out into the corridor.

The dance was already in full swing when Picard arrived with Dr. Crusher on his arm. There was a slight decrease in the volume of music from the ever-popular Federation Horns, in deference to the captain's appearance—and partly out of acknowledgment of the stunning medical officer on his arm. Then the music went back to its previous levels, and other couples continued to flow into the holodeck. The Horns struck up a slow waltz time.

A rather intriguing scenario had been created for the evening's entertainment, one that would make the Tizarin feel at home. The walls, the ceiling, even the floor looked like a glistening starfield. Couples were, in essence, dancing in space. Of course, some variations in the holodeck environment had been made. It wouldn't do to have guests freezing to death or suffering from explosive decompression. The aim was for romance, not deadly realism.

The floor of stars was solid beneath them, but nevertheless it was disconcerting for Picard to look down and see an endless drop beneath his feet, yet not be in any danger of falling. It took a few minutes of getting used to, but after that initial period he was effortlessly gliding across space, Beverly Crusher in his arms.

She matched his steps with artful gracefulness. She moved like liquid silk against Picard, and for a brief moment his face softened as he thought, *God, how lovely she is.* Then he remembered who he was, and who she was, and his expression returned to the polite but faintly distant look that he usually maintained in such instances.

Beverly was aware of the rapid "in and out" of the captain's attitude and sighed inwardly. *Jean-Luc, you brilliant fool,* she thought, and reflected on it no more.

Instead her gaze wandered across the "star room." Couples sailed across, and Dr. Crusher felt that if there was indeed a heaven, this was probably some inkling of what it was like.

Then she noticed something and murmured, "Jean-Luc."

"Hmm?"

She tilted her head just slightly in the direction she was looking, and Picard turned to follow her gaze.

He saw Kerin dancing suavely with some girl of the house of Nistral. He seemed to have eyes only for her, and standing off to the side, looking immensely annoyed, was Sehra.

"That," murmured Picard, "does not seem to bode well."

"Oh, they're young," said Crusher. "They'll work it out."

"I certainly hope so. The last thing you want when you have heavily armed ships on either side of you—manned by individuals with a long-simmering feud—is to have a situation that's going to antagonize them."

Deanna and Riker entered, Deanna having changed from her red pants outfit to a flowing turquoise gown.

She glanced around quickly and said, "I don't see them here."

Riker sighed. "Are you going to spend the entire evening worrying about your mother? Deanna, if she's not worried, I don't see why you should be. She's a grown woman."

"A grown woman with an increased sex drive and garnering the attentions of a godlike being with unknown intentions. Will, how am I supposed to—"

He picked up a date and popped it into her mouth. "Shut up and dance, Counselor," he said, and swung her away.

Ensign Charles was with a number of other young crewmen. Their dates were standing nearby, chatting among themselves. Charles was chuckling to the others, "Told you he wouldn't be here."

"I don't see why you're so worked up about him," said Lieutenant Dini, munching on a carrot stick. "Unless you're interested in the girl."

Dini let out a low whistle, and Walter Charles glanced around to see what he was whistling at.

Wesley Crusher had just entered, and on his arm was the blue-skinned woman with the red hair. Wesley was formally dressed, but the woman—

"Oh my God," breathed Charles.

The vast majority of her dress wasn't there. It was composed of several strips of glimmering metallic material, strategically placed, and a long, shimmering cape swirled off her shoulders. Her blue skin seemed iridescent.

Wesley nodded once in the direction of the young officers. "Gentlemen," he said simply, and then he took the girl in his arms and started to swing her out onto the dance floor.

She stepped on his foot.

Wesley's back was to the others, so they didn't see

this. He jammed his top teeth into his lower lip to prevent a cry of pain.

"Sorry," she murmured.

"No problem," he gasped back.

Beverly glanced over Picard's shoulder and almost tripped. "Ohhhh my goodness," she said.

"What now? Bride and groom about to shoot each other?" asked Picard.

"Wesley is here."

He turned and looked and raised an eyebrow. "It seems your son has done quite well for himself."

"I'll say. What in the world is keeping that dress on?"

"The eyes of every young man in the holodeck, I would wager," said Picard.

Riker was pouring punch for Deanna, when he spotted Wesley's date.

"Will," said Deanna softly.

"Yes?"

"I think that's more than enough."

Riker pulled his gaze away from the dancing ensign and gave a startled utterance. To say he had overfilled Deanna's glass would be to understate matters. It was pouring over the sides and splattering onto the vastness of space.

"I'm sorry!" said Riker. "I was . . . distracted."

"I know. You've always been easily distracted," said Deanna, not without amusement.

He turned back to Deanna and grimaced slightly. "That's always been our problem, hasn't it."

"Not *our* problem, *your* problem. I've come to accept that about you, which is why we will forever remain *Imzati* . . . but no more than that." Despite her problems, she smiled. "Besides, Commander . . .

154

it's not as if I've been sitting about, waiting for you . . ."

Her voice suddenly trailed off as her eyes widened.

"Deanna, what is it?" said Riker, suddenly alert.

"They're coming," whispered Deanna.

Wesley felt a tap on his shoulder and he turned. Ensign Charles was standing behind him. "May I cut in?" asked Charles.

Karla looked at Wesley curiously. "Cut in?" she asked.

"He wants to dance with you," said Wes.

Charles sucked in his gut, silently matching his rather impressive physique against Wesley's. "Right, sweetheart. You see, I know the real story between you and Crusher here, and I thought you might be interested in exploring other opportunities."

Wesley felt his cheeks flush and he started to turn, but the blue girl held him firmly in place.

"I don't know what 'story' you've heard," she said, in a voice of such iron that it startled Wes, who had only heard her speak in soft, seductive tones. "But stories change. As for a dance . . . or anything else . . . I'm afraid not. You see, I'm too much woman for you. Only Wesley Crusher will suffice."

She turned back to Wesley, took his face in her hands, and kissed him passionately, and this time Wesley did not resist in the least.

Charles backed off, a beaten man. He returned to the others, shaking his head, and they were snickering loudly. "Dazzled her with your charm, Casanova?"

"I can't get over it," said Charles, in shock.

Charles's date, Lieutenant Clarke, pinched him soundly on the arm and he yelped. "Some women," said Clarke in annoyance, "like a man with brains."

Dini chuckled.

"Dry up," Charles told him.

Meantime, Wesley was coming up for air. He looked at her, her eyes glistening with adoration for him, and he said, "I . . . uh . . . thank you."

"He wanted to take me away," she replied. "As your servant, I couldn't allow that."

"Look, Karla, I don't need a servant, but maybe if—"

And suddenly there was a blinding flash of light.

Beverly Crusher, over the shoulder of Picard, was watching her son be on the receiving end of an impassioned embrace. She wanted to say something, but wasn't sure what, and then suddenly she and Picard, along with all the others, reacted to the abrupt spectacle.

In the middle of the dance floor, it seemed as if a sun had gone nova. Illumination burst forth from an undetermined source with a roar like a cosmos being born. At first the light was blinding white, and then it dissolved into a spectrum of colors, whirling about like a madly pulsating rainbow. People shielded their eyes and yet couldn't help but gaze at the dazzling display that was being played out before them.

And then, from within the heart of the light, two figures began to take shape. The colors surrounded them and then congealed, and Q and Lwaxana Troi stepped out as if through a dimensional portal. The moment their feet hit the dance floor, the spectacular doorway collapsed in on itself, depositing the two of them in the middle of the holodeck.

There was a low murmur of astonishment as everyone stared, whispering to each other, trying to figure out what they had just seen.

Mrs. Troi, arm encircling Q's, patted his forearm and said, "Does he know how to make an entrance, or what?"

Deanna put her hand to her forehead and moaned. Riker's lips thinned in annoyance.

Picard took a step forward. "Q," he said firmly, "that was not amusing."

Q sighed loudly. "Picard, the list of things you find unamusing is truly staggering. Someday I might actually find something to crack that stoic facade."

"Someone might have panicked," Riker confirmed.

"Gentlemen and ladies," called out Q, turning towards them with a theatrical wave, "and lower life forms of all sorts, your opinion of my pyrotechnic display?"

The Tizarin and the majority of guests burst into spontaneous and approving applause. This prompted Q to turn back to Picard, a satisfied smirk on his face. "They're clearly petrified, Jean-Luc."

"Don't . . . do it . . . again," said Picard with barely contained fury.

Q sighed with excess boredom. "As you wish, *mon capitaine.*"

"Mother, are you all right?" demanded Deanna, coming to her quickly.

"Oh, I've never been better, Little One," she said. She looked up at Q with undisguised adoration. "Never better."

Q extended his arms to her. "Would you care to dance?"

"Absolutely," said Lwaxana, and sailed into his arms.

The Federation Horns struck up a faster waltz this time and Q danced off with Mrs. Troi.

Deanna walked quickly to Picard and said, "Captain, stop them."

Picard turned to her. "What would you have, Counselor? That I chastise Q when he is obnoxious *and* when he behaves himself?"

"I don't know," she said in frustration. "And I hate not knowing."

Picard watched Q and Lwaxana waltz across the dance floor. "Damn," he murmured. "The one thing I was most afraid of."

"What?" said Deanna urgently.

"Q is a superb dancer."

"Of course," Riker said dryly. "You can't be omnipotent and have two left feet, now can you?"

"Incredible," Picard said. "I've never seen Q so consistently polite, even respectful, of a human being. Is it possible that he's actually falling in love with her?"

"I don't believe it," was Riker's firm response. "He *must* have an angle. He's just playing his cards closer to his vest this time."

"We'll have to see now, won't we?" Picard said. "And it would seem that until we do, we're depending on Lwaxana Troi to keep him in check."

Kerin watched Q and Troi with rapt attention, and then he heard a voice at his side. He turned and there was Sehra. "I'm sorry, what?" he said.

"You haven't danced with me," she said pointedly. "Not the entire time."

"I've been busy," he said.

"Busy with every other female here," she replied, and tears began to sting her eyes. "Why do you hate me so much?"

And Kerin began to feel like a total creep.

"Oh, Sehra, I'm sorry," he sighed. "I'm . . . you know, protocol and everything. I have to pay attention to others, but it's all duty and things. The other girls don't mean anything."

"They do when you attend to them and totally exclude me."

"You're right, you're right."

"And I just get—"

He took her by both arms and said firmly, "Sehra, I said you're right. That means you win the argument and we can stop."

"Oh," she said in a small voice. "You sure they don't mean anything to you?"

"No other female attracts me the way you do, and I never think of any other female the way I think of you." He ran his fingers through her long hair. "That's the truth."

She smiled at that, satisfied. Then she suddenly said, "Oh, look! Come on, Kerin," and she grabbed him by the hand and dragged him firmly behind her.

"Wesley!" she called out.

Wes worked on prying Karla off him. She seemed to adhere to him like a second skin. "Sehra! Kerin!"

"I hope you like my gift to you," she said.

Wesley managed to twist Karla off and said, "Yeah, I meant to talk to you about that . . ."

"She's been a good servant," Sehra told him. "It broke my heart to give her away. But the mark of a good gift is that it pains you to give it."

"There's a little problem, though," said Wes. "You see—"

"I hope you're not refusing her," said Sehra firmly. "That is a tremendous insult in Tizarin custom."

"Could lead to war between the Federation and the Tizarin," Kerin confirmed.

Wesley looked from one to the other. Then he looked back at Karla.

"I want to bear your children, Wesley," said Karla.

He looked back at Sehra and Kerin. "Let me get back to you," he sighed.

Q turned across the dance floor, the picture of elegance. Lwaxana looked as comfortable in his arms as if she had been born into them.

"No one trusts you," she said.

"There's no reason they should. In the past, I've treated them like the inferior life forms that they are, and they've taken umbrage at that."

"I'd have expected better of them."

"That's the difference between us," said Q. "You expect to see the best of humanity on display, whereas I always anticipate the worst of humanity. Somehow I always seem to get it."

"Perhaps they live up to your expectations. You are, after all, a god. They behave in the way they think their god expects them to act."

Q frowned at that. "You mean they don't want to disappoint me?"

"Exactly."

"Amazing." His eyes widened. "My insight into humanity grows by quantum leaps when I'm with you. Your uncanny perceptions are invaluable. Obviously, Lwaxana Troi, our meeting was destined."

"Do you really think so?"

"I know so."

"Oh, Q," she sighed. "You make me feel light-headed."

There were gasps from around, and Lwaxana said, "Light on my feet too."

"There's a reason for that."

Lwaxana looked down and now she gasped as well.

They were dancing in midair, high among the "stars," the rest of the guests looking up and pointing in amazement.

And inside Lwaxana's head, she heard, *Mother!*

*I'm fine, Little One,* she sent back. *Never better.*

"Your daughter is concerned," said Q.

"You sensed our communication?"

"Of course."

"And yet I can't sense anything of you," said Lwaxana. "Why is that?"

"Because you're not of the Q," he said simply. "Does it trouble you?"

"It attracts me," she told him, as they moved across the sky of the holodeck, going higher and higher. "There's something about a man whose every thought is hidden from me; it makes him a challenge. It makes him someone I want to investigate . . . deeply."

"Deeply?" said Q.

"Incredibly deeply," breathed Lwaxana Troi.

He spun her around in ever-widening arcs. "Do you trust me, Lwaxana Troi?" he demanded. There was iron and challenge in his voice.

She hesitated.

"Do you?" he asked again as the stars twirled around her.

"Yes," she said firmly.

"Good." And with that, he danced her right through the unseen wall of the holodeck, with a kind of distant popping sound that was drowned out by the shouts of astonishment.

"I'll kill him," said Deanna Troi.

Lieutenant Commander Data was incapable of surprise. He could, however, register when something unexpected had happened, and react accordingly.

Such a time was now, as he looked up from the ops station at the bridge and saw what was on the forward screen. "How interesting," he said. He glanced at the sensor readings to confirm what his eyes were telling him.

Chafin looked up from his station, as did Burnside from hers.

There was dead silence for a moment.

"You know," said Chafin thoughtfully, "I understand there are ships that go along for months, even years at a time, without once seeing unaided people cruising past them in space. We see it twice in a week."

Pirouetting across the front viewscreen were two people, their feet moving across an invisible floor, dancing to silent melodies.

"Shows how quickly something can become old hat," observed Burnside.

"Bridge to Captain Picard," Data said briskly, observing procedure.

"Picard here," came the captain's voice. He sounded considerably older.

"Captain, there is—"

"A couple dancing in front of the ship?"

"Yes, sir."

"Specifics, Mr. Data?"

Data studied the screen. "They appear to be performing a classic waltz step. Quite smoothly, actually."

"Thank you, Mr. Data."

"Upon closer magnification, it would appear to be Q and Mrs. Troi."

"I surmised as much, Mr. Data."

"Shall I order a shuttlecraft dispatched, or perhaps the transporter . . . ?"

"No, don't bother," sighed Picard. "I suspect they'll come in when they're damned good and ready."

"Breathtaking, isn't it, Lwaxana," said Q.

She looked around at the stars that whirled about her. "It's like a dream," she whispered.

"All of life is a waking dream," said Q. "And in death is the final awakening."

She should have been cold. She should have been dead. Instead, all there was was the remarkable silence of space. Never before had she realized the awesomeness, the immensity, the sheer power of empty space. And here she was in the arms of one who was greater still than space. One who could effortlessly resist its ravages, its demands. One whose power was beyond the ability of space to touch.

And he was sharing that power—and himself—with her.

*Her.*

It seemed fair and just. It seemed what she deserved, what with her status and rank. Yet she still felt an overwhelming, numbing sense of gratitude.

"Am I going to die?" she whispered. "Am I already dead?"

"Not at all," said Q. "No one, and nothing here, dies until I say so."

"I can live with that," she said.

They danced among the stars, and the stars seemed close enough to touch. "I feel," she told him, "like I could reach out and gather them all in my hand."

"You mean, like this?" he asked.

He stepped back from her a moment and stretched out his clenched fist. When he opened it, it was filled with glittering balls of light. They leaped from his hand and spun about in intricate circles, incandescent phantoms against the black satin of infinity.

They whirled faster and faster, and Lwaxana's eyes were wide. She was mesmerized by the spectacle. The stars filled her entire field of vision. She heard a low laugh—the sound of Q—and for a moment, just a moment, the laugh sounded full of menace and wicked amusement. Then it passed and she was swept away, the stars an overwhelming kaleidoscope, and they were everywhere—in her eyes, in her body, in her mind, exploding within and without . . .

She closed her eyes, gasping, reaching out.

And then she heard something—a low rumble, a soft humming.

Slowly, almost fearfully, her eyes opened and she saw the inside of her quarters. Q was nowhere in sight.

On unsteady legs she rose from the bed she was sitting on. She let out a long, quavering breath, realizing only at that moment just how long she had been holding it. Then she looked down at the pendant that still hung from her neck, glittering with faint impressions of the stars that had filled her.

She shook her head.

"He certainly knows how to show a girl a good time," she said.

# Chapter Sixteen

AFTER ASCERTAINING that her mother was back on the ship and unharmed, Deanna went straight back to her quarters. Riker, seeing that she was clearly concerned, followed her. By the time he got there, she was already pacing back and forth.

He had never seen her like this. He knew, from personal experience, that there was something about parents that took the most mature, level-headed and stable of individuals—which Deanna Troi most definitely was—and reduced them to a state of confused near-infancy.

"No one knows how to deal with parents, Deanna," said Riker soothingly. He sat on a chair and watched her circle the room like a caged cat.

"I should," she said. "I can help utter strangers, and yet I'm helpless to aid my own mother."

"Maybe it's because parents always look at their children and see them only as the mewling infants they were at birth. They don't acknowledge expertise and maturity."

"How can she not! I am mature!" cried Deanna with an impatient stamp of her foot. "I am! I am! Oh God . . . listen to me." She sank into another chair, holding her head in her hands. "Listen how crazy she's making me."

He moved from his spot and crouched next to her. Taking her hand, he said, "Deanna, you're going to have to deal with this."

"Don't you think I'm trying?" she said. "But I know she's making a terrible mistake. Why won't she listen to me?"

"Tell me something," said Riker. "What did your mother think of your involvement with me?"

She frowned. "I don't remember."

"I think you do."

"She said—" Deanna's face clouded and then cleared. "She said that it would never last. That you'd never be able to settle down, that your first love would always be Starfleet, and that it would never work out."

"And did you listen?"

"Yes, I listened, but . . ."

"But what?"

She sighed in unpleasant admission. "I did what I wanted anyway."

"And . . . ?"

"But it did work out, Will," she said urgently. "We're still the best of friends. We're . . ."

"Not what we were," said Riker. "She was right. In the respects that she was focussing on, it was a mistake. Besides, she had her own fiancé picked out for you."

She waved it off. "It's ancient history, Will."

"History has a way of repeating itself," admitted Riker. "And just as you had to be free to make your own mistakes and own successes, so must she be free also."

"But she came to accept you," Deanna said. "Besides, it's totally different. I was young. But she's . . . mature. It's not the same thing at all."

"It never is."

She frowned. "You are so smug, Will Riker. Wouldn't you rather have Q off this ship?"

"Undoubtedly. But I'm not the one he's dating."

"They're not dating!" she said. "They're . . . I don't know what they're doing." Her hand flew to her mouth as she envisioned Q and her mother together. "Please . . . don't let it have gone that far. Will, she's been completely taken in by him, and everyone is just sitting around letting it happen. Letting it *happen!* And it's all my fault!"

"Your fault?" said Riker in surprise. He was becoming more and more concerned about Deanna's fractured state of mind. Was it possible that somehow she was empathically linking with her mother, and her mother's chaotic body chemistry was wreaking havoc with Deanna as well? Certainly anything was possible when dealing with as powerful a telepath as Lwaxana Troi, and as skilled an empath as her daughter. "How could it possibly be your fault?"

"It's the blasted Ab'brax," she said. "The mourning for my being unmarried. If it were just her being in phase, she could probably handle that . . ."

*I wouldn't bet on it,* Riker thought.

"But she's in mourning for my single status as well. She dwells purely on what she doesn't have: a mate of her own; a married daughter. Emotionally, she's at loose ends. If I were married, she could fuss over my husband. She could fuss over grandchildren. I can just hear her. 'Me, a grandmother! Impossible!' And she'd wail and complain about getting old, and all the time she'd be loving it. Will, if anything happens to her because I was unable to prevent it, I don't know what I'll do. Standing there and watching it happen, as if she had some sort of terminal disease that no one could cure. Oh, Will, I don't . . ."

He took her firmly by the shoulders. "Deanna."

She looked up at him, her confusion and frustration practically leaping out of her eyes. "What?"

He took a deep breath. "Want to get married?"

Sehra sat in her room, staring at the walls.

Kerin had apologized. She had won. But . . .

But she had envisioned her wedding celebration being one long, joyful experience. She had not anticipated any strife, any confusion, any problems.

But Kerin had been difficult. So difficult. And even though he'd apologized, there had still been that . . .

That what? It was nothing she could put her finger on.

She flopped back on her soft bed, and pulled a pillow out from under her head. She sat up, staring at the full-length mirror across from her.

She stared at her reflection.

She hated it. Her nose was entirely too long, her forehead too high. Her hair hung there like lifeless string. And she was fat. Fat and ugly.

She drew back her arm and hurled the pillow at the mirror.

A red-clad arm extended out from the mirror and caught it.

She gasped and skittered back on the bed, her hand flying to her bosom. She made little noises but wasn't able to get out a coherent sentence, or even a comprehensible word.

Her reflection was gone from the mirror, replaced by the image of . . . of that man! The one from the party! The one who had been dancing through the air and then had vanished like mist.

"You should be more careful," he said scoldingly, and extended first one leg and then the other. As if swimming, he eased himself through the glass, which actually shimmered at his passing. The glass closed, sealing around him, and when he stepped clear, there was no mark whatsoever in the glass to indicate that he had ever passed through there.

"How," she gasped. "How did you . . ." Her voice faded for a moment, then she found it again. "Are you a wizard?"

"In a sense," said Q. "A wizard at understanding what makes the minds of mortals function. My dear child," he said, kneeling before her, "I am both a great teacher and a great student. I am always trying to learn and understand. And there is much that you can teach me."

She looked at her mirror, which now displayed only her homely reflection once more. "That *I* can teach *you?*" she asked in wonderment.

"Absolutely," said Q. "For example . . . I am most interested in the concept that you Tizarin have. A number of human cultures have it as well—the idea of loving one, and only one, person."

"Yes," she said slowly. "Yes, we believe in mating with one individual, for life." She got up and went to the mirror, running her fingers over it. "How did you—?"

He didn't appear to notice her curiosity over the mirror. "So you agree to love no one except your mate for the rest of your natural lives."

"That's right," she said.

He looked at her skeptically. "Truly?"

"Oh yes," she said fervently. She still wasn't sure how he had come through the mirror, or what he was doing here. There was an air of unreality about the whole encounter that gave it a dreamlike aspect. It made her wonder if any of it was really happening. "Yes, if it's true love, you need no one else."

"I don't understand," Q said. "If you meet another individual who is as attractive to you as your mate, you are forbidden from loving this person?"

"You can feel deep affection for them," she said.

"Can you love them?"

"Not in the same way."

"And your people," said Q, leaning forward, interlacing his fingers thoughtfully. "Your people can control their emotions so thoroughly?"

"We believe in 'one man, one woman,'" she said.

"And when do you acquire this ability to control such base emotions as lust, desire, et cetera, et cetera?"

"Generally," she said, "from the time when you fall in love with her or him whom you will marry. Your love for them totally consumes you."

"A stream full of earth piranha would accomplish the same task, and it would seem far more merciful," observed Q. "So your Kerin loves you with total devotion, eh?"

"Oh, yes."

"Odd. That's not what I perceived."

She frowned. "What do you mean, 'perceived'?"

"What? Oh," he sounded almost laconic. "My powers are . . . well, there's no other way to say it . . . the be-all and end-all of human comprehension. And your fiancé, Kerin, seemed to have some rather significant things on his mind during the dance this evening."

"What sort of significant things?" she asked slowly.

Q pointed to the mirror, and Sehra turned to look at it. She gasped.

There was Kerin, locked in a passionate embrace with a girl from the Nistral.

"I don't believe it," she said firmly. "That's his old . . . I mean, he feels nothing for her anymore. I don't believe he was thinking that."

"Or this?" asked Q.

The Nistral girl faded, to be replaced by another, who had also been at the dance. Kerin had danced with her as well. Yet another girl that Kerin had confidently said he was not interested in as anything other than mindful host.

Mindful. He certainly seemed to have a mind full of her, all right.

"You're making this up," she said, but this time there was far less certainty in her voice.

"This one, then?" he asked, and there was Kerin again, chewing on the ear of yet another girl. "This was all in his mind. I didn't fabricate it. I didn't have to. I just wanted to know if this was what you meant by his being singly interested in you. Or maybe this is," and another girl appeared, "or this, or this, or . . ."

*"Stop it!"* she shrieked. "Stop it! Stop saying these things! Kerin loves me. He does. He does!"

"Oh, I'm certain," said Q serenely. "Although it's curious. He envisions all these females . . . except you. He seems endlessly intrigued by the physical side of a relationship. Perhaps propelled by hormonal curiosity. Yet he doesn't seem to exhibit any interest in you. As if there were no mystery. Why would that be, do you think?"

She turned cold eyes on him. "I don't know," she said. "And I think you're doing nothing but lying."

"Nobody, dear girl," said Q, "can lie quite as well as we do to ourselves." He tipped an imaginary hat at her. "Good day," he said, and stepped back into the mirror. In an instant he was gone, the only thing left behind being the tear-stained reflection of a teenage bride-to-be.

Deanna blinked and drew an arm across her face. "What?"

"You heard me."

She actually smiled. "You can't be serious."

"No, really." He was now circling Deanna's quarters, and he didn't seem to know what to do with his arms. Sometimes he had them folded across his chest, other times he draped them behind his back. "I've . . ." He cleared his throat. "I've been thinking about it lately, and perhaps . . . well, since we're on the same ship, and there's no one I feel closer to, and . . . it would take your mother's mind right off of Q. It would probably be for the best . . ."

"You *are* serious!"

"I think I am."

Now she laughed. Laughed loudly and delightedly.

"Having never made a marriage proposal, I wasn't sure what to expect," said Riker, sounding slightly annoyed. "I wasn't expecting total amusement."

"This is a conspiracy," she said, shaking her head. "Whenever I fall into deep depression over my mother, a male member of this crew takes it upon himself to cheer me up. First Wesley and his 'difficulties,' and now this."

"Deanna, I mean it! I love you, and we should get married!"

"Oh, Will," she sighed. She went to him and took his bearded face in her hands. "I know you love me. I know I love you. But this isn't the right time."

"It may never be the right time," he said.

"Then, it never is," she said easily. "But not this, Will. If you entered Starfleet with the same conviction that you made this . . . offer . . . you'd still be sitting

172

in drydock somewhere. Will . . . I take this as a sign on your part of how devoted a friend you are. And how anxious you are to spare me pain. And if you look deep down into yourself, you'll realize that this proposal, as well intentioned as it is, isn't truly what you want."

"How do you know . . ." He shook his head. "Forget I said that."

"It's forgotten. All of it is forgotten," and she kissed him on the cheek, "except your good intentions. *Imzati* forever."

"Forever," he sighed. "I just hated to see you like this, Deanna. You're usually so . . ."

"Stable," she said. "A rock. And that's how I'll be again. Perhaps Q has managed to turn my mother's head, but he'll no longer be able to affect mine. You've brought a great deal into perspective for me. A dash of cold water, as it were."

"That's what I was always hoping my first marriage proposal would be like: an emotional slap across the face," he said dryly.

## Chapter Seventeen

WESLEY CRUSHER stretched in bed and turned over.

A female face smiled back at him, barely an inch away from his.

He gasped in surprise and skidded back across the bed. "Karla, do you mind?!" he said.

She sat back on her knees. "Good morning, Wesley," she said brightly. She pointed. "I brought you breakfast." Over on a table was a cup of juice, and sunny-side up eggs.

"I could've gotten breakfast myself," he said, rubbing the sleep from his eyes. He desperately tried to straighten his hair. It always stood up in the morning and he hated the idea of someone seeing him like this. He adjusted the blankets around himself. "Why aren't you in your own quarters, anyway?"

"My place is with you, Wesley," she said softly. "That is where Sehra wishes me to be."

"And what about what you w—never mind," he sighed. He'd been through this with her before.

She looked downcast. "I thought you liked me, Wesley."

"I do," he admitted. How could he get upset with her? At least she was wearing a robe and not walking around in the cheerful nakedness that he found so disconcerting. And she was serving him breakfast, after all. And her performance at the dance last night had impressed the others, that was for sure. And afterwards . . .

"Sure, I like you, Karla. I mean, isn't it obvious?"

"Not really, no."

"Look, I'm sorry, okay?" he said. "I'm just a little new at this, you know? So . . . so look, breakfast sounds fine."

She nodded eagerly, turned, and got the breakfast, which was on a glistening tray. She started back towards Wesley . . .

And tripped on a stray bedsheet.

The juice hit Wesley first, drenching him, followed an instant later by the eggs. They hit him full in the face, ran down his chest and onto the bedsheets.

"Oh!" cried out Karla. "Oh Wesley! I'm so sorry!" She grabbed up the far end of the bedsheet and brought it around, trying to clean him off.

"It's okay! It's okay!" he said, trying to get the mess off him. "I always like to wear my breakfast instead of eat it. Keeps you thin."

She dabbed at his back. "I'm so sorry."

"Really, it's all right," he said in exasperation.

Her fingers dug into the bottom of his neck. "You're so tense."

"Now, I wonder why that is?" he replied, unable to keep the sarcasm out of his voice.

She brought her other hand up and started massaging his shoulders. "Let me take care of that."

"No, please, that's . . ."

And his head started to hang loosely. In spite of

himself, he smiled. "Hey, that feels pretty good," he admitted.

"I'm an expert massage artist," she said.

"I can tell. I didn't realize how tense I was."

"You're a very aggressive, very determined individual. I can tell these things. Someone like you always has tension. But I can keep you relaxed."

His head swayed back and forth gently. "I can believe it."

"Lie down," she said, "and watch what I can really do when I get started."

Wesley did as she said.

And a few minutes later, anyone walking past would have heard incredible howls from within Wesley Crusher's quarters.

Ten-Forward was empty, except for Guinan who—as near as anyone could tell—never left. She was checking over her stock in brisk fashion, when suddenly she looked up. "All right," she said in annoyance. "You might as well show yourself."

There was a bright flash, and Q materialized in the middle of Ten-Forward. He stood there, smug and confident. "What does one have to do to get a drink around here?" he said.

She shook her head in disbelief. "I'm not going to serve you," she said.

"And you call yourself a hostess," he said. "At least, that's what you call yourself now."

"These are good people," said Guinan from behind the bar. "Why do you insist on tormenting them?"

"What torment?" said Q expansively. "I have been on my very best behavior."

The door of Ten-Forward hissed open and Deanna Troi entered. She stood there a moment, regarding Q. "I knew you'd come here," she said.

"And here is someone who can attest to my behavior, can't you, Deanna?" he asked silkily.

"It's over, Q," she said calmly.

He raised an eyebrow. "Whatever do you mean?"

"I can read you." She took a step forward. "I can sense every maggot-ridden thought that's crawling through your mind."

"No, you can't," he said calmly. "My mind is a closed book to you."

"It's an open book, and every page is torn," she told him. She continued towards him in slow, measured steps, the picture of calm. "Obviously, whatever your powers once were, they are diminished."

"Nonsense. I am every bit as omnipotent as I ever was," said Q.

"You are as omnipotent as a cheese wheel," she informed him, "and substantially less decorative."

The carefully conceived mask that Q wore started to slip just slightly. Danger glimmered. "I do not take kindly to such words."

"I know your every move," she said. "You intend to humiliate my mother. To torment her, for no other reason than that she had the poor judgment to be attracted to you. You are setting her up for a colossal fall, simply because you want to show that you can. Your pathetic existence has dwindled down to your ability to show your power over lesser life forms. But you've overestimated yourself this time, Q. You, the superior life form . . . your every move is plain to me."

"You're lying." His voice was harsh, his anger growing.

"I don't have to lie. I'm here to inform you that I'm not afraid of you."

"Really." The air was starting to get dark.

"Yes. And I'm here to inform you that not only is

my mother not helpless, but neither is her daughter. I love my mother, and if you cause her harm, if you cause her pain . . . I will make certain that you suffer."

"You!" And he started to tremble with unrepressed fury. "You think you can threaten me! You . . . you . . ."

"I will step on you," she said quietly, "like the bug that you are."

He took a step towards her, his brow clouded, his eyes smoldering.

Immediately Guinan was in between them. Her hands were outstretched in a defensive posture. Deanna wasn't precisely sure what sort of defense Guinan could possibly construct against this creature, but the Ten-Forward hostess definitely seemed to have something in mind.

What that might have been, Deanna Troi would never know. Because as suddenly as the storm gathered, it passed.

Q collected himself, his fury ebbing, his anger dissipating as if it had never existed. Within seconds he had restored his placid, amiable exterior.

"You claim to love your mother," said Q, "and yet she is happy with me, and you would deprive her of that happiness. So this love business would seem to hinge a great deal on personal selfishness."

"Loving someone means being concerned for their well-being," said Deanna.

"Does it also mean," he asked, "that you start making decisions for the one you love? That sounds rather patronizing to me. If you truly know what I am thinking, Deanna Troi, then you are aware that I believe you are having trouble believing in your mother's intelligence. And that, dear woman, sounds a great deal more like your problem than mine."

With that parting shot, he vanished.

Deanna sighed and sank down into a chair.

Guinan walked slowly over to her. "You couldn't read him."

"No," said Deanna.

"It was a bluff."

"Yes."

"And you were deliberately baiting him."

"That's right," sighed Deanna.

"Mind telling me why?"

"Because," said Deanna reasonably, "if he had attacked me, assaulted me . . . my mother would have been aware of it. She would have sensed my distress immediately, and the cause of it. The more heinous attack I could provoke, the more of a shock it would be to her. I wanted her to be aware of just what Q is capable of."

"In other words, you were willing to sacrifice yourself. That took a lot of class, Counselor."

"Thank you."

"Not a lot of brains, mind you."

"Thank you again," she said, a bit more sardonically this time. "Guinan . . . is it possible that he's telling the truth?"

"I was wondering that earlier. Frankly . . . I don't think so. The only question is, how much hurt is he going to cause while he's spinning his lies?"

"I don't know," said Deanna. "But at this point, I've done everything I can. Matters are simply going to have to run their course now."

"Let's hope we can all keep up with it," Guinan said.

"I'm sorry," Karla kept saying as she helped Wesley down the hallway.

Wesley had thrown a robe on over his pajama pants and was leaning heavily on Karla's shoulder. Pain was stabbing through his torso with every step. "It's okay," he gasped, for what seemed the hundredth time.

"You must hate me," wailed Karla. "You must detest me. You must loathe the very sight of—"

"Karla, shut up," moaned Wesley. "You're not helping."

"I'm sorry, Wesley."

"And stop apologizing."

"I'm sorry for apologizing, Wesley."

He would have sighed deeply, except it caused him too much pain.

And just as they rounded the corner to sickbay, there, naturally, coming from the other direction— displaying timing that bordered on the supernatural —was Ensign Charles.

Wesley moaned, partly out of pain, partly out of embarrassment. Charles's eyes widened as he saw the two of them, and Wesley said to him, "Don't say anything. Not a word. Not a smart remark. Nothing."

"What the hell happened?" said Charles.

And Karla, all upset, explained, "We think I broke a couple of his ribs." With that, she ushered him into sickbay and the door closed behind them.

Charles watched them go and then whistled. "She's an animal," he whispered to himself enviously.

Wesley lay on the exam bed, his mother passing a tricorder over him. She nodded briskly and glanced at the concerned young woman standing just nearby.

"Second and third ribs, upper left," said Dr. Crusher. "It appears to be a clean break."

"I'm very efficient," said Karla. When Beverly Crusher's expression demanded further explanation of that remark, Karla said, "That's probably why it's clean. I'm tidy that way."

"Look, go tidy up somewhere else, all right?" Wes pleaded.

"Should I clean your room?"

"Yes. *No!*" he quickly amended. "Don't do that. Don't do anything. Don't serve me. Don't rub me. Don't . . . just don't. Go back to your quarters—*your* quarters—and wait for me there, okay?"

"Whatever you say, Wesley," and she walked out of sickbay.

Wesley allowed his head to drop back on the medical bed. Beverly Crusher stared down at her son, not exactly sure what to say. "Look . . . Wes," she said, as she reached for the instruments she would need to heal the break. "As your mother, I know that there are certain lines that I just should not cross. At the same time, as chief medical officer, I have responsibilities for the health of this crew."

"Mom . . ." sighed Wesley.

"Now, under ordinary circumstances, your . . ." She hesitated on the word a moment and then forced it out. "Your sex life is your own business . . ."

*"Mom!"*

She was speaking very quickly, anxious to get it out. "But if you're getting injured as a result, then perhaps certain procedures should be reviewed to—"

"Mom, it had nothing to do with sex."

She stared down at him. "It didn't?"

"No."

"But then—"

"Promise you won't laugh."

"Wesley!" said his mother with mild annoyance. "I am the chief medical officer ascertaining an injury to a crew member. It is hardly a laughing matter."

"Promise."

She looked heavenward and in an annoyed little singsong said, "I promise I won't laugh."

"She was giving me a backrub."

Beverly Crusher looked at her son skeptically. "You're joking."

"I wish."

"She broke your ribs giving you a backrub?"

"She was doing it with her feet."

Beverly sat down, the instrument forgotten in her hand. "How did she rub your back with her feet?"

"By walking on it."

Beverly Crusher put her hand to her mouth, and her sides started to shake.

"You promised!" moaned Wes. "What *is* it with women! Deanna promised she wouldn't laugh, and then you—"

"Deanna? She was there too?!"

"Yes, mother!" Wesley blew up, ignoring the pain in his side. "Deanna was there. And Guinan. And Sonja Mendez. And every female in the cadet class at Starfleet Academy was there, and the entire female population of Angel One. I just couldn't get enough, okay, mother? *Okay?*" He sank back, exhausted, the pain a dull ache.

"I'm sorry, Wesley," said Beverly with only the mildest twitch of her mouth. "I didn't mean to upset you."

"She's killing me, mother. Slowly. Painfully. There she was, walking on my back, and then she started to fall off. I started to turn over, just out of reflex, and the next thing I knew I felt this cracking in my chest. And then she landed on me and . . ."

"You'll be as good as new when I'm finished." She looked at him oddly. "What's that in your hair?"

"What color?"

"Kind of yellow."

"That would be egg yolk. The white is the rest of the egg, and any orange is juice."

"Busy morning."

"Mother, what am I going to do? She's driving me crazy."

The first thing that occurred to her was that he should wash his hair, but she knew that was hardly the

182

advice he was looking for. "Can't you send her back where she came from?"

"No," he sighed. "It would be an insult."

"If it's a question of insult versus compound fractures, I'd risk the former."

"Yeah. Yeah, so would I."

# Chapter Eighteen

THE BICKERING was becoming louder, more constant, and more incessant. It had gone from disagreements to cold looks to out-and-out fury. And everyone among the Tizarin was beginning to wonder whether this was far more than a case of simple pre-wedding jitters. It appeared as if this once-loving couple was at each other's throats.

No one could figure out why. It wasn't as if Kerin had suddenly sprouted horns, or Sehra a tail. Yet now, when he looked at her, it was with a cool and critical eye, as if seeing her in a new light. And when she would look at him, it was with a burning suspicion that invariably would set the two off again. Eventually the arguing would subside, and they would apologize to each other. Increasingly, though, it seemed that these apologies were coming more from a sense of form and a reluctance to call a halt to ceremonies for which they had so devoutly fought.

"It will pass," Graziunas said confidently to his

wife, but it was not a confidence he felt in his heart. He had seen the love light in his daughter's eyes, and now something was eclipsing that light. He tried to speak to her of it, but she was cool towards him. Her attitude was not something he took especially well to, but he had no idea how to deal with it. Sehra had always been an obedient, loyal child, and he'd rarely even had the need to raise his voice to her. So this new attitude of hers—this antipathy towards her husband-to-be—left Graziunas confused.

After one angry spat, Graziunas sandbagged his daughter and demanded an explanation. "Has he said something to you?" he demanded.

"Nothing specific that he said, no," she replied sullenly.

"Something he did, then. Some action."

"Nothing he did."

"What, then?"

She paused. "I just don't like the directions his thoughts have been going," she muttered.

"His *thoughts?* Gods, girl!" Graziunas threw up his arms in frustration. "A man is supposed to police his very thoughts now in order to satisfy a woman? Doesn't that seem just a *bit* unusual to you? Doesn't that appear to be a tad unreasonable?"

"I suppose . . ." she said reluctantly, but she was still uncertain.

Similar discussions took place between Kerin and his father, as Kerin spoke of coming years and deterioration, and his father—in his frustration—spoke of splitting his son's head open wide, like a ripe melon.

And at night, a voice whispered doubt and uncertainty into Kerin's ear, and into Sehra's ear, even as it spoke words of affection to Lwaxana Troi.

That night, Graziunas and Nistral were visited as well. The visits took on a decidedly unreal aspect to them, and each of the men was not certain what had happened to them in their sleep. They only knew that they awoke the morning of the sanctification ceremonies with their hearts hardened towards their opposite numbers, and their tempers on hair triggers.

"Isn't it beautiful?" asked Lwaxana Troi.

Q and Mrs. Troi stood at the edge of a cliff overlooking a vast jungle. "The Genesis Planet," said Lwaxana. "A thing of beauty, created by human hands."

"It's edifying to witness this," Q said, "since it always appears that human hands exist only to destroy, rather than to create."

"There you go again," said Lwaxana, shaking her head. "It's statements like those that put people off, you know. If there's one thing that humans hate to be reminded of, it's their limits."

"It's hard not to," Q protested. "There are so many."

"Oh, honestly . . ."

"It's true!" said Q. Lwaxana walked along the edge of the cliff and away from it, up towards a clearing. Q followed her. "Think of it. There's frailty of form. Vulnerability to aging and death. Dependence on technology. Warlike tendencies . . ."

She raised a scolding finger. "Not any more."

"Oh, nonsense," scoffed Q. "They give lip service to that conceit, but underneath, they're as warlike as their ancestors. If they truly believed in peace, they would carry no weapons."

"Then, they would be unprotected!" protested Lwaxana.

"Throughout the history of mankind," Q replied, "there have been a relative handful who have been genuinely peaceful. And they are notable for being willing to die rather than lift a hand against their fellow man. They would not carry weapons because they would *rather die than use them.* Those were true men of peace. Picard considers himself an idealist, but he would not be willing to die on behalf of his ideal."

"Well," said Lwaxana, "if the *Enterprise* had no weapons, then my daughter would be unprotected. I can't say that I'd be pleased about that."

"You could protect her," Q said.

She stopped and looked up at him. "What do you mean?"

"It's every mother's dream," he said. "The ultimate expression of love. Don't tell me that there haven't been nights when you lie awake, thinking of your daughter out in the middle of deep space. Facing unknown danger at every turn. Her only protection being a—" and he glanced around, "a shell of metal that's only as good as the human hands that made it. There you are, night after lonely night, knowing that this ship could become her coffin just like that," and he snapped his fingers. "Don't tell me you haven't thought about Deanna meeting some hideous death deep in the airless reaches of space. And you might not even know for—"

"I'd know," she said darkly. For the first time all of her confidence and her "bigger-than-life" airs evaporated. She touched her temple. "I'd know here," and she tapped her heart, "and here. A part of me would just . . . just shrivel and blacken and die. Don't think I haven't thought about it. Don't think I haven't dreaded it. She's chosen her life, and I support it, and whenever I see her I . . . I do anything except let slip to her what really gnaws at me. A day doesn't pass that I don't think about getting that feeling. A feeling I don't even know, yet which I'd recognize immediately. The feeling that tells me that my baby will never come back. So I . . . I busy myself with . . ." Her hands moved in vague circles as she looked around the lush and thriving tropical world. "I busy myself with rituals and duties and Betazoid society. With dusting a pointless clay pot, or keeping the Holy Rings shiny. Holy Rings," she laughed sourly. "No one cares about them. Not even me, really. They're in a box in the back of my closet. I tell myself it's for security reasons. And it's all so that I don't dwell on my own loneliness, and on the hideous inevitability that I might, someday, be lonelier."

She was silent for a long moment. "I've never spoken to anyone of this, not even Deanna. It shows how much I trust you."

"It's comforting to know that someone on this ship does," he sighed. "All the others think a world of evil of me, despite all the good I can do."

She watched a bird sail overhead, making a distant, cawing noise. "What you were saying before . . . about always protecting Deanna . . . what did you—?"

He didn't seem to hear her. "They don't trust you, either. They don't trust us as a couple."

Her breath caught in her throat. "Are . . . we a couple?" she managed to get out.

He turned towards her. "This world is supposed to represent beginnings? The start of something?"

"Yes."

"This world . . . this room," and he made an impatient noise. "The computers of the *Enterprise* try to imitate the abilities of the gods. Of beings like myself. They create something from nothing and applaud themselves for their skill. Phaw! It's like a human child learning to crawl and congratulating himself on achieving the be-all and end-all of existence. Picard and the others take arrogant pride in this, yet would have no truck with me and my 'arrogance,' even though I'm capable of far greater than this with the barest wave of my hand."

He went to Lwaxana and took her by the shoulders. Where once he had seemed reluctant even to touch her, now he seemed quite comfortable with it. "You need your consciousness raised, Mrs. Troi."

He gestured.

The holodeck seemed to explode around them and then coalesced into a shimmering tunnel of colors that sped by them at blinding, even frightening, speed. The air was filled with a roar, a scream: the scream of a universe dying and being born, all within the same moment.

Before her eyes, within her mind, stars crashed together and leaped outward once more. Suns burned bright, cooled, and collapsed into themselves all within the blink of an eye. Planets crackled into existence, and there were life forms—gods, so many, all at once, overlapping and throbbing with newness and age. There were amorphous beings that undulated across orange ground, a green sky hanging in the background. There were entities the size of mountains whose hearts beat once every century, who took a breath every millennium, who had existed from before the beginning and would be there beyond its end.

And she saw the innate insanity of life in the galaxy, arguing over borders and frontiers. How could there be any part of space that "belonged" to any specific species, because space had always been and would always be, long after the races that had staked their claims had vanished.

Space spun outward, ever outward. There were galaxies beyond reach, galaxies beyond understanding, populated by beings that redefined the word *alien*. Expanding ever outward, tickling the infinite, waltzing with eternity. Life, and more life, and beyond that was the unknowable, the incomprehensible, except, my God, she was beginning to understand, and it was all so *simple* . . .

Lwaxana Troi sat down hard.

She felt the jolt from the bottom of her spine to the top of her head, and it snapped her eyes into focus. She looked up, and there was Q.

He was eating a nectarine.

"That," he said, "is an inkling of what it is to be me."

The holodeck had returned to the jungle setting that was in quiet preparation for the sanctification ceremonies due to begin shortly. It was as if the visions had never been, and indeed, maybe they hadn't. Lwaxana's heart was pounding, her mind racing desperately to keep up. "I don't . . . that's incredible . . ." she began.

"It is, isn't it. I once shared a fraction of my power with Riker. His mind, of course, did not have the strength or subtlety to come to terms with the full ramifications. But you, Lwaxana Troi—I would share far more with you. Imagine. If you shared in this power, you could be aware of your daughter at all times. Be there to help her in an instant, if she needed it. Constantly safeguard her, and all who accompany her. The possibilities are endless for you to protect your ungrateful daughter . . ."

"Ungrateful?" Lwaxana looked up. Her voice sounded thick to her, as if she had rocks in her mouth. "What do you mean, ungrateful?"

Q sighed loudly. "Your daughter . . . everyone on board this ship, really . . . would love to take your freedom of choice from you. Without so much as a by-your-leave, they would have me leave. They don't want to expose you to me. They don't want you to be with me. They hold before them the shield of love. They're doing it all for love; love is their great motivator. Love that would deprive you, dear Lwaxana, of your right to choose. What I feel for you, however, is unselfish."

"Are you saying you . . . love me?" Her voice was low and hesitant.

"Need you ask?" said Q.

She moaned softly, the world becoming a soft haze around her.

"All this," Q told her, "all that I have shown you—you can be one with it. Your so-called loved ones drown you with selfishness and offer you nothing. But I give to you unselfishly, and offer you everything."

"Why me? Why, in all the cosmos, have you chosen me?"

"Gods need no explanations," Q told her archly. "When you become one, you will understand. I warn you, though. If you do accept this offer—you will see the others for what they really are. They will seem small, even insignificant, to you. When you stride through the great road of eternity, you'll see the small bumps along the way for what they truly are. You'll realize the truth of all things, and that can never be undone."

She smiled. "Will you tell me why a nectarine holds the answer to the secrets of the universe?"

"My dear," he said, "you won't even have to ask. So . . . do you want it?" He took her hands. "Are you ready to leave behind the petty concerns of mortality?"

"I . . . I don't know," she said. "I mean it's . . . it's such a big step, I . . ."

The waterfall nearby hissed open.

Lwaxana pulled her hands from Q as she spun. Standing there were Picard, Riker, Deanna, various ambassadors, and all the members of the Tizarin wedding party. Deanna reacted with surprise as Picard said, "Mrs. Troi! Anxious for the sanctification ceremonies to begin?"

She felt a flush of guilt, as if she'd been caught in the

act of something. "Oh, yes," she said. "We certainly are."

"We?" said Picard with curiosity.

She glanced behind her. Q was gone. She turned back to the captain and smiled lopsidedly. " 'We' as in 'all of us.' "

"Yes, of course," said Picard. He didn't quite understand Lwaxana's slight jumpiness, but on the other hand, at least Q wasn't around. At least the sanctification could go smoothly, and tomorrow would be the wedding, and they would be done with this business already.

Ten minutes into the ceremony, all hell broke loose.

# Chapter Nineteen

PICARD SMILED at the assemblage before him. All were elaborately dressed in the colors and robes of the Tizarin, their respective colors declaring their house allegiance. Diplomats and other spectators stood off to the side.

The captain held in front of him the Tizarin sacred book of matrimonial procedure. All of the ceremonies were spelled out there in depth, in twenty-seven languages including English. It was not surprising for such an aggressively star-spanning race as the Tizarin to be alert to the language requirements of all walks of life.

Picard's finger automatically paged through to get an idea of the length of the ceremony. He sighed inwardly. *About thirty pages. This is going to take a while.*

As required, he stretched out his right arm in the gesture of a benediction. "Good people! All who are assembled this day in the sight of the gods of the

Tizarin—the only real and true pantheon of gods in the cosmos . . ." He paused and glanced at the fathers. Graziunas shrugged slightly. Nistral offered a game half-smile.

*Stay in the spirit of it,* Picard told himself. ". . . in the cosmos," he continued, "are brought here to witness the sanctification of this place," and he gestured widely to encompass the entire holodeck scene. "It must be duly sanctified and cleansed, so that the spirits of matrimony and childbirth can enter this place and bless the wedding."

"If they can stand the humidity," murmured Fenn.

Nistral moaned. "Mother!" whispered Sehra between clenched teeth. "I *told* you . . ."

"Sorry," whispered Fenn back.

"Computer, reduce humidity by thirty percent," Picard said briskly. Fenn nodded her appreciation.

"I knew she'd cause problems," Kerin murmured.

"Kerin, she's my mother," Sehra shot back.

"Yeah, I know."

"Excuse me," said Picard, flipping the pages. "But we have a good deal of ground to cover. May we continue?"

"By all means, Captain," said Nistral.

Picard cleared his throat and said loudly, "All of the assemblage will bear witness to the good feelings that pervade this place. To the affection. To the devotion. To the deep and abiding love between this man and this woman. For this love is too powerful to suffer any evil spirits to survive. This love will last throughout eternity. From now through old age and beyond . . ."

Kerin made a slight noise. It was hard to tell exactly what it was. Not so much a moan, or a gasp. More of a slight choke. Nothing really. Nothing at all.

Unless, of course, someone was listening for it.

Sehra turned to him and said, "What do you mean by that?"

194

"By what?"

"That noise you just made."

Graziunas took a step forward and said in a low, embarrassed tone, "Sehra, there's *people* here."

"I want to know what that noise was he just made."

"I didn't make a noise!" said Kerin in exasperation. "I was just clearing my throat."

Now Nistral came towards them. "He just cleared his throat, Sehra. That's all."

"Well, naturally you would take his side," said Sehra.

"Gentlemen, ladies," began Picard, now quite annoyed. "We're supposed to be making certain that the site of tomorrow's marriage is going to be harmonious. If there is some sort of problem, could it be settled elsewhere and elsewhen?"

"There's no problem, Captain," Kerin said. He fired a look at Sehra. "Is there, Sehra?"

"I will thank you," Fenn said crisply, "not to take that tone of voice with my daughter!"

"What tone of voice?" Nistral said. "The boy didn't do anything wrong, and I see no reason why you and that daughter of yours keep carping on him!"

"That daughter of *hers*, Nistral, is also a daughter of *mine*," said Graziunas sharply. "And if anyone should be reconsidering tones of voice, it's you."

Picard closed the book with the sound of a cannon shot. "That's it. This goes no further. You obviously—"

"My tone of voice is perfectly within acceptable limits," Nistral said, "which is more than I can say for you. You've never known how to curb your excesses, Graziunas. Never."

"My excesses!" snapped Graziunas.

Kerin turned on Sehra. "Look, if you have a problem with me, I don't see why you have to drag your parents into it!"

"I don't have to drag my parents anywhere," said Sehra fiercely. "They go where they please and do what they please."

"Then, maybe I should do the same thing!"

"Oh, of course!" said Sehra, throwing up her hands. "Because once you're tied down to me, you can never go anywhere or do anything again, isn't that right!"

"Yes, that's right!" shot back Kerin, now only a couple of inches away from her.

The guests were milling about in confusion. There was no confusion, however, for the wedding parties of the respective houses. They started drifting towards their house leaders, their faces set and determined.

"If this does not stop instantly, I shall call security!" thundered Picard.

His was a voice in the wind, blown away by the torrent of emotions that had been kept submerged but were now bubbling, fully, to the surface.

"You'll never be able to see other women! That's what's really eating at you, isn't it!" snapped Sehra.

"No!" retorted Kerin. "It's that I'm going to have to see you at all!"

Sehra stepped back as if struck. And now Graziunas stepped forward, snarling, "You little cretin! How dare you—!"

"He was provoked is how he dares!" shouted Nistral. The veins against his silver forehead were starting to stand out. "She's a master of provocation, Graziunas. She gets it from her father!"

Riker was trying to get between them. "That's enough!" he snapped, with as much authority as he could muster. But it was like trying to stop a tidal wave with a sponge.

Picard tapped his communicator. "Security team to Holodeck 3, immediately."

"I've never provoked anything in my life!" Graziunas bellowed.

"What? You're joking! What about when you undersold me in that deal with the Byfrexians!"

"Undersold you, my ass! I can't help it if you were overpriced for the same goods!"

"You sold at less than profit just to get back at me," said Nistral furiously, "because I landed the entire Skeevo system! That stuck in your craw!"

And now one of the members of the Nistral shouted, "Everyone knows that you can't trust the Graziunas!"

"If anyone knows about untrustworthiness, it's Nistral," shouted back one of the Graziunas. "If they want to see a double-crosser, all they have to do is look in the mirror!"

"Parasites!"

"Cheaters!"

"I can't believe you're letting this happen!" wailed Sehra at Kerin.

"Me! You started it!"

"I didn't!"

"You did!"

Security charged in, Worf at the head. Their weapons were drawn. They started looking around in confusion, unsure of what to do because everyone was shouting at once. The air was filled with insults, shouting, and fury.

"I'm glad!" Nistral was shouting. "I'm glad this happened, before my son got stuck with a humorless harridan like your daughter—!"

He actually only got the beginning of the word *daughter* out, because Graziunas had swung a furious punch that caught Nistral square in the mouth. The leader of the house of Nistral went down flat on his back, clutching at his injured jaw.

The security team started forward, now focussed on something they could deal with. Before they could get there, however, Kerin had leaped forward and landed square on the back of Graziunas. Graziunas turned, grabbing at his back, trying to pry off the boy who was pounding on his skull, but before he could get to him, another member of the Nistral had smashed into his legs. Sehra screamed as her father went down and she jumped towards a random aggressor, swinging her hands forward and clawing at his face.

Within seconds there were a good thirty people slamming into each other, pushing and shoving and falling over one another in a frenetic free-for-all that was as appalling as it was unexpected. All were screaming epithets. Disputes long forgotten were being dredged up for the sole purpose of providing excuse for revenge.

It took the security team close to two minutes to restore some semblance of order. The combatants stood apart, their chests heaving, their eyes glowering. Their nice formal clothes were hanging in shreds, their faces were torn and bloodied. Since they'd been fighting on the holodeck-provided forest setting, their gleaming skin was caked with dirt and filth from rolling on the ground. There were occasional sounds of choked sobbing, although it was impossible to discern the source.

In as clear and concise a voice as possible, Picard said, "Get off my ship. All of you. You have abused even the most liberal definition of hospitality. And you will not be welcome until you cool down and are ready to behave like civilized beings . . ."

Nistral took an unsteady step forward. Blood covered the lower half of his face. He stabbed a finger at Graziunas, who looked decidedly less the worse for wear, but still like someone who had been in a fight. "We have no need of your ship, Captain. We need only our own. And what we need it for, we will quickly finish."

"Blood feud," snarled Graziunas. "You've long had

it coming, Nistral. You and your underhanded tactics, your airs, your arrogance . . ."

"Blood feud it is," shot back Nistral. "You're a blight, Graziunas. I have tolerated you for far too long, for the sake of our young ones. But I tolerate you no further!"

"Let us out of here, Captain!" shouted Graziunas. "We have business to attend to! Final business!"

"I want you to cool off—" Picard began.

"It's no longer your affair, Captain," said Nistral. "It's ours to settle, and we will. I suggest you get your ship to safe distance, because shortly there is going to be a fight."

"It will not be a fight," said Graziunas. "It will be a slaughter. A great, glorious slaughter."

Within minutes the Tizarin had emptied out of the holodeck, leaving the *Enterprise* senior officers and a group of stunned ambassadors looking at each other.

And Lwaxana Troi staggered forward, bleeding from the split lip that a stray elbow had caused. "Anyone for coffee and cake?" she asked thickly.

# Chapter Twenty

WESLEY CRUSHER returned to his quarters, still nursing his sore ribs, but determined to get his uniform and head up to the bridge. He'd heard scuttlebutt that something was going on, that the wedding had fallen completely apart. Whatever was happening, he was bound and determined to be a part of it.

He entered his quarters and stopped. Karla was sitting on the edge of his bed, her blue face streaked with tears. She looked incredibly waiflike.

"Look . . . Karla," he began.

"I'm sorry, Wesley," she said softly.

"Don't apologize," he said for what seemed the hundredth time. He started towards her. "There's something we have to—"

"I must return to the Graziunas."

He paused in midstep and immediately suppressed an urge to shout *yes!* "What?"

She went to him, putting her hands on his shoulders. He fought the impulse to flinch from her. "Blood feud," she said, "has been declared. My people are at war with another family. It's a long and tangled rivalry, Wesley. No one even remembers how it all started, really. It's just there, and now there's no going back. And in a blood feud, all able-bodied members of the house line must return. Any other ties are secondary."

"Well, you . . ." He took a deep breath. "You do what you have to."

"My people are very angry. They've ordered all communication with the *Enterprise* be . . ." She choked on the word. ". . . severed. I'm being taken back. Oh, Wesley!" she wailed and threw her arms around him.

He let out a brief cry of alarm, but fortunately she didn't seem to dislocate any portions of him this time around. Awkwardly he patted her on the back. "It's okay," he said soothingly. "Everything will work out."

"Wesley, I know how this must make you feel . . ."

"Oh, I don't think you can begin to imagine," Wes told her.

"I'll think of you, always. Forever," she told him.

"And I'll be thinking of you, every time I break a rib."

"That's soooo sweeeet!" she wailed and threw herself into the embrace with him with such force that she knocked him off balance. She caught herself, but Wes, his arms pinwheeling, stumbled back and fell. His forehead crashed against the edge of the bureau, and he sagged to the floor, moaning.

She started towards him. "Wes, let me help y—"

*"No!"* he shouted, stretching out a hand. It had blood on it. "Stay away from me! Please!"

"It's hard for you, I know."

201

"Don't make it any harder!" He didn't want to even look her in the eyes, for fear that, in her instance, looks could genuinely kill. "Just go, okay? Go!"

"Whatever you say, Wesley," she told him with the voice of one who is truly damned for all eternity. She started to leave. Her footfall slowed as she approached the door.

"Keep going!" he admonished her. "Don't look back! Just keep going!"

She paused in the door, which had opened. She called out at the top of her lungs, "There'll never be another like you, Wesley Crusher! Never!" And with that she turned and headed for the transporter room, where her belongings already were.

And Ensign Walter Charles, who had once again happened to be passing by, shook his head and went straight to Wes's quarters. He stood in the doorway, looking at Wesley's crouched back, and said desperately, "How do you do it, Crusher? What's your secret? How do you get them to come back for more? What should I be doing?"

Wesley slowly, unevenly, pulled himself up and turned to face Charles. Charles's eyes widened as he saw blood streaming from the nasty cut in Wesley's forehead.

"Get me to sickbay," Wes told him. "That's what you should be doing."

# Chapter Twenty-one

"THE QUESTION IS, What should we be doing?"

Picard faced his senior officers in the conference lounge, the question hanging in the air. No one had an immediate answer.

"The ambassadors are having fits," Picard continued after a hesitation. "All of the respective governments are demanding to know what we are going to do about it. Everyone except," he amended, "the government of Betazed. Mrs. Troi has kept her own counsel in this matter, and frankly, Counselor, I must say I'm somewhat grateful. I'm being badgered enough already."

"What would they have us do?" demanded Riker. "The Prime Directive is clear on this matter. We can urge the Tizarin to settle this peacefully. We can provide them with the facilities and support mechanism to do so. But we can't twist their arms or put guns to their heads."

"Perhaps if we did, they would listen to reason," Worf said sourly. "Captain, from a security standpoint, perhaps it would be best to relocate the ship. As it is, situated between the Tizarin house ships . . ."

"We may be caught in the crossfire," Picard admitted. "A calculated risk, Mr. Worf. If we simply leave, it may seem as if the Federation sanctions this entire blood feud business. By maintaining a presence here, we give a subtle message that we most definitely do not approve and want to see this thing settled immediately. Counselor, how did you perceive the situation?"

"A bubbling over of the repressed anger I told you of earlier, Captain," Troi said. "At the same time, I sensed a degree of confusion, even regret, that matters had come to this. No one is truly happy about this turn of events, but there is too much pride involved for anyone to turn back now."

"Too much pride," murmured Picard, shaking his head. "I don't understand. Why were they all on such short fuses?" His eyes narrowed. "What is the possibility that Q had something to do with this?"

"Captain, Q wasn't even there," Riker pointed out.

"Physically, no. But perhaps the master complicator was there in spirit somehow. I don't know," said Picard impatiently. "All I know is that a once-anticipated event has deteriorated into armed camps about to enter a state of war, and I'm looking for reasons that seem in very short supply."

"Perhaps, Captain," Data said slowly, "Q was not there because whatever he had done, he had already attended to."

"I don't follow, Mr. Data," said Picard.

"It is entirely possible that—"

Suddenly the yellow alert klaxon sounded throughout the conference lounge. Immediately everyone rose from the table.

"Hold that thought, Mr. Data," said Picard. "It seems matters are moving ahead without us."

They stepped out onto the bridge as Burnside said briskly from the ops station, "Shields just came up, sir. The Tizarin ships have begun firing on each other."

"Type of weaponry?" asked Picard, taking the command chair. Riker and Troi assumed their places on either side.

"Standard phasers. They are presently firing at one-half strength." Burnside rose to allow Data to resume his station.

"Warning shots," murmured Worf.

"They're flexing their muscles," agreed Riker. "And they're giving us a chance to get out of the way before being hit by something that could cause us damage."

"Hailing frequencies," Picard said. "Let's make one last effort to talk this insanity through."

"They are not responding," Worf said.

The *Enterprise* suddenly rocked slightly.

"I think that was their response," Riker commented.

"Hit on rear deflectors," Data reported, checking his instruments. "From the trajectory, I would surmise it was a stray shot rather than aimed directly at us. No appreciable damage."

"Get us out of here," said Picard. "Set heading at—"

"Captain, we are clear."

"That was quick," said Picard in surprise.

"We and the two Tizarin ships had been moving at steady impulse," Data told him, "but the Tizarin have abruptly ceased their forward motion. Consequently, we kept going out from in-between them. We are at present 10,000 kilometers away and increasing."

"Bring us around, heading of 118 mark 3. Put us in

orbit around the ships. Maintain a presence without getting too close. We want them to know we're here."

"What difference will that make, Captain?" asked Riker.

"Frankly, Number One," said Picard stiffly, "probably not one damned bit."

Sehra lay stretched out on her bed, her breast heaving in great, racking sobs. Next to her was Karla, sharing in her unhappiness, awkwardly patting the back of her mistress.

Sehra turned over onto her back, trying to stop the flow of tears. "How?" she asked Karla. "How did it all go wrong? What happened? First one thing was said, and then another, and everything seemed to feed on itself. Hatred instead of love, chaos instead of consideration."

Karla shrugged. "I don't know, mistress. I don't know much of anything, I'm afraid. I didn't even know how to make Wesley Crusher happy."

Her mother stuck her head in. "Sehra?" she said softly. "Please don't be upset."

"How—?" She managed to compose herself and start over again. "How am I not supposed to be upset? I was supposed to marry tomorrow, and instead we're in a blood feud! Mother, what happened?"

Fenn entered and indicated, with a nod of her head, that Karla should give them privacy. With a small bow, Karla got up and went into the adjacent room. Fenn sat down next to her daughter and stroked her long hair. "You have the most lovely hair, you know. You always did. When you were small I could brush it for hours and you would never complain. Not once."

"Mother . . ."

Fenn shrugged. "Things happen, my dear. This goes beyond your abortive engagement to Kerin. It goes beyond your father, and even your father's father.

Generations ago, the houses of Graziunas and Nistral were fast friends. That was when the pact of coexistence was first signed, and the two houses joined to face the harsh existence of the spaceways together. As time went on, though—as with anything, I suppose—familiarity resulted in a certain degree of contempt for the other. Relations deteriorated, but out of a sense of tradition and continuity, the families stayed together. Gods know, we've been patient in these matters. Nistral has done more heinous things to your father, pulled more cheats, spoken such harshness—it's really nothing short of miraculous that this hasn't occurred earlier. In a way, I suppose we have you to thank for bringing matters to a head. Finally this will be disposed of, one way or the other."

"I don't want it disposed of! It's all my fault! I want things to go back to the way they were! I can't live with the knowledge that all this is happening because of me!"

Fenn's eyes darkened. "I've told you, you silly girl, it has nothing to do with you."

"I'm not a 'silly girl,' mother!" she said furiously. "I'm a young woman. I was going to be a married young woman! How am I supposed to act as if none of this is my responsibility?"

Her mother stood, shaking her head. "I can see, this is becoming pointless," she said sharply. "You can't go back to the way things were, Sehra. You can only go forward."

"I don't want to go forward! Don't you understand? I want Kerin!"

"This is beyond your control, Sehra. You can't have him." And she went out, the door shutting behind her.

Sehra turned and stared into the mirror—the reflection was of a frightened and angry young woman . . .

A silly girl.

"If I can't have Kerin," she said with a voice that sounded much older, "then I don't want myself, either. There's no point to living without him. I've been such an idiot. And even if I went to him now, he'd probably hate me. No . . . it's better this way."

Karla slowly emerged from the side room. "Do you want me again, mistress?"

"Yes, Karla," said Sehra with renewed confidence. She turned and went to her handmaid quickly. "I want you to go down to ships stores and get a fighter uniform. And a helmet. Bring it here quickly, and you are to tell absolutely not a single member of the Tizarin about any of this."

"But . . ."

"Do as I say."

Karla shrugged. "Yes, mistress. Whatever you say."

Kerin was standing in full gear on the flight deck of the Nistral ship. Others were running past him at full speed, making last-minute checks on their ships.

His father strode up to him, fully outfitted in his black-and-silver jumpsuit with the additional crest on it. He clapped him on the back. "Ready, son?"

He turned to his father. "Father . . . when I launched my 'assault' on the Graziunas ship, in order to press my suit for Sehra's hand—I felt determined, certain. I know that I never could have made it if I had felt the way I do now."

"It's understandable, son. You loved this girl, or thought you did. And now you're about to battle her kin."

"I didn't think I loved her, father. I know I do . . . did . . . do . . ." He shook his head in exasperation.

"It's not your fault, Kerin. Obviously you had second thoughts, and instead of being supportive, she became a shrill and accusing bitch."

"She didn't!" Kerin said with unexpected heat. "She's beautiful and young, and who cares what she'll look like years from now—?"

His father spun him around and looked at him firmly. When he spoke, it was with a voice of iron. "Kerin . . . everything we have done we have done in accordance with your wishes. When you wanted to marry her, even though every fiber of my being said it was a bad match, I supported you. And when your better sense took over, I supported you. And when that bastard Graziunas began to insult us, I supported you. That one was easy, I'll admit. Graziunas has been an arrogant, egotistical ass for as long as I can remember, and I've longed to pound some sense into him. If I have to blow him to dust to do it, then that's what I'll do. But you can't start having second thoughts yet again. We've gone too far. We've mobilized our forces, and they stand ready."

"Can't we call them off?" said Kerin. "Can't we—"

"No! Damn it, Kerin. Someday you will carry the name of Nistral. Someday you will succeed me, and bear the responsibility of leadership on your shoulders. Do you seriously think that anyone will follow you if you're known as someone who can't make a decision? Who gets himself into situations without thinking and doesn't have the heart or guts to see it through? I can't let you do that to yourself, Kerin. Now, get ready to fly."

"Father, I—"

"Do it!" said Nistral with barely restrained fury.

And Kerin, the future Nistral—should he live that long—hung his head and said, "Yes, father."

# Chapter Twenty-two

WORF TURNED TOWARD PICARD. "Captain, the Nistral have launched attack vessels."

"Keep trying to raise them, Lieutenant," said Picard sharply, rising from his command chair, his fingers flexing in helplessness. "We've got to do something. Get them to reason together in a sane, rational manner."

"The Graziunas have now launched retaliatory vessels," Worf informed him.

"It would seem," said Riker quietly, "that we've just run out of time."

Sehra climbed into the cockpit of the fighter and scanned the controls. The first thing she found was the button to close the cowling, which slid over her head and sealed her in with a loud *ka-klack*. It felt like a coffin. She put that out of her mind as she went back to studying the arrays in front of her.

She had not flown in ages, and then only under the

careful supervision of her father. In the house of Graziunas, there was a very specific division of labor between male and female, and females most definitely did not fly fighters into combat. Least of all, the daughter of the house head.

There was a loud rapping on the cowling, and she looked up. On the other side was the annoyed face of the fighter pilot whose ship she was in. He was shouting something at her that she could not make out. It didn't matter. She was reasonably sure that with the encompassing helmet she wore, he didn't recognize her. Certainly the loose-fitting jumpsuit had concealed her form more than adequately.

She fired up the main engines. The pilot, seeing what she was doing, gave an alarmed yelp and jumped free of the ship. All around them, ships were leaving the hangar, launching themselves into space for head-to-head battle with the Nistral. So one more ship leaving wasn't going to attract any attention.

Sehra waited until the pilot was clear, although he was still wildly gesturing, clearly, that she should get out of the fighter ship. She appreciated the sentiment but, unfortunately, was not going to be able to comply.

The ship rolled forward. It was not all that difficult for her—much of the work was computer-aided, and the things she had learned to make a flight even smoother easily came back to her.

"This," she said with an air of finality, "is to make up for starting this mess. This is to make up for losing the best thing I ever had." And the ship hurtled forward and launched, with a final roar of engines, into the silence of space.

Worf looked up. "Captain, we're getting an incoming audio message from the Graziunas house ship."

"This is Captain Picard," Picard called out.

"Graziunas, I am pleased that you've taken the initiative to—"

And a quavering female voice filtered through the air. "Uhm . . . is Wesley Crusher there?"

Picard looked at Riker, who shrugged. "Who is this?" demanded Picard.

"My . . . uhm . . . my name is Karla. I have to speak to Wesley immediately."

"Young lady, this is the bridge of the *Enterprise,*" said Picard stiffly. "We do not allow personal calls. Worf, cut off the trans—"

"It's an emergency, damn you!" came the hysterical voice. "I have to talk to Wesley! It's life and death!"

"Captain—" began Deanna. "Perhaps—"

"Yes, yes, anything! Just get her off the blasted frequency."

"Computer," said Deanna, "locate Wesley Crusher."

"Wesley Crusher is in sickbay," the computer replied briskly.

"Again?" said Riker in surprise. "He's becoming somewhat accident-prone, isn't he?"

"I'll explain later, Commander," said Deanna. "Computer, transfer incoming message to Wesley Crusher immediately."

"Complying."

Beverly Crusher finished sealing up the gash in her son's forehead, and she made a good-natured scolding noise. "With the amount of business I'm getting from you," she told him, "I should be giving you quantity discounts."

"At least it won't be happening anymore," said Wes with relief. "My own personal disaster area is back with her own people."

"How did you manage that?"

"She went back on her own because of this war that's broken out," said Wes. He gripped the edge of the table he was sitting on. "I can't say I'm pleased that it took something as terrible as a war to get rid of her. I'd've preferred something less drastic. But at least she's gone. And I should be getting back up to the bridge. If there's trouble, that's where I should be."

"Where trouble goes, Wesley Crusher follows," said Beverly with amusement.

And from nearby another voice said, "I know exactly how he feels."

Wesley turned and saw Lwaxana Troi coming out of another room in sickbay. "Mrs. Troi! What're you doing here?"

"She suffered some damage in that rather unfortunate brawl earlier," Beverly informed him. "I had a medic fix her right up."

"I would have preferred," Lwaxana told her, "that the chief medical officer attend to me, rather than an assistant. Especially since the damage was done to my face. When you have to operate in an ambassadorial capacity as I do, looks are extremely important. I'm sure you understand that."

"Oh, fully," said Beverly through thinned lips. "I can assure you, however, that my staff is the best."

"There's no mark?" asked Lwaxana, pointing at her mouth.

"None."

"That's fortunate," she said, "because I can assure *you* that if—"

Wesley's communicator beeped and he touched it. "Crusher here," he said.

"Wesley? Wesley, is that you?" came a familiar, dreaded voice.

His eyes widened. "Karla? *Karla?* How did you get on my comm frequency?!"

"That man on the bridge connected me to you—"

"You called *the bridge,* looking for me?" His face was in his hands.

"Wesley, it's Sehra! She's going to be killed!"

He looked up. "What?"

Lwaxana stepped forward as well. "What is she saying about Sehra?"

"She made me promise not to tell any of my people. I can't go against her wishes. But I can tell you. I trust you, Wesley. You have to do something! She has no combat training! She won't last five minutes!"

"I'll do what I can."

"Thank you, Wesley! I knew you could help! Goodbye!"

"Wait!" he shouted. "We could communicate with them over your— Hello? Blast! Crusher to bridge."

"Bridge here," came the crisp reply of the captain. "Are you done chatting with your girlfriend, Mr. Crusher?" He did not sound happy, and at that moment, Wesley realized that there were bigger things in the galaxy than making sure that the captain was happy.

"Sir, Sehra of the Graziunas is in a fighter ship, without the knowledge of her parents. She'll be killed!"

"A lot of the Tizarin are going to be killed, Mr. Crusher. But we'll inform them. For all we know, it might make a difference. Bridge out."

Kerin's fighter knifed through the vacuum. Hovering before him, in the distance, was the home ship of the Graziunas. Rising up to meet his wing squad was a brace of Graziunas fighter ships.

No games, this time. No weapons at partial strength. Man to man, one on one. That was the way of the blood feud. The opening salvos had been fired,

214

and now it was time for the fighter ships to settle matters once and for all.

The prospect of facing death was not as horrifying as the thought that Sehra would not be waiting for him back home, waiting to embrace him and congratulate him on his victory. Instead he was going out to battle his loved one's kin. How had it all become so horribly, horribly wrong.

He loved her and hated himself for refusing to stand up for what he believed. He and all his people were being punished for his cravenness. And even now, he was going to face the void, and all he could see was the face of Sehra in the stars before him.

Kerin felt his throat closing up and shoved the fear down and away into a remote portion of his mind. Through his comm unit, there was brisk chatter from his squad as they checked position.

"A and B wing with me. C wing run back up, E and F wing close at 280 mark 3. Punch it, men."

Kerin's squad dove towards their targets, other squads coming in right behind them with blinding speed.

Lwaxana was pacing her quarters, feeling helpless and frustrated. Everything had fallen completely apart. It was the greatest fiasco of her diplomatic career—not that she had caused it in any way, but still . . .

And that poor girl! She remembered that sweet, innocent face and pictured her dying in the cold of space. Would she feel anything? Would death be instantaneous, or would there be long moments of agony? And the girl's mother! What hell would she live through—

Would any of them live through! The Tizarin were going out to fight and die, and it was all so senseless . . .

"Q!" she cried out. "Q, please! Do something! If you love me, do something!"

"What?"

She spun and he was there, leaning against a wall, looking calm as anything. "What would you have me do, Lwaxana?"

"Still trying to raise the Tizarin," said Worf. "They are not responding, even to the message about the girl."

"They're refusing to receive it," said Picard tonelessly. "The fools."

"We could fly right in between them," Riker said. "Try to break it up that way."

"We can't interfere, Number One! You know that! If they want to blow themselves to hell and gone, that's their right, damn it all!" Picard was barely restraining his fury. "A waste. A massive, insane waste."

Sehra didn't know where to look first.

*So many ships! Gods! Hundreds, thousands . . .*

Instruments flashed at her, computers gave readouts. Everything was coming at her with unbelievable speed. She didn't know where she was supposed to be, or what she was supposed to be doing . . .

She'd hurled herself into the void out of a grand sense of responsibility, coupled with a bleak despair that life was hopeless, pointless, and flat-out not worth living anymore. This feeling of hopelessness lasted until the depths of space reached out to encompass her. With death now staring her in the face, Sehra began to blink excessively.

She thought her heart was going to leap out through her throat. Her hands were shaking, her breath coming in short gasps.

And then bleak despair settled over her.

*They'll miss me when I'm gone,* she thought darkly. *And Kerin will miss me most of all.*

With that black sentiment supporting her, Sehra angled upwards towards the descending Nistral ships.

"Make them stop fighting, Q!" Lwaxana begged. "You have the power! You can do it!"

"Of course I *could,*" Q told her, but he sounded extremely sad. "The problem is, dear woman, that I mustn't."

"Why not, in heaven's name?"

"I've sworn to my fellow Q that I would not use my powers to force my way into the affairs of mortals," he said simply. "I can interact, of course. Talk. Try and gain knowledge. But not 'bully,' as it has been called. They would be very upset if I just muscled into the Tizarin dispute, much as that dispute pains me."

"But you would be doing a great service! You would be helping mortals, not hurting them! You'd be saving lives!"

Q paced slowly, his hands behind his back. "It's not the actions that are disputed, Lwaxana. It's the principle. The principle is consistent, you see. I wasn't told by the Q that I could butt in only when it was 'right.' That's a very subjective interpretation, you see."

"That girl is going to die!" said Lwaxana. She went to him and put her hands on his chest. "And hundreds more like her. Please! You must stop them!"

"I can't," he said simply.

Lwaxana sagged against a chair.

And then Q said slowly, "However . . ."

She looked up hopefully. "However what?"

"Well, *you're* certainly under no such obligation, are you?"

For one of the few times in her life, Mrs. Lwaxana Troi didn't know what to say.

* * *

Wesley walked onto the bridge quickly, still catching his breath from having run from sickbay to the turbolift. His ribs and head still ached him somewhat. Picard turned in his chair. "Your information was timely, Mr. Crusher, but unfortunately, the Tizarin don't seem interested in listening to it."

"That's crazy!" said Wes, even as he took his station.

"Unfortunately, Mr. Crusher, people do not have to be sane to kill each other," Riker said dryly.

Worf looked up from the sensors. "Captain," he said in a deathly voice, "the fighter ships are opening fire on one another."

There, on the viewscreen, they could see the flashes of light that indicated blaster fire. The battle was joined.

Picard slid down slightly in the command chair and felt a little of himself die with every shot.

Kerin dove through the air, dodging incoming fire with brilliant precision. His wing guard was with him, and they opened fire on the oncoming ships. On the first pass, all shields held on all sides, but a few more attack runs would take care of that.

Then Kerin noticed something out of the corner of his eye. One of the Graziunas ships had broken off from formation. It was spiralling towards the house ship of Nistral at breakneck speed. Moreover, Kerin's sensor array quickly told him that that renegade ship didn't have shields.

He tried to come up with a reason for it, and couldn't find one, except that it was some sort of bizarre trick.

"Wing Flight, break off. Reconnoiter," he checked quickly, "at 143 mark 14."

"What's up, Kerin?" came the question.

"Have to chase down a raider," he said crisply. "Won't take a minute."

He swung about and set off in pursuit of the Graziunas ship that was evidently on some sort of suicide run.

Sehra had gotten totally turned around.

She couldn't believe how easy it was to become lost or off course. But her attention had wavered for a moment, and now she'd lost her bearings completely. She couldn't see the other ships. She couldn't see . . .

There! Ahead of her was a house ship. The immensity of it drew her towards it before her mind fully realized that it was, in fact, the Nistral ship. She tried to reset her course, but she was starting to lose control. It was getting hard to breathe, and the cockpit was cramped, closing in on her. She felt panic bubbling up through her, beyond her ability to handle.

An instrument in front of her flashed a warning. She wasn't sure what it meant. Then she looked up. A Nistral fighter ship was hurtling down towards her.

*I'm going to die,* she thought, *I'm really going to die. Oh gods. Kerin, I'm sorry.*

And suddenly she didn't want to die. There in the coffinlike crampedness, there in the blackness of space, she had had more than a taste of death and decided that it was more than enough.

Her shields would protect her enough to break off and get the hell out of there—

Shields.

She hadn't activated the shields.

Kerin spun towards the Graziunas ship. He was about to kill his first person. He had trained for it, known, as a defender of Nistral, it would come sooner or later. But he had always believed it would be against some marauding outsider. Ferengi or Orions, perhaps. Not against his own people.

He was about to kill one of Sehra's kin.

And he had no choice. The attacker was heading right towards the Nistral ship and had to be stopped —now.

Kerin targeted the ship.

"I'm sorry," he whispered.

Sehra reached desperately for the shield activator. Then there was a flash just above her and she knew what was about to happen.

"I'm sorry," she whispered.

The wingboard blasters spit out death and Kerin's aim was perfect. The diving ship below him was blown to pieces, random bits spiralling out into space. Of the pilot of the ship, there was nothing left.

# Chapter Twenty-three

ON THE BRIDGE of the *Enterprise,* there was a flash of light and a sound that was, oddly, noiseless.

Picard was immediately on his feet, anticipating who it was. "Q—!" he began angrily, about to tell the all-powerful entity that now was most definitely not the time.

It wasn't Q.

There was a long moment of silence, and then Deanna Troi slowly rose, holding the edge of her chair for support. It was a good thing it was there, because otherwise she would unquestionably have fallen over.

"Mother?" She could barely get the word out.

Lwaxana Troi stood before them, a soft haze around her. She was smiling beatifically, and there was a calm about her that seemed totally alien to her nature.

"Mother, I—" Deanna couldn't find the words.

"Hello, my dear," said Lwaxana. When she spoke, her voice was low and melodious, and seemed to come from everywhere at once.

"Mrs. Troi . . . what's happened?" said Picard, although he strongly suspected he knew.

"I can't feel her," said Deanna. She walked slowly towards her mother. "I can see her, but I can't feel her. In my mind. In my heart, I can't feel her."

"Oh, but I can feel you, Little One. I know it will be hard for you to understand but . . ." She smiled. "Your mother is cosmic now."

Nistral was monitoring the battle, Dai at his side. Suddenly the lights flashed wildly throughout the control rooms. Everyone was looking around in confusion, not understanding what in the world was happening.

On the house ship of Graziunas, the exact same thing was occurring. No one could comprehend it. Just like that, communication with everyone was being lost.

"It's a trick!" shouted Graziunas. "It's some sort of Nistral trick! Some sort of weapon—!"

"Sir!" shouted one of the monitor men. "We're receiving transmissions from the fighter ships!"

"What's happening out there!" demanded Graziunas. "Tell me!"

"It's not a matter of 'out there,' sir," said the monitor. "Nothing's out there anymore."

"What in the gods are you talking about?! If the ships aren't out there, where are they?"

At first Kerin thought he was hallucinating. There had been absolutely no warning. One moment he was swinging his ship around to re-enter the battle, and the next . . .

He looked down at his instrument board—dead. The great engines were silent.

He could hear shouting now, bellows of confusion

and anger. As if not believing his own senses, he scanned the instruments once more, giving them a brisk rap with his fist. Completely dead.

He settled back in his seat and shook his head.

"Some star jockey," he muttered.

Riker finally voiced what everyone already realized: "He's given her the power of the Q."

Picard got to his feet and straightened his jacket, the better to give him a few moments to collect his thoughts. Lwaxana was waiting with what seemed infinite patience.

"Lwaxana," he said slowly, carefully. He felt as if the least wrong word might send her hurtling off into the ether. "Lwaxana, I truly think you should reconsider this. Q gave the same 'gift' to Commander Riker, and it nearly destroyed him."

"Oh, but my mind is far stronger than Commander Riker's. No offense, Commander."

"None taken," he said evenly.

"Lwaxana," Picard started again, "to take on the powers of Q—you'll become like him. You'll believe that you're superior to all life forms."

"Jean-Luc, honestly," she said dismissively. "I've always felt superior to all life forms. Now, I simply will be."

Data turned towards Picard. "She does have a point, Captain."

"Not *now,* Data," Picard said icily.

"Mother, please stop this," said Deanna. "You have no idea of what could happen."

"Of course I do, dear. I will be all-powerful and accomplish great good."

"Or great evil," said Worf darkly.

"Oh, nonsense, Worf," she said. She blinked over from one side of the bridge to the other, so that she was standing next to Worf. The Klingon took a step back in surprise. "Just because I'm omnipotent, that doesn't mean I'm no longer a nice person."

"She's starting to sound like Q already," Worf muttered.

"Stop it!" she said with a stamp of her foot. "Stop criticizing him! That's all any of you have been doing. If Q was the hideous creature you've all made him out to be, then why would he have given me the power to take action?"

"Take action?" said Deanna. "Mother, what are you talking about?"

"Captain," Data suddenly said. "The fighting has stopped."

"What? You mean they're no longer firing at each other?" Picard's eyes searched the screen and he frowned, not quite understanding.

"No, sir. They are no longer in space. They have vanished."

Picard turned towards Lwaxana. "Mrs. Troi," he said very slowly, very formally, "where are the ships?"

"I put them back where they started," said Lwaxana. "It was so easy. It barely required any thought at all. I just thought about it and—*poof*—everything is attended to."

"Mother, you can't do that!" said Deanna. "You can't just step into the middle of people's disputes and—"

"No, Little One," Deanna cut her off sharply. The air in the bridge seemed to crackle. "*You* can't step in. I can. I can do what I wish. It's a free galaxy, and you're going to have to realize that your morals are not always pertinent to the issue at hand. I wanted to save lives. I saved them. Q offered me the power to do it, and I took it. And if he were to offer it a hundred more times, I'd take it a hundred times. I trust him. I trust him implicitly. He's brought me up to his level, and it's as if I've been blind all my life, blind until this very moment. There!" She pointed at thin air. "I just saw a molecule fly by. I decided to see one molecule, and there it is. And if I wanted to, I could make it do whatever I wanted."

"Mother, please! Listen to me!" said Deanna urgently. "You're already changing! You're already becoming something you're not! You've got to tell Q to take this power back!"

"Why? Because you're having trouble coping with it? That, my child, is *your* problem. But for the first time in my life, I'm alive! You're asking me to give that up? To give up the wonders of this new state of mind? To make me like . . . like . . ."

"Like us?" Deanna finished.

"Yes!" She pointed at Deanna. "Yes, exactly. To make me like you. You can't begin to realize the differences between Q and you. Between me and you. Don't you see? I never realized what I was missing until now. Life is a banquet! And most poor bastards are starving to death!"

"I've heard that before," said Deanna.

"Of course you have, dear. I've said it on many occasions." She patted Deanna on the cheek and Deanna trembled. It was her mother, and yet the touch felt . . . wrong. "I know what the real problem is. I know what's most on your mind. But I can assure you, Little One, I will still love you, even when I'm a goddess."

Kerin was removing his helmet, when his father ran up to him and grabbed him by the shoulders. "What are you doing here!" he practically shouted at his son. "How did all the ships return to the landing bay!"

"I don't know!" shot back Kerin. "I was hoping you had some idea."

"Oh, I have an idea, all right," said Nistral.

Other pilots were gathering around them now, looking to Nistral for leadership. Everyone was shouting at once.

"Graziunas!" someone was saying, and others took up the shout. "It must have been Graziunas!"

"No," said Nistral sharply. "It wasn't, because their ships disappeared too. No, this stinks of some sort of Federation hypocrisy. And they'll pay dearly for it."

Sehra opened her eyes, expecting to find herself in the afterlife. She wondered momentarily what that would look like. Somehow, she had not thought that it would look like her room, but that was indeed what she saw when she dared to look.

The door opened and Karla entered. Her hands flew to her mouth as she gasped in shock. Sehra still wasn't focussing on what had happened. "Karla—?"

"I knew it!" Karla cried out. "I knew that Wesley Crusher could do it! He can do anything!"

Picard couldn't think of a thing to say in response to Lwaxana's profession of undying maternal love, even now that she was a deity. So he felt a flash of relief when Worf said, "Captain—incoming message from the Nistral," he paused, "and the Graziunas now as well. They are demanding an explanation. They think we did something with our transporters to send them back where they came from."

"The ingrates!" Lwaxana said stridently. "I stopped them from killing each other! I stopped that young boy from unknowingly blowing his own lover to bits . . ."

"You saved Sehra!" Wesley asked excitedly.

"Of course I did," she said. "It was child's play."

Picard moaned inwardly. "Worf, tell them all concerned parties should meet here on the *Enterprise* within the hour. Everything will be sorted out then."

"If they don't agree to that?"

"They had better! Or I'll personally dismantle their ships a piece at a time," snapped Picard.

"Jean-Luc," said Lwaxana, "I can arrange that, if you wish."

He felt a chill cut through him. "That is not funny, Lwaxana."

"It wasn't meant to be, Jean-Luc," she said mirthlessly. "It wasn't meant to be."

# Chapter Twenty-four

GRAZIUNAS AND NISTRAL glowered at each other across the conference table until Lwaxana Troi entered. Then they glowered at her. Picard, Riker, Worf, and Deanna were already there. Seated nearby, but also on opposite sides of the table, were Kerin and Sehra. They couldn't even look each other in the eye.

Nistral stabbed a finger at Lwaxana. "Let me understand this. You're saying that this woman was responsible for stopping our blood feud?"

"She dared to interfere?" boomed Graziunas.

"I don't believe it," Nistral began. "I simply don't . . ."

"Believe it," Nistral finished. And looked around to see that he was standing in the *Enterprise* engine room.

Geordi La Forge turned in surprise. "Excuse me, can I help you?"

Before Nistral could say anything, he vanished.

Geordi stood there for a moment. Then he tapped

his VISOR a couple of times, shook his head, and went back to what he was doing.

In the meantime, Nistral reappeared in the conference lounge. The entire thing had taken only a couple of seconds, and when he did come back, it was to the open-mouthed astonishment of the other Tizarin in the room. To the *Enterprise* crew, of course, this was becoming standard operating procedure.

"Convinced?" asked Lwaxana calmly. "If you need more, I can send you into orbit around Vulcan."

"That would be fine with me," Graziunas said.

"All right," snapped Nistral. "But she is here as a representative of Betazed, and of the Federation. Her actions were unspeakable."

"Her actions saved lives!" snapped Picard. "Including, Graziunas, the life of your daughter."

"My daughter?" Graziunas turned towards her. "What are you talking about?"

Lwaxana pointed at Kerin in an offhand fashion. "She was in a ship, and he blew it to pieces."

Kerin and Sehra looked at each other in shock. Together, they said, "That was *you!?*"

"Yes," said Picard. "Do you young people see? And do you—you elders? Do you see as well?"

"Sehra, if I had . . ." Kerin couldn't even get the words out. "If I had . . ."

"I didn't want to live!" she wailed. "I didn't—"

"I don't care what happens!" said Kerin. "I don't care what you look like when you're old!"

"I don't care if you think about other girls! It doesn't matter! I just want you!"

"Not again!" shouted Nistral. "First it's on, then off, then on! I won't tolerate this!"

"It's what I'd expect from your son!" bellowed Graziunas. "Women twisting him around their little fingers! He hasn't a mind of his own!"

"Shut up!" bellowed Kerin. "Both of you, shut up!

We love each other! That's all. We do! And if I hadn't been so damned gutless—"

"It wasn't just you," said Sehra. "It was me. We let ourselves be pushed around and—"

"Not anymore," said Kerin. He grabbed Sehra's hand and held it so firmly she thought her fingers would break, but she said nothing. It was the best pain she'd ever felt. "We've listened to all of you," said Kerin. "We've listened to others. We've listened to everyone and everything except our own hearts. No more!"

"Get your hands off my daughter," said Graziunas.

"You're humiliating me!" Nistral said fiercely.

"No, I'm standing up to you. Get used to it. That's the way it's going to be."

Nistral was seated near Picard, and he started to get up out of his seat. To the surprise of all present, Picard grabbed him by the shoulder and shoved him back down into the chair with such force that his teeth rattled.

"That is more than enough!" said Picard, his voice ringing. "It seems to me that what we have here are two young people with more brains than their parents! Kerin and Sehra are ready to put their disagreements and problems behind them. But you . . . you two . . . are unwilling to let go of your hatred!"

"You don't understand—"

"Wrong, Graziunas. I do understand. I just do not care. Not about your rivalries. Not about your blood feuds. Not about your houses. A plague on both your houses! All *I* care about is that we started out with a young couple who wanted to celebrate a joyous union. And instead what we have is anger, jealousy, vituperation, accusations, hatred, and poor spirits. Now, what do you call that sorry state of affairs, eh?"

"Why, Jean-Luc!" came a voice like the screech of a thousand bats. "It's what you humans call 'love.'"

230

Q had materialized in the middle of the conference table. He stood above them, his arms folded, his smile lopsided.

Lwaxana extended a hand. "Q!" she said. "How wonderful to see you, my love!"

He glanced at her disdainfully. "Oh, puh-leeese," he said.

She shook her head, not quite hearing him properly. "What?"

But now Kerin and Sehra were pointing at him. "That's the man who showed me that you were going to be old and wrinkled and ugly," said Kerin. "And . . . and it upset me, and I didn't know how to deal with it, because I didn't think I could even look at you when you're old . . ."

"And he told me that all you cared about was other women! That you'd never stop wanting them . . ."

"Q!" said Picard angrily. "So you have been meddling after all, despite all your protests to the contrary!"

"Is pointing out the truth meddling?" demanded Q. "Is doing these young people a favor meddling? I ask you."

"Kerin," said Picard, ignoring Q's protests for a moment. "Yes, in years to come, Sehra will age. So will you. That is inevitable. What you don't understand is that you will grow old together and cherish those years. And when you behold her, you will not simply see some old woman, but instead the woman you've shared many long and joyous years of married life with. You will look at her with love. And Sehra, yes . . . Kerin will doubtlessly look at other women. Being married doesn't mean that you stop noticing beauty. But if he were to lose his ability to appreciate the more beautiful things in life, then how could he possibly continue to cherish you? Cherish the beauty in your face and form, and the beauty in your heart?"

"Oh, bravo, Picard!" Q said sardonically, clapping his hands in slow, sarcastic applause. "Bravo! Try to justify this nonsense as best you can, and it will all boil down to the simple truth that the human concept of love is a total sham."

Lwaxana came towards him, her dark eyes concerned. "Q, I don't understand what you're saying—"

He shot a look at her. "Woman, you could attend me for a thousand lifetimes and still barely begin to grasp the subtleties of my greatness."

Lwaxana gasped and stepped back, thunderstruck, her hand to her breast.

"Is this why you've come then, Q?" demanded Picard.

"Of course, Picard!" sneered Q. "The entire ship was filled with spirits of love, love, love. It was nauseating. You humans are so obsessed with love. You're always looking for it, or you're in it or out of it. Or you're singing about it, or writing poems about it. So I decided to examine it, to see just how durable this supposedly most enduring of emotions is."

Picard came around the table to face Q. All of his fury and energy was directed towards Q, towards this unknowable being who presumed to judge humanity in all its aspects. "In the cause of love, civilizations have risen. For lack of love, civilizations have crumbled. It's the most glorious and ennobling emotion of humanity."

"Then humanity is in even worse trouble than I surmised," Q told him. "Your most glorious emotion? My dear Jean-Luc, it's your most positively ludicrous! It's selfish and self-directed. Possessive and spiteful. It encompasses everything that you humans are always claiming that you're above, and yet it's cloaked in this charming storybook idea that people loving each other is a good thing. You think that your race surviving war is your greatest achievement? Nonsense! It's that your race has survived love, the most overblown, ridiculous excuse for a positive emotion that any race has ever encountered."

Lwaxana was ghastly white, as if her soul had been ripped open. "I . . . I don't understand . . . you said . . ."

Q rudely blew air from between his lips. "Are you deaf *and* stupid, woman? How painfully clear do I have to make matters for you?"

"Stop it!" said Deanna. "Leave her alone!"

"Q, get out of here!" snapped Picard.

But Q ignored them. Instead he walked down the length of the conference room table, towards Lwaxana. Every step was swaggering arrogance. "Oh, of course. I forgot to add self-deception to the list." He laughed once, that ugly, unholy sound. He hunkered down to bring himself on eye level with the ashen Lwaxana Troi. "Woman, you have been, and always shall be, merely another bit of data for my study. Another rat to go running through the maze. I wanted to see how, in the name of love, you would interact with your precious daughter and vice-versa. I wanted to see if this wonderful emotion would blind you to everything that was dictated by common sense. And it did! How splendid."

"You love me!" said Lwaxana, desperately, urgently.

"And still you continue! This is excellent. You're more self-involved than I thought. So much so that you ignored the advice of the daughter you love and the people you respect, just so you could fall in love with a being you just met and who every other person you encountered claimed had no capacity for love. They were right, *dear* Lwaxana. You are nothing to me. Humans are nothing to me, except when sometimes they can provide me with some amusement. And you, Lwaxana," Q's voice fell to a sarcastic, harsh whisper, "you have provided me with the most amusement of all. Thank you very, very much, you ignorant cow."

Lwaxana sank to a chair.

"Q, I am telling you to leave," said Picard.

"A joke," Lwaxana murmured. "It's all been a joke. A scheme. An experiment."

"I hardly think you're in a position to issue commands to me, Picard," Q said.

"He gave me the Q powers," Lwaxana said evenly.

"I am in a position, and my command is for you to leave. Now!"

"He gave me the powers of the Q," Lwaxana said more loudly, and she looked up. There was something in her face. Something unpleasant. Something dangerous.

Deanna took her by the shoulders and said urgently, "Mother, let's go—"

"A joke," and now when Lwaxana spoke, it was with a voice that sounded like thunder rumbling over the tops of mountains. "A plot to deliberately humiliate me. And you gave me the power of the Q . . ."

"An interesting wrinkle, I'll admit," said Q. "I wanted to see if you'd choose power over the love of your daughter. For you would have lost that love, woman. In a shorter time than you can imagine, they would have come to hate and distrust you as much as they do me. So imagine my lack of surprise when you chose power."

"Power in order to be near you!" she said. "Power out of love for you, you ungrateful, no-good . . ."

Sounding bored, Q said, "Your name-calling is meaningless to me. I'm above such things. This little experiment is over. Love does not conquer all. Only conquest conquers all. Only the kind of power that is generated by weapons and strength, not by the pointless display of a useless emotion."

Lwaxana clenched her fists. "You *used* me! You made me look like a fool!"

"Nature did that," said Q. "I simply gave you an audience."

Her entire body trembled in mortification and shock. And then came a scream, the sort of agonized scream of a fury to which hell had nothing remotely comparable. The fury of a woman scorned.

"Very impressive, Lwaxana," said Q. "Now, if you don't mind, I'll retrieve my powers and be on my way."

Her face darkened, her body stiffened. With a slow, measured tread she started towards him, her fists clenched.

And Q blinked in surprise. "Lwaxana, give me the powers back. You cannot keep them."

Lwaxana was seething, the air crackling around her.

"Mother?" said Deanna nervously.

No less nervous, suddenly, was Q. He stretched out a hand as if yanking something away. Instead there was a sound like energy building up.

"Lwaxana," said Q, looking decidedly less sure of himself. "I don't know what you're doing, or how you're doing it. But you can't have those powers anymore. You can't resist me. *Lwaxana!* You're making me angry! And since I'm above human emotions, that's not possible." He strode towards her, trying to look confident. "So before this goes on any further, give them back to me—now! This is my last word on the subject!"

Lwaxana Troi blew him through a bulkhead.

# Chapter Twenty-five

THE BRIDGE SHUDDERED as Data suddenly called out, "Hull integrity breach! In the conference lounge."

Burnside looked up from her station in surprise. "What? Are we under attack?!"

"Apparently," said Data, "the impact was from the inside out." He rechecked his instruments. "The breach has just been repaired."

"Look!" called out Wesley Crusher, pointing at the screen.

Q was floating in front of them, spinning around, looking confused and dazed.

"Someone outside?" said Chafin, utterly nonchalant by this time. "That old chestnut again."

"Mother!" said Deanna in shock.

Picard took a step forward. "Lwaxana," he began.

She spun and Picard saw the look in her eyes. He took a step back and began again, "Lwaxana . . ."

She didn't hear him. She was beyond hearing,

beyond caring. The only thing she was able to hear was Q's mocking tone. The only thing she could see was his sneering face. The only thing she could do was go after him. And she did.

In an eyeblink she was outside the ship, behind him. "Q!" she shouted, and naturally he heard her. He turned and Lwaxana's arms extended wide. Energy leaped from them and enveloped Q. He shrieked, twisting and writhing in space, his body snapping about like a stringed puppet.

He flipped backwards and vanished.

"You can run, but you can't hide!" shouted Lwaxana Troi, and vanished as well.

Graziunas and Nistral looked at Picard in astonishment.

Picard shrugged gamefully. "Lover's quarrel," he said.

Q dashed down outside of the right nacelle like a sprinter. Lwaxana was right after him. He spun, took a stand. "Lwaxana!" he bellowed. "I don't know how you're doing this! But I want those powers back!"

"How am I doing it?" She advanced on him. "You gave me powers equalling your own. But my mind was already superior to yours, and you heightened it that much further when you empowered me."

"Your mind was never superior to mine! No human mind can be superior to mine!"

"This is no human mind!" she screeched. "This is the mind of a daughter of the Fifth House!"

She reached out and she didn't even have to touch him as she brought her hands down. Q was smashed right through the warp nacelle.

There was pandemonium in the engine room. Q had just hurtled down into the matter/antimatter mix.

Alarms were sounding and technicians were running every which way. Geordi was madly trying to shut down all power on the ship, because in ten seconds everything was going to blow.

Q staggered out of the containment area, miraculously leaving all the radiation behind him. He looked dazed, punchy.

A hand clamped down on his shoulder, and from behind a deadly voice continued, "Holder of the Sacred Chalice of Riix!" He turned and Lwaxana swung a right cross that smashed him through the nearest wall. With a gesture she repaired it, and the damage to the mix. Just as quickly as the danger had arisen, it was past.

Q was running, tearing headlong down a corridor. He was desperately watching behind his shoulder, and so ran straight into a fierce kick to the crotch. He went down, gasping.

Lwaxana stood over him, boiling mad. She kicked him over and over for emphasis as he twisted on the floor, trying to get away, as she bellowed, "And keeper [kick] of the Holy [kick] Rings [kick] of Betazed!" and she booted him once more, sending him skidding down the corridor.

Picard, Riker, Worf and Data barreled down a corridor, following the trail of carnage. To their shock, Q came running from the other direction. He skidded to a halt and shouted, "Warn her, Picard! Warn her that she cannot treat me in this manner! She's unleashing forces she doesn't understand!"

"She hasn't listened to me since this whole business started," said Picard calmly. "What makes you think she'll listen now?"

Suddenly Q vanished.

They looked around, certain that he had dematerialized once more, and then abruptly they heard a high-pitched cry of alarm. They looked down.

Q was six inches tall. He was running around on the floor, shaking his teeny fists in impotent fury.

Lwaxana burst into existence above him. "Hello, darling!" she snarled, and brought her foot down.

Q ran frantically, right and left, dodging the pounding feet. "Picard!" he howled in soprano. "Picard!"

She suddenly reached down and grabbed him up. "Got you!" she snarled, and vanished.

The *Enterprise* officers looked at each other.

"She's really beating the stuffing out of him," observed Riker. "What do you think we should do?"

"Sell tickets," rumbled Worf.

Everyone else had left the conference lounge except for Kerin and Sehra. They sat there, holding each other's hands, and Sehra said, "I'm so proud of you."

"If I'd injured you . . . gods, I can't even imagine it. I should never have doubted us. Doubted anything. I'm sorry for everything. Will you give me another chance?"

"If you will for me."

"Of course I will." He grinned. "Isn't being in love wonderful?"

"Computer," said Picard, "locate Lwaxana Troi."

"Lwaxana Troi is in the rocketball court."

Riker blinked in surprise. "What's she doing there?"

Lwaxana swung the glowing paddle with confidence and smashed Q against the wall.

He ricocheted off it and spun backwards, out of control. Lwaxana was waiting for him and with a brisk backhand, whacked the miniature god again. He screamed as he careened once more into the wall.

The *Enterprise* officers ran into the spectator area. Mr. Homn was already there. He was sanguinely eating popcorn, watching the "match." When he saw the others, he extended the bag and offered them some.

"No, thank you. Mrs. Troi!" called out Picard.

Q snapped back to his normal size and hurled headfirst into one of the glowing walls.

Lwaxana spun angrily towards Picard. "Jean-Luc! You ruined my concentration!"

Q vanished. Lwaxana vanished after him.

"Here we go again," said Picard.

Crew members were running everywhere, shouting in confusion. Great, horned beasts were charging down the hallway, bellowing their defiance, and barely two steps ahead of them was Q.

He dove right through a corridor wall, leaving the frustrated beasts behind.

He kept on going, passed through to the other side and stepped out into a corridor on the other side of the ship.

Lwaxana was waiting for him. She was clad in full, bristling body armor from ancient Betazed. She was wielding a long weapon that was hooked at one end and spiked at the other. The hooked end lashed out, grabbing Q by the leg and hurling him to the floor. She reversed it and slammed the spiked end down right where Q's chest had been, except he had already melted through the floor.

Lwaxana pushed back her visor. "Damn," she muttered.

Q staggered down a corridor, his mind and body reeling.

He couldn't comprehend any of it. Lwaxana Troi was massacring him. He hadn't been able to mount any sort of offense at all. She just kept on him and on him . . .

Suddenly he saw her waiting for him at the end of the corridor.

He lashed out at her, energy leaping from his fingertips. Lwaxana stood there, weathering the barrage, her hands outstretched. She staggered slightly but otherwise showed no signs of difficulty.

"Give up!" cried out Q. "You can't beat me! I'm Q!"

"You were Q!" shot back Lwaxana. "Now you're going to be an ex-Q."

Q's body suddenly began to stiffen. He lost control over his arms, finding himself unable to move them. He tried to run, but his legs wouldn't budge, either. He looked down in horror and saw why—they had taken root. His fingers were becoming small branches. There was a cracking sound like wood splitting, and within seconds, Q had metamorphosized into a tree.

He tried everything he could do to move. He unleashed the full power of his mind, but it was as if something were hanging over it, dampening it. He couldn't counter any of the moves, couldn't focus his strength, couldn't . . .

He heard a sharp, wissing sound. His neck, although wood, was still capable of moving, and he managed to look up.

Lwaxana Troi was coming towards him, wielding a massive, glistening *deelar*, a Betazoid weapon that bore a remarkable resemblance to an axe. It glistened, and for extra effect, blood dripped from it. There was a satisfied grin on her face.

"No!" shrieked Q, almost surprised to see that his voice still worked.

"Now," said Lwaxana firmly. "Now we cut you down to size."

"Mother!" came an alarmed shout.

Lwaxana didn't even glance behind her in response to her daughter's shout. "Not now, dear. Mother's chopping some wood."

"Please don't do this, mother!" She grabbed her by the arm, being certain to keep her fingers clear of the *deelar*'s blade. Several feet away, Q's branches trembled. "Enough! You've made your point! He knows you're angry."

"He humiliated me! I can never have anyone's respect again."

And now Picard was there, and he said, "That's not true, Lwaxana. You've earned all our respect!"

"I, for one, would certainly not wish to have you angry with *me*," Worf informed her.

"He has to apologize," said Lwaxana.

"Q, apologize!" ordered Picard.

Q was silent.

"Q," warned Picard.

"She couldn't really hurt me," Q said uncertainly.

"Are you willing to bet life and limb on that?" Riker demanded.

"Forget it," said Lwaxana. "Stand aside, Riker." She swung the axe back, and it was clear that the first stroke was going to be in Q's nether regions.

"I'm sorry!" howled Q. "I'm sorry! All right? I'm sorry I did it! It was reprehensible! It was hideous! I shouldn't have even contemplated it! I'll never think of it in the future! I don't know what I could have been thinking! I am a terrible and vile individual, not fit to exist in the same universe as the splendid Lwaxana Troi! There, are you happy?!"

She paused, considering it.

"I don't think you mean it," she said, and swung the axe back once more.

But Picard put a firm hand on her shoulder and said, "Enough, Lwaxana. *I* mean it. Enough."

Slowly she lowered the axe, and then it vanished.

"I really would have done it, you know," she told him.

"Yes, we all know that," said Picard.

An instant later, Q transformed back into his normal state. He staggered and stumbled against a wall, confused and gasping.

Lwaxana strode up to him and he flinched. "You hurt me," she said. "You hurt me in ways I didn't even think it was possible. You're so disdainful of humanity. Of mortals. You keep saying you're above our emotions, and hold them in such disdain. You know what I think? I think you're not worthy of them. I think you're not good enough to feel love." Her voice was trembling. "You're just not good enough." And she turned on her heel and walked away.

Deanna started to follow her, but she heard a sharp, *Leave me alone, Little One* in her head, and she stayed where she was.

Q sat on the floor, trying to compose himself. He looked up in irritation and said, "What are you sneering at, Worf?"

"Nothing," said Worf with satisfaction. "I am sneering at a great big nothing."

"You know, your insults are meaningless to me," said Q. "Everything you say is meaningless to me. But that woman—that . . . that damned woman!" His voice was shaking with fury. "She is the most aggravating, infuriating individual I've ever met!" He was getting to his feet, and his body was literally trembling with rage. As opposed to the cold arrogance with which Q usually cloaked himself, now he was clearly angry. "I cannot remember when I've met someone who has actually aroused in me a feeling of such total fury! It is truly staggering! I see her face in my mind, and I just want to grind it beneath my foot! This is truly amazing! I loathe her! I *despise* her! It's not just that she so thoroughly beat me through means that I still cannot even guess. I was humiliated just as badly when I lost my powers, but I didn't feel anything like this . . . this mind-numbing feeling of bile in my mouth! I—"

And Picard, the picture of calm, said serenely, "You will find, Q, that an extreme of one emotion usually indicates that an extreme of another emotion is present."

"What are you blathering about?" demanded Q.

"You see, Q . . . those we love the most are also the most capable of driving us to complete distraction. Because we've left ourselves open and vulnerable, you see. In other words, it's quite possible that you do indeed feel love for her, which is why she is able to make you as angry as she does."

"That's ridiculous. That's . . ." His face fell as he thought of it. "I'm . . . I'm certain that's ridiculous. That can't be. I couldn't actually *be* in love. I'm a being with power far beyond yours. To be laid low by the pathetic emotion you call love, that would be . . ."

"Very human," Riker said, turning the screws.

"Face it, Q," Picard told him. "You've been hanging around humans too much. Your system has not been able to build up proper immunities to us, and we're becoming contagious. You're coming down with a terminal case of humanity."

"Picard," said Q, with a bit of the old arrogance. "Get some hair. Your brain has caught cold." And with a burst of light and sound, he vanished.

"Good riddance," rumbled Worf.

"Oh, I don't know," said Picard slowly. "I hate to admit it . . . but I'm starting to get used to him."

"Captain, you're joking!" Riker said in horror.

Picard turned towards him. "Oh, of course I am, Number One." But he wasn't entirely sure that he was.

\* \* \*

Lwaxana sat in her cabin totally alone, totally depressed. She stared into her mirror, taking a close look at herself.

How pathetic she was. How ridiculous. Here she was, with the power of a goddess, and she couldn't even get herself to smile.

Her eyes brimmed with tears, and Lwaxana Troi began to cry. She put her hands to her face and sobbed deeply, caught up entirely in her own misery.

"Here," said a voice.

She looked up.

A slim, blond man was standing in front of her. He was wearing a simple green jumpsuit and was extending a handkerchief. "Here you go."

She took it gratefully and blew her nose. "I'm sorry, I didn't hear you come in. Who are you?"

"Q," he said.

She stared at him. "That isn't funny. I know what Q looks like. I'll carry that knowledge to the grave, or I would if I were ever going to die . . ."

"Oh, you'll die, in your own time," he said. "Trust me on this. I know he was Q. I'm Q too."

"Q Two?" she said in confusion.

"Whatever," said Q Two. He looked at his hands in approval. "Nice to know it all still fits."

"Let's assume for a moment I believe you," said Lwaxana. "What are you doing here?"

He strolled around her quarters, picking up objects and examining them out of idle curiosity. "We've been keeping an eye on Q, watching to make sure he doesn't use his powers in the same annoying way he did before."

"You mean what he was saying before, about not bullying people . . ."

"Oh, that was quite true," said Q Two. "But you see, instead of those same annoying ways, he's trying to find new annoying ways. Nothing that we could discipline him for, but nothing that we considered to have much redeeming social value. But when he tried to take the power he gave you back again, well, I thought I'd take the opportunity to teach him a lesson."

"You helped me keep the power?" she said incredulously.

"Long enough for you to give Q a taste of his own medicine, yes. I must admit," he smiled, "you were very imaginative. I took lots of pictures. I can't wait to show them to the others in the Continuum . . . particularly that business with the paddles. Very imaginative. Worthy of the Q."

"Thank you," she said, and she smiled. "It was rather clever, wasn't it."

"Oh, extremely," he said pleasantly. "And for Q's own good, really. Maybe he'll remember what it's like to be on the receiving end, for once."

"I certainly made him think twice about treating people so badly." She actually started to grin, and then she laughed, a deep, throaty, lovely laugh. "He'll think long and hard about it, yes indeed."

"Got to take the powers back now," said Q Two, and he snapped his fingers.

Lwaxana sagged slightly as she felt something disappear from within her, as if someone had turned off a light switch. "Ah well," she said sadly. "I did so like the idea of being able to keep watch over Deanna . . ."

"Sounds to me like you could easily have begun to smother her."

"I suppose you're right. It's probably best this way. You seem very wise, and very capable." She regarded him thoughtfully. "And I must say, you are a rather attractive individual, you know."

He put up a warning finger. "Don't even think it," he said, and vanished.

Lwaxana Troi shrugged. "Can't blame a girl for trying."

Q stood atop the Nistral home ship, watching the *Enterprise* from a safe distance. When Q Two appeared next to him, he didn't even bother to turn. "I should have known you were responsible."

"You did it to yourself," remarked Q Two. "He struck pretty close to home, didn't he."

"Who?"

"Picard. Of course, you now owe him for saving your life. I'd start trying to think of ways to make it up to him someday, if I were you." Q Two regarded him with tremendous amusement. "She really did get to you, didn't she? Not just physically, which she needed my help for. I mean mentally."

"Faw. She was nothing."

Q Two hunkered down next to him. "You can't lie to me, Q. Maybe to them, maybe even to yourself, but not to me. You felt something for her."

Q looked up at Q Two. "I can't have. I'm beyond love."

"Perhaps not. Perhaps no one is. Perhaps it's so powerful a force, and perhaps that's what Picard was trying to tell you."

"And perhaps you talk too much."

"Between you and me, Q. It'll go no further. Not even to the Continuum."

Q looked back at the *Enterprise* which, for some reason, seemed even more distant.

He sighed.

"She was magnificent, wasn't she?"

"Yup," agreed Q Two.

"And she'd never want to see me again, even if I wanted to see her."

"You said some pretty despicable things. I doubt she would."

"Well, good," said Q, drawing himself up. "That's the way it should be, then. She is, after all, only human."

"Aren't we all," said Q Two.

Q shot him a look and then vanished, and Q Two laughed silently into the airless void of space.

# Chapter Twenty-six

"AND SO," Picard said, smiling, "by the power given me as captain of the U.S.S. *Enterprise,* and with the blessings of the gods of the Tizarin, I now pronounce you married."

Kerin and Sehra turned towards each other, and he took her face in his hands and kissed her. A cheer went up from all around, and applause, and a general sigh of relief. Picard closed the great book with finality and gave silent thanks.

Shortly thereafter there was a grand reception that had been set up under the shady trees of the Genesis Planet. The Federation Horns were playing a bossa nova while a holodeck-created bird watched them with curiosity.

Wesley took the opportunity to approach Grazi-unas, who was getting good and drunk along with Nistral. "Sir," said Wesley slowly, "I need to talk to you, man to man."

"Man to man, young sir!" boomed Graziunas, feeling no pain. He draped a heavy arm around Wesley's shoulder. "What would that be about then, man to man?"

"It's about Karla . . ."

"Karla! The girl my daughter is always trying to get rid of?"

Wesley's eyes widened. "What?"

"The girl is a total fumblefingers. She's always dropping things, or knocking into things or people. She once broke my right big toe by stepping on it! Can you believe that?"

"Easily," said Wesley.

"My daughter keeps trying to pawn her off as a gift to unsuspecting souls. But she always winds up being returned to us."

"And you're not insulted?"

"Insulted?" said Graziunas in confusion. "Why should it be any great insult to return a gift? And in Karla's case, it would certainly be understandable. What's this all about, young man?"

"She lied," said Wes wonderingly.

"Women always lie. That's so men can hear what they want to."

"I just . . . I thought if you were planning to give her back to me, now that the fighting's over, I . . ."

"You want her?"

*"No!"* Wesley had actually wanted to head off any plans of her coming back to him as some sort of token of gratitude. "Not at all."

"Well, that's fortunate. Seems Sehra has become fond of her. Some business about Karla helping to save her when she went off on that insane jaunt in a ship. Craziest thing, that. Women, eh?"

"Women," agreed Wes.

250

Graziunas squeezed Wesley's shoulder. "Tell me, young sir, do you arm wrestle?"

Wesley felt the strength that was gripping his shoulder and had the depressing feeling that he was going to wind up in sickbay again shortly.

Lwaxana was back wearing black. "Mother, enough is enough," said Deanna, nursing a drink. Riker, Picard, and Data were standing nearby, taking it all in with amusement. "I want you to stop this mourning business."

"What choice do I have, Little One?" sighed Lwaxana. "You make it so difficult for me."

"I make it difficult?"

"That's right," said Lwaxana firmly. "There are so many men on this ship who would be a fine catch. And furthermore, I . . ."

Deanna sighed deeply and looked down, as if she'd been caught with her hand in the cookie jar. "All right, mother," she said. "I can't hide it from you. I have, in fact, been discussing just that topic and . . . well . . . we're now prepared to announce our engagement."

Lwaxana looked up in surprise. "To whom?"

Deanna turned and walked towards the *Enterprise* officers. Lwaxana saw her heading towards Riker and clapped in delight.

Deanna reached out and took Data firmly by the arm. She pulled him forward, to the laughter of Picard and Riker. Data looked around in polite confusion.

She hauled Data in front of her mother and said, "Him."

Data looked from the firmly smiling face of Deanna to the blanching face of Lwaxana. "This will be very interesting," said Data. "I look forward to the experience. And should, by some chance, there be children, we would very strongly consider naming them after you, Mrs. Troi."

"Call her 'mom,' Data," suggested Riker.

"Mom," said Data obediently.

"I'm going to get a very, very stiff drink," said Lwaxana, and she did so.

# STAR TREK ®
## THE NEXT GENERATION ™
# Technical Manual
## Mike Okuda and Rick Sternbach

The technical advisors to the smash TV hit series, STAR TREK: THE NEXT GENERATION, take readers into the incredible world they've created for the show. Filled with blueprints, sketches and line drawings, this book explains the principles behind everything from the transporter to the holodeck—and takes an unprecedented look at the brand-new U.S.S. *Enterprise*™ NCC 1701-D.

## Coming Soon From Pocket Books

POCKET
BOOKS

The First Star Trek: The Next Generation
Hardcover Novel!

# REUNION

## Michael Jan Friedman

Captain Pickard's
past and present
collide on board the
U.S.S. *Enterprise*™

POCKET
BOOKS

Coming Soon in Hardcover
from Pocket Books